PART I

The Middle of a Wish

by Heather Conrad

Copyright © 2020 by Heather Conrad

Published in the United States by Lightport Books
www.lightportbooks.org

All rights reserved. No part of this book may be reproduced in any form or by any means, electronic or mechanical, including photocopying, recording or by any information storage or retrieval system, without permission in writing from the Publisher. Inquiries should be addressed to Lightport Books, PO Box 7112, Berkeley, CA 94707

ISBN 9780971242586   GTIN 09780971242586

This is a work of fiction. Names characters, places, and incidents either are the product of the author's imagination or are used fictitiously. Any resemblance to actual persons, living or dead, events, or locales is entirely coincidental.

Credits

Cover art by deForest Walker
The publisher would like to thank the following for permission to reproduce their material. Every care has been taken to accurately credit copyright holders. However, if there is an unintentional error, we apologize and will, if informed, correct it in any future edition.
In Part I, Compass: Aukland Museum, posted on Wikimedia Commons, http://api.aukland museum.com/id/medi, under the Creative Commons Attribution 4.0 International license. No changes were made to this image.
In Part I, Starfish: Stephen Pavlov, posted on Wikimedia Commons, under the Creative Commons Attribution-Share, Alike 4.0 International license. No changes were made to this image.
All other photographs in this book: Heather Conrad

Author Acknowledgements

My heartfelt thanks and appreciation for the insightful and valuable guidance I received while writing this novel from Kate Colwell, Alisyn Neat, Ginny Orenstein, Sandra Treacy and deForest Walker

For the children

I'm writing this with a pencil, in a paper notebook from decades ago. It's strange to write something that can be so easily erased, or burned, or disintegrate—that can be destroyed as if it never existed. Something not stored in the cloud for them to spy on and manipulate and use against me. The cloud—such a perfect metaphor—ever-changing, eternal, opaque.

It's raining finally. The "real" clouds appeared yesterday. Mackerel clouds, like white fish scales blanketing the sky. The sky itself had been white for weeks. Nuclear winter, I call it, though no bombs have exploded here. It's simply the usual pollution. Muted, nearly invisible colors, no shadows. And now for the first time in eight months—rain.

And finally. Finally! We are on the road. The years of waiting, frustration and hopelessness are behind us.

I hear a trash can caroming down the asphalt against the wall. Bam-bam-bam! A pause, and then again. The wind is fierce.

I don't mean we are on the road literally. We're huddled here in the shelter waiting out this storm. Mentally, though, we are finally on the road.

I am seventy, so I remember. There were beautiful flowers near my home. Fragrant flowers with a sweet delicate scent not synthetically reproduced yet. I doubt they will ever manage to do it, but then no one will remember that scent anyway. Does it matter?

There are only persons who identify as female in this shelter, along with their children. We have been here three days, our second stop on the way to the Capitol. Star looks at me now and smiles. She has been in a good mood for days. It's wonderful to see. My daughter has not had an easy life. My husband and I had named her Eva but at eleven she changed her name to that of her favorite video hero. We acquiesced.

That's how it was decades ago in our milieu, parents granted their children's identity choices.

Star is a survivor of the identity wars. She wasn't yet born when some white women in America talked about their "visceral" reaction to the image of a black woman as First Lady of the White House. Nor when a black woman told a gay black man on the news she had a "visceral" reaction to seeing two men kissing. Visceral reactions meant outrage or repugnance back then. Unattractive women had always felt men's visceral reaction to their presence, while attractive women used it to advance themselves. It was the basis of men's great power over us. I suppose we have A.I. to thank for making the human body so much less relevant now.

Star fortunately did not participate in the opioid epidemic, although one of her friends was addicted to OxyContin. He was in one of the state programs that focus on arts and crafts for export. He painted ceramic tiles used for decorative siding on stilts elevating lowland housing. He loved seaweed and tide pool motifs. His anemones were actually in high demand.

Star is too ambitious for opioids. Even at thirty, now, she believes in herself and her plans. She was simply born that way. Dale and I always said we had nothing to do with her unusual power.

I was especially proud of Star when she threw away her iPhone after the second wave of surveillance scandals. She was in middle school and life without social media wasn't easy. She threw it in the ocean. I wish she'd recycled it but I understood the importance of the drama. Star is a bit of a drama queen, I'd have to say.

Remember No-Drama Obama? I laugh silently to myself when I think of this. Not many recall those years.

We will be "marching" toward the new Capitol tomorrow. Today is for final preparations. I can hardly believe it's happening.

When we arrived at this shelter days ago I saw a dozen or so red-winged blackbirds flying low over the wetlands, their fiery red wing-patches lit by the afternoon sun. They seemed to be heading straight along the line of where the highway used to be. The line we will be following in rafts until we get to the peninsula.

The sight of the birds made my heart soar. It's a sight one might have seen hundreds of years ago. Birds in flight, beautiful and with purpose. They don't know our names or our history, nor care. Except perhaps for the different distribution of resources, and how the landscape has changed. Not a creature nor a plant has been exempt from the changes.

Even the millions of cloned cattle, chickens, pigs—you name it—on farms around the world. Or perhaps especially them. It was Star who first told me about the farm in Oklahoma owned by a neurosurgeon who had cloned dozens of Black Angus cattle back in 2009! I had asked her why she had become vegan. When I heard her answer, I became vegan myself. Dale was not so susceptible and continued his usual omnivore diet right until the end.

In some ways, I admired the way Dale pooh-poohed a lot of trends and what he considered fads or bogus ideas or "fake news." He was nothing if not rational and evidence-based in his thinking. I found this to be grounding and very helpful when I simply did not know what to make of a situation. My mind often caught on odd details or subtle signals that led me to weave a story out of the unspoken half-thoughts that many people choose to ignore. My interpretations of events often baffled Dale. But they were not always inaccurate. In fact, the unconscious can tell us a great deal about what is not immediately evident.

The collective unconscious, as Jung named it. Or "the knowing" as I've called it myself. It's astonishing how much we actually know but are not aware of.

Dale wasn't impressed with this kind of thinking, although he did grant that occasionally my "intuition" revealed a grain of truth about whatever goings-on we were discussing. But he wouldn't go so far as to believe my theory that every being in the universe is as a cell is to a whole organism—containing all the knowledge, like DNA, and yet being only a tiny part of the whole organism, at the same time. Of course he believed in DNA and all the rest. He was a biologist. But not the part about omniscience.

It sounds like Dale and I may not have been well-suited. But we were. He calmed me. When my imaginings and premonitions began to make me feel I was disintegrating in a phantasmagoria, he set me firmly back into the specific context of the moment. And I—what did I do for him? I suppose I made him feel—what? In charge? Always a benefit a woman can provide for a man. I am actually of a generation where most girls around the world were instructed by their mothers to let boys think they are the smarter and stronger sex. This was especially important for less "marriageable" girls. For girls who were a ten on the beauty scale, though—anything goes. They did not generally have to kowtow or subvert themselves. But they were not immune from assault and abuse. There was a remarkable social uprising when Star was an infant, the "Me Too" movement which revealed an astonishing level of men's abuse of beautiful women. The abuse of less beautiful women had been more well-known, or such was my impression.

I've learned to qualify a lot of what I say like that—a survival technique for living with Dale. Or just in general. In fact, most people seemed to find me quirky, I confess. I would "speak my truth" as we were taught to do in the second wave of feminism and also the Me Too movement, and people would crinkle their foreheads or give me a look like WTF? And when I would describe the particular facial expression I'd seen someone make or the snippet of conversation I'd heard that led me to form my impression, they would shake their head or laugh. That didn't happen all the time, just now and then.

But Dale often loved my imagination and perceptions. He loved my artwork. And he respected me. I got a lot done. And there were many subjects we could converse about for hours—natural history, the arts. We had a happy marriage.

Dale died four years ago. Cardiac arrest. It's still hard for me to talk about that time.

Star wants to show me something. She beckons to me from a small group of young women she is standing with near the firepit. The rain is still falling in sheets outside making it hard to hear. I walk over to them.

"Mom," she says. "Look at this." She has a paper torn from a notebook with a hand drawn map. "The marsh road's closed. JoJo boated there at dawn and there's a wooden sign blockin' the way. We have to go west around the delta. The sign says a levee broke."

"We can't use the rafts?"

"They could get stuck in the shallows. We'll have to leave the rafts at the north beach like we planned, but walk west instead of north on the perimeter road."

I take the map from her hand and study it a moment. Somehow it looks like a child's Escher derivative to me but I don't tell her that.

"Okay," I say.

"We're going to have to reorganize our supplies and packs for a longer trek." She looks at me. "You okay?"

"I am." I smile. "Thanks for getting this all worked out, Star. You're doing a great job." Ever the parent. I really don't have a clue.

I decided to go along with the young people several years ago. To follow their lead. They have so much more at stake. At first it was so encouraging, and a relief, to see their "woke" energies. That's what it was called when the changes first began: being "woke." After so many generations of ignorance and self-interest in the U.S. The "me generation" coming of age in the '80s. The angsty self-absorption of "Generation X"—my generation. Of course I sympathize. It was the beginning of the decline when we were young, although everyone pretended otherwise, except for the tattoos and piercings. Then the Millennials— a far more populous version of the same. At first, until they finally noticed what was going on. When the Millennials became engaged in causes, it was almost like the '60s. Except that it wasn't, because of the internet, among other things. And then came Star's generation. A harder, sadder, more determined generation. iGen.

Anyway, you know all that now. I don't want to dwell on it because then the despair begins, and these are hopeful times.

We wake at dawn and begin to finalize our preparations. I can hear crows outside conversing. *Caw Caw Caw.* Call and response. The chortling and clicking. They are as loud as we are quiet in the early morning light that filters through the high windows. The rain has stopped. I'm glad we waited it out. I don't hear the wind; it must have died down. One of the children is crying, but softly as the women comfort him. There are twenty-five of us. Twenty adults and five children, only two of whom are very small. I see Star's flowing dark hair as she moves about getting the dry foods packed.

I risk opening the door and look outside. No one stops me. The sun is out and the wetlands glisten, colorful and alive. One would never guess acres of concrete parking lot and a shopping mall lay beneath. What a joy to see it now. I remember that shopping mall. Decades ago. Walking there with a friend, I felt I needed sunglasses just to get through the glitz. The bright fluorescent lights everywhere the eye traveled. So many dayglo pinks, the glaring white linoleum, chrome the color of tinsel, infinite plastic, hundreds of thousands of items packing every inch of space screaming for attention. Groups of people walked along the glistening white floors in the blinding light surrounded by masses of stuff, talking and minding their business, sometimes laughing, sometimes glum. I was one of the glum ones. It horrified me even then. It was the peak of the glut of goods from China, before the trade wars and the virus. Outside thousands of cars sat in ordered diagonal rows, their shapes muted and colorless in the white-gray sky.

I look out at that expanse now, the old sight visible only in my mind's eye. And then it shifts, to its present form. The tide is high and streams of brackish water ripple through reeds, sedge, bulrush and cattails. The wide sky above is blue. A testament to the undying resilience of the natural world.

But the most blessed element is the silence. Embracing, yet distant; I can expand into it with all of my being. My mind dissolves across the horizon where the palest pink wisps of clouds take my eye. And then I recall that parking lot. Remember leaf blowers? Hahahaha

I realize I'm laughing out loud and stop. And a sadness fills me as it does sometimes when I feel myself dissolving into the ether. And it's at times like this that I really miss Google. Where does that word "ether" come from, and what does it really mean? What would Wikipedia say? Well, to me it means the "isness" of everything, the beyond the beyond. I felt it, after Dale died. It was so obvious he was no longer in his body and, as if he were telling me himself, I realized he was not "up above" but beyond—beyond anywhere we know.

Sometimes I wonder if my despair at the "end of nature" in the last years before the "first pulse," as some call it, wasn't largely fear of my own death, the "end of me," not nature. Nature will never die. Will it become uninhabitable for most plant and animal species on our particular planet? It was heading that way. Until now.

A snowy egret soars by and I watch him recede into the wind. I look out at the wetlands again and rest my eyes in the peaceful expanse. The distant horizon.

Someone comes up quietly behind me and suggests I close the door. It's Millie, the one other woman close to my age in our group. She is kind and unblaming. I don't think

someone sent her over here to get me in line. Of course, I shouldn't be standing here gazing out at the early light with the door wide open. Oh well. No one is perfect. This is my new mantra. My excuse for myself. Because sometimes I feel rather desperate—to do what I want, to ignore the group and the rules and everyone's needs. I'm an American, right? Of course, I'm a mother and know all about putting others' needs first. I remember this as I quietly shut the door and return to an area by the back wall of the shelter. We have somehow all claimed certain spots in this warehouse room as our own. Like members of a club who always end up sitting in the same seats at each meeting, though nothing has been assigned. I think this used to be a Costco. There are still holes in the cement floor where the scaffolds of shelving were riveted. If I close my eyes I can so easily go back to myself wandering these aisles to buy huge packages of toilet paper, and disposable diapers for Star, big bags of cookies and lettuce, all kinds of things. And of course the random impulse purchase. Maybe a gadget for cleaning dog hair off furniture. There are two dogs here.

One of the dogs belongs to Millie. They say dogs look like their owners, and it's true Millie has gray/white hair like her little terrier. But the similarity stops there. The terrier has been a godsend because he's a ratter. His take is already seven and we have only been here five days. The rats are not very fat, not like the ones you used to see hanging from a bird feeder gnawing at the tiny holes where the seeds fell. Remember those?

The other dog is a shepherd mix, a stray that one of the young women found as she was making the trip here. She actually got her into her boat; the dog—we call her Honey—has a limp and a bad bite on her foreleg, probably from a coyote. Maybe a fight?

It was decided the dogs will come with us. Jen, the young woman who found Honey, has said she will make a dray for her if she can't keep up. Of course it will be important to have the dogs to sniff out predators. Though we really don't expect to see too many people. Most have moved far inland. And we have heard that in the interior, "the Heartland," there are still towns and even cities operating as if it were still 2025. Cars! Lights on day and night. Supermarkets and box stores. Though on a diminished scale. There was not a great effort to change in the interior. Only to adapt as minimally as possible. But those adaptations have added up over the decades. There is simply so much less stuff! A lot of it has been swept out to sea and some has been incinerated. Entire towns burnt to the ground. Starting with Paradise, California, decades ago. No one ever commented, to my knowledge, on the irony of its name.

Shanika is motioning for us to gather by the high windows on the south wall. I hear a sudden whoop of excitement. Two teenagers are hovering over some device and apparently have gotten a signal. The first in several days. Shanika insists they look for a weather forecast but they're frantically looking for messages. The withdrawal has been brutal for them, for everyone under fifty. Until a few years ago we still had the internet, for the most part.

And I can't claim immunity. I, too, had become unable to read for ten minutes without interruption. That restlessness of the mind. I even started hearing dings and beeps and whooshes when there were none.

Shanika is actually wresting the device away from the kids. I stand back. I've seen some nasty fights over devices. It looks like a Generation XXV neck chain. I haven't seen one of those in quite awhile. Shanika has it now. And she and Star and Tania are hovering over it. The teens are livid for a second but then seem to get some perspective. Kids are growing up so much faster now. The last year or two are probably the first time most of them have lived without devices. I wonder if they have discovered their own minds and memories. Possibly not. We have, as a species, evolved to incorporate the infinite electronic brain as our own.

Homo Electronicus. I remember when it was "announced" by the academy that our species designation had changed from *Homo Sapiens* to *Homo Electronicus.* They didn't even try to find a Latin word for it---humanity's embodied internet and A.I. How could a dead language describe who we are now?

It was controversial. Many academics refused to accept the change just as they refused to accept "Anthropocene" as the name of our current geological age. And really, now—I agree with the dissenters. The Earth is not defined or governed by Man, by Anthro. It is still for us to adapt or go extinct. The Earth will go on. But I suppose that's understood. Our junk is still everywhere, and that's the point. The fossil record will show man's effects everywhere. Yet the Anthropocene may simply be a very short geological age.

Shanika seems to have connected with an inland weather station that is still standing in the desert, despite the winds. Star looks at me and mouths the word, "Grim." What does that mean, I wonder. Or maybe she said, "Him?" But no—did I mention that the young people refer to others with only the pronouns "they" and "them," which have morphed into "ze" and "zir" in recent years. A change I haven't adapted to. Fortunately, I and my generation can say he, she, him, her, without judgment, for the point here is tolerance.

Shanika is speaking, something about the satellite picture. I move closer and peer at the screen as she holds up the device for us to see. It appears there is a cyclonic cloud formation covering most of the southwestern United States. Heavy rains at the eastern periphery for some 600 miles. It will be sure to wash away more lowlands. Clear skies where we are, but not for long. We need to get into the boats. People start moving. Millie has already put her terrier, Dot, into a carrying sling. And Jen has Honey on a leash. The children are holding the hands of their mothers and caretakers. I quickly go to get my pack.

I have to say, after staring at the satellite image just now of the atmospheric conditions of the U.S. that was created in outer space by A.I.—that it is godlike, to have this knowledge. You can understand the hubris of the Anthropocene. But, I, for one, don't miss computers— "devices." I was so sick of them. I was sick of living in "the world according to engineers." They were always thinking up new "user friendly" hints and gimmicks and complexities that…what? Took over. They took over our brains.

And when the last satellite is defunct, fried by the sun's radiation, there will be no more. I hadn't realized the internet doesn't work by satellites anyway, it's the fiber optic cables stretched across continents and along ocean floors. Star explained this to me, and that, like satellites, they have a shelf life. They are deteriorating and they are not being replaced. It's just a matter of time.

We are gathering by the door and I join in the back of the line. Again we, almost meekly, find our places without direction. I suppose it's by personality. There are those who instinctively go to the front and those who instinctively hover in the middle, and those that fall to the back. Star, of course, is in the front with Shanika, Tania, Chela, Fae, JoJo and Kamala. Jen and Honey, Millie and Dot, the five children and the women caring for them are all in the middle. I am with the handful of women in the rear. I was not, nor probably were any of us, one of those students who sat in the last row of seats in the classroom. And I am eager to get outside! I suppose we are the deferential ones. The people pleasers. Oh no, you first. Go ahead. Smile. Although I wasn't always that way. It's probably age. As I said, let the young people lead.

Star

I can hear Taddie cryin', the youngest kid, Chela's— pickin' up on all our nerves. The day is very clean out there, I can see a horizon. It's gonna be alright.

I turn around to get everyone's attention and I see Mom slinkin' around in the back. What is zir problem! Ze's been like this since The Fail. It's not like it was the first time we fell off the grid and the economy collapsed, but it wasn't global before. And it slammed zir and ze's different now. Ze looks up and smiles at me. Oh god. I nod, turn to the people in front.

"Okay! We're gettin' outta this box. Now we know why they called these things 'box stores.'" People kinda laugh. I'm tryin' to keep it lite.

"Shanika." I look at zir. "You wanna tell 'em the route?"

"Listen up," Shanika calls out cuz kids are makin' noise. The parents get 'em quiet and then ze says: "We're gonna do the rafts. Kelly left them behind this building last night. We'll take them up the tide flow to the old hiway and walk east from there. It's about ten miles so we gotta stay synced. Kelly said ze can meet us there and show us the next shelter."

Shanika gives me a look with a smile, then turns back to our group. "So are we ready for this!?" ze shouts.

Everybody shouts back, "Yes we are!" There are some hoots and whoops and we're all gettin' excited. It's okay. Everybody'll calm down once we gotta wrestle with those rafts. Everybody hefts up their stuff—there's not much of it—and Tania leads the way thru the high wet grass, findin' the least muddy footholds. Of course, after a couple minutes, one of the kids slips and gets soaking wet. Ze doesn't scream or cry tho. We've all been thru too much to cry about little stuff.

The rafts are on some high ground out back tied to a window latch. There's three of 'em, all bright yellow. They're old tho. They coulda come from this very box store. But Kelly found 'em up north at a park station and towed 'em down here for us last night. Ze's such a great person. Ze's only nineteen and knows so much about everything. Gotta say, it's how people grow up so fast now.

Shanika, Tania and I each grab a boat and get it in place so people can board. We gotta have six or seven people to a boat not countin' the kids. One of us will always be outside the boat draggin' it along. It's only gonna be for a mile or so 'til we get to the old hiway and start to walk. Everyone knows where they're supposed to sit, cuz we told them already. We made sure there's a couple people from each group (the front-of-the line types, the middle types, and back-of the-room types) in each boat. Everybody's real cooperative, even the kids.

Tania pulls out first with zir boat. I wish I had those waders. Tania got 'em from zir dad who liked to fish, ze told me when I saw 'em last week. I asked why zir pack was so fat and ze pulled 'em out and showed me. They're high and shiny black and go all the way up to mid-thigh. I've got red rainboots. It's been really hard to find any boots the past years. For one thing there was a lot of scarcity issues after The Fail, almost eight years ago now since that economic crash.

Shanika gets zir boat out next. Ze's got the tow line and drags it up almost next to Tania. The stream is wide here cuz we're close to New Bay. We're maybe 200 feet from where this stream flows into the open water, but you look up ahead and see it narrows pretty quick, like maybe a quarter mile. That's where we're gonna have to really haul these things, maybe two, three people are gonna have to grab the ropes and pull thru the narrow spots. So blessed it's a clean day and the air is pretty dry and anyone who doesn't have good boots can dry out fast enough. We'll all deal with our feet when we get to the hiway.

I pull my boat out next and we're barely movin' forward. Can't tell you how slow we're goin'. Some of us are laughin'. It's like, really? We really think we're ever gonna get anywhere? Shanika looks back and gives me a look, Who're we kiddin'. I shrug. But then Tania looks back at us both with squinty eyes. I see how set ze is, like this is absolutely no joke and ze's right. And that's when I see the snake and there's a lot of shouts and splashin'—thank the powers we all gathered those long sticks cuz JoJo and Caylee in the middle boat put 'em to good use. Somehow they jab at it while a couple people in each boat jump out and help us pull and we're sloshin' and splashin' outta there so fast. So much for pacin' ourselves like we'd planned. Who cares. We gotta get outta here. It was just a little snake about three feet long and probably scared. I'm watchin' the people with sticks real close cuz all we need is a puncture. I don't know how long it took Kelly to get these boats inflated, or maybe they already were, but there's only one repair kit per boat and I am determined to get these boats to the pick-up place at the hiway so they're good for Kelly's next trip. I will not let Kelly down, cuz ze has never let us down.

After about fifteen minutes, when we have slowed down again and are catchin' our breath and people are back in their boats and dryin' themselves as best they can and the kids have calmed down mostly, I tell myself the truth. That was a juvenile sea snake, one of the more aggressive kind, maybe a *Hydrophis ornatus*. So many sea snakes have come up from way south of here, years ago. People see them in the strangest places cuz they are so adaptable, tho they still don't come on land. I look up ahead and see Tania's makin' sure nothing fell out of any of the boats. I nod at zir. It's okay. We've got the first aid kits all high and dry.

I think I see the rise of the land bed where the hiway is about a half-mile ahead. I hope that's it cuz we're comin' up on the narrows. The water's so calm today, that's how we saw the snake as clear as a video shot. I used to love those videos in school. I only had two years left to get my biology degree but I had to drop out right before The Fail, things were already bad and school was a crazy luxury. Mom was so sad I couldn't finish. Ze knew I wanted to be a naturalist like you can't even know.

Oh god, Tania's boat is already stuck. "Hold up!" ze shouts and both Shanika and I plonk down on the front cushion of our boats to slow 'em down. I see Mom up in

Tania's boat tryin' to look around people to see what's up ahead. Ze looks back at me then. Mom always knows when I'm lookin' at zir. Ze gives me a brave smile. I nod, then look behind me. It is blessedly beautiful. We've come up far enough northeast of the "box" that I can see the whole expanse of the wetlands out to New Bay which is maybe the bluest I've ever seen it, it's like dark blue green, and the creek is muddy brown and then gray as it gets wide at the Bay. All of a sudden about thirty or forty birds rise up in the far west, too far to see exactly what they are. What a joy to see so many of 'em. I hear Shanika say something and turn around. Everybody's out of Tania's boat, even the two kids, and they're liftin' it up. Oh no, it's tiltin' pretty bad. Tania's strong tho and hoists it over and straightens it out. I see how they're all single file pretty much cuz the creek is so narrow here. We just have to hope it widens again.

Shanika and her group are out of their boat too now and I start gettin' mine ready to follow. "Make sure the gear is tied down," I say to JoJo, who seems to have the most energy and least fear right now. I'm checkin' the other gear. The only kid in this boat is a ten-year old and ze's doin' fine. Ze clambers over the side and hops knee-deep into the creek, lookin' around. I do a quick, intense scan for snakes.

We're all in line now with the rafts overhead, startin' the slow slog toward the hiway. There's some slippin' and slidin' but mostly we make progress. I'm wonderin' if we're just gonna have to abandon the rafts but I really don't want to. We need to get 'em back to Kelly.

I also wonder if at this rate we're gonna get to the next box shelter before dark. We can hike on dry land in the dark, especially if it's still clear. The moon is waxin' gibbous now and we've been waitin' for that. It should rise just after sunset. It can be as bright as daylight with no ambient light, which there is none of in this part of the Westlands.

Tania and her group lower their boat. Shanika does the same and signals for me to also. We've gotta rest. We're all pretty strong but our upper body strength is not really up to this kinda portage. All our hearts are poundin'.

I shout up to Tania, "What's up ahead?"

"Looks like it might open up in about a hundred yards," ze yells back.

We're all silent as we stand and look around. You wouldn't believe the silence. I hear one of the kid's snufflin' and that's all, and then the distant cry of a bird. That lifts my heart, cuz I believe they're comin' back, I don't know from where. Maybe it's like Noah's ark.

I start thinkin' about before The Fail which I try not to do much, but in my mind it's like twenty plus years ago and I'm a kid sittin' on the couch watchin' tv. Mom's in the kitchen puttin' stuff in the microwave. It's winter and dark outside. Then there's a big FTTTZZ and the tv goes all pixelated— white dots and then black. I'm just sittin' there thinkin' WTF? I hear Mom say, "Oh no," then, "Must be the wind." But it's windy all the time, I'm thinkin'. Mom opens drawers lookin' for something and ze comes up with a flashlight, and then ze finds some candles and et cetera. That was one of the first times with no explanation. It was another year before it became a weekly thing.

We're on the move again and I check my watch and wind it a little, it's 9:45. I'm not sure it's right tho cuz it's kinda wet. After awhile we rest again, and then move on, rest, move on again 'til we get to a place where the creek widens out and we get back in the rafts. I'm gettin' pretty tired, haulin' this boat, liftin' and carryin'. We move so slow. I'm thinkin' maybe we're gonna have to camp on the roadway tonight. I look up at the sky and there's not too many clouds, just some low ones to the north—tho that's where we're headed. My feet feel kinda numb and they must be all wrinkled up. I hear a couple people in Tania's boat argue about something, but then one of 'em gets out and helps Tania and Chela pull on the ropes.

It's after 11:00 a.m. when we get up to the hiway. We all whoop and holler and hug each other, and then regroup. The asphalt is a cracked and potholed mess but it's dry. Everyone has unloaded the rafts and Tania, Shanika and I drag 'em over to the place Kelly told us about. We double check the map about where to tie 'em up, then we do all kindsa double knots and make sure they're secure and then we rejoin the group. Mom and some others have spread out a big towel with the lunch on it and people sit and stand around to eat. We've got dried fish, dried apples, and a lot of grapes. Lots of vineyards are underwater but a lot more aren't and they still produce fruit after all these years, partly cuz some people lived and farmed there 'til recently. So grapes are a crop that grow abundantly and are easy to come by. We filtered a lotta water during our long wait in the box shelter so we're set with that for a few days.

People calm down some now that we're on dry land and have some calories. Everyone starts to heft up their packs and gear, even the kids. At 3:00 we'll stop again to look for a signal. We can use some battery then cuz Kelly said there's power at the next shelter from a windmill and generator they put there last year.

After the fires in the Heartland way back, people built windfarms all over, miles and miles of 'em—and they have power there all the time, I heard. Here in the Westlands we've got solar more than wind and we've got birds comin' west away from the windmills. But who'd've thought, Mom always says, that the Heartland would go green first.

Mom

I don't want Star, or anyone, to know and I don't think it's noticeable. But something happened last night, a small stroke, or? I feel very tippy today, having to catch myself constantly in order not to fall. Luckily no one is asking me to do a lot of lifting or balancing of the rafts or gear. I feel it behind my left eye. And I tip to the left. Just a hint of wooziness. Last night I woke to a sudden "zap" in my brain—that's the only way I can describe it. Like the kind of fzztt sound that happened with an electrical outage in the past. I felt the sudden noise and then a blankness in my head and I woke, my heart pounding. Immediately I sat up and put my arms over my head, smiled, said my name. I remember that from my mother, how to test for a stroke. They taught everyone in her senior home.

It was so dark in the shelter. And there were only the sounds of soft snoring, people sleeping. I lie back down. And as I often do when I wake in the night, I said the prayers I like to say. Soon I was asleep again. But this morning I am so unbalanced. I'm hoping I will find a dry stick somewhere along the roadway. There are still oak trees, though so many died years ago from Sudden Oak Death. I've heard the Glendors are doing a reforestation project at the new snow level of 6,000 feet, going all the way down to the valleys.

I see a small stand of trees ahead. And are those song birds flitting from tree to tree? Star will be thrilled. I glance behind me. She and her group are bringing up the rear. I see her rhythmically scanning the horizons, 360 degrees. There are predators, of course. Human, feline, canine, reptilian. That incident with the sea snake was a bit scary. I don't know, though, if it was one of the more aggressive or venomous ones. I'll have to ask Star. After the rains so many days we were in the shelter, there will be plenty of creatures looking for sunshine and dry land. And food. And open, high ground to get a signal.

Oops! I shouldn't look up and then back down quickly. I had to catch myself noticeably and I do not want to be noticed. I need to focus on the road and the stand of trees— find a walking stick. Star is behind me and if she sees me bobbing around, losing my balance, it will distract her from her focus.

I laugh a little to think of that. We are all so focused now. The age of distraction is behind us. I remember how Star couldn't even read through one page of a book without grabbing her phone, checking for "notifications." All kinds of inane alerts. My brain groans to even contemplate the excess of stimuli. I am thankful every day for the return of nature to human consciousness. Though I may be in the minority for that, or certainly I was in the early years after The Fail.

The incident last night, the short-circuiting in my brain. It felt like something I might have experienced before The Fail. Say, after a day of constant screens—at work, at home, tv, devices, signage, ATMs and car dashboards and control panels on appliances, news feeds and broadcasts on the many televisions in every restaurant and store. Hardly a moment went by without electronic input. And my electrified brain, like an overheated wire back in the days of wires---FZZTT. Spark. Blank. Really, doesn't that say it all? Isn't that what The Fail was? A global short circuit? Of course there were many factors: The preceding outages and cyber-attacks on grids, peak oil, the water shortages, pandemics, extreme weather, climate refugees, governmental crackdowns and collapses. You were there.

I see a small declivity along the roadway beneath the trees and bramble, a trickle of a stream running along. And yes, there, a fallen branch, small but with possibility. I step out of our line to look at it. It will do. I pick it up and break off some of the twigs and leaves, test it. It's sturdy. I can feel a couple of the others watching me. I look up and smile at them.

"A walking stick," I say. It's a novel idea for them. I rejoin the line, resisting the urge to glance back at Star. Later I'll tell her my knee was a little achy, no problem.

I was hoping we might see Kelly at the raft drop off, but no sight of zir. I have to use the young people's pronouns when I talk about Kelly because I truly have no idea what gender ze is. Ze is an attractive person, in the old sense of the word, with flowing dark hair and large amber eyes and the usual mix of clothing people in these parts wear now. Fashion is definitely a thing of the past here. Although I hear people are setting trends in the Heartland. Here, it's whatever castoffs you might come across at the shelters, or at the farmers' markets—where occasionally you can find handmade items if you're so lucky as to be the first there. Gender neutral, one size fits all—though some of the garments are very creative. I prize a knitted, sashed tunic I found a few years ago, made of many colors and gauges of yarn that must have been someone's old stash, or perhaps unraveled scarves or sweaters. I traded my nylon market bag for it! It was a relatively clean and sturdy bag. Nowadays you see quite a few totes and wallets made of woven plastic from old shopping bags that wash up on beaches. A group called the Weavers makes them. Most of those old plastic bags are from before the bans. They're quite valuable because it takes awhile to collect the bags. And of course they never deteriorate—they're all out there somewhere, billions of them. But we can't really retrieve the plastic bags in the landfill. Although sometimes they bubble up out of the dump sites that are underwater now.

And there is more clothing available in the northern valleys, Kelly said, where little farms are still occupied and worked. Ze was up that way last fall during the harvests. So many old vineyards still cover the landscape. What a cash crop that was. It's hard to get the pesticides out of the soil, and the aquifers have not recovered. But Kelly is hopeful.

I love this walking stick! I'm feeling more stable. Remember Pilates? Hahaha. The kids thought it was a word out of the Bible when I mentioned it awhile ago. I call them kids but they're all in their twenties and thirties, except for the little ones. And Millie, of course. I wonder if Pilates has made a comeback in the Heartland. That's where we're headed, you know. After the Capitol. We'll join up with all kinds of others. We are the latest wave of climate refugees. Will they welcome us? That region has such a history of exclusion. A bastion of white patriarchy in the past. The young people can hardly believe some of the news stories I recall from my youth. I don't know if it's really that they don't want to believe them because the Heartland is our best hope now. If we can get over the mountains. I suppose I should be grateful that the snow level is so high now. Nothing like our ancestors faced two centuries ago. I doubt if we'll be munching on each other at Donner Pass. I'm sorry, I don't mean to be morbid, or irreverent. Or ridiculous. And anyway, they say there's a train. Fusion powered. The Italian inventor Andrea Rossi is supposed to have invented the fusion device decades ago. It may just be a rumor, I fear.

I've also heard there are wood-burning steam trains powered by old slash from felled dead trees. They say there is one in the northern Rockies where millions of dead trees are easily harvested. The pine beetle bug epidemic lasted forty years in western Canada, spreading east slowly and inexorably. In our region it was drought that killed so many trees in the mountains and foothills.

As the rumor goes, old steam locomotives from train museums are refurbished and pulling passenger cars from abandoned diesel trains, and light freight too. All headed east. Like a reverse migration of the settlement of the western United States after the first Civil War.

Or I suppose it started a decade earlier than that, with the gold rush in California. You know I have to say, what really shocks me is how little history the young people know. True, a lot of them weren't able to finish their education, like Star. That was a heartbreak. But I think the bigger problem when Star was school-age was twofold. People couldn't read that well anymore, nothing longer than a few hundred words before changing the subject or generally losing attention. And secondly what they call the post-truth era. Every image was digital, and every image was altered. In a sense, it was like reverting to before the photograph when all representations were rendered by artists and accordingly subjective. Not that photographs hadn't always been somewhat subjective. But they were not photoshopped until this century, and the manipulation of the photographic image became relentless before The Fail. Not just oversaturated colors, but people's heads on different people's bodies, that kind of thing. It was impossible to tell what had really happened. At first the journalists reported the false information put forth by whatever hack or corporation or politician, followed by various disclaimers and fact checks, but it became very muddled. Everyone knew to ignore most data by the time of The Fail. How many had died in a chemical explosion? Could be the 179 number reported or 1,000 or 10,000. Remember how some people thought the first moon landing had been staged in a movie studio? There's an old fringe conspiracy theory—the kids probably don't even know about it. But that's what I'm talking about, that kind of doubt became the norm.

There are old rotting, fallen telephone poles—we used to call them that—every few hundred feet along this roadway. Even some shredded wires here and there. I'd heard most of the poles had been scavenged for levees or to shore up the shelters. We may be too far out toward the sea. Not many people venture this far west anymore. When Star and I finally left New Bay after the last king tide flowed so far east last month, we were some of the last holdouts there. Star had already joined the Caretakers—Tania and Shanika's commune. When they decided to leave, we joined them. Tania has been Star's best friend since childhood.

I see Tania has stopped up ahead and has an arm raised, beckoning. Shanika heads to the front of the group. I look back to see Star has stayed in place, still scanning but with an eye on Tania too. The sun is high overhead and hot. Many of the women have stripped down to their underclothing—t-shirts, shorts. Some of the t-shirts are very old and have sayings on them. Sexy kitten. Peace Now. Big John's Brewery. Women's March. SPCA. MAGA. They seem surreal. Whatever you can scavenge, though. I think of World War II and the French countryside. Or the South after Sherman's march. So many abandoned homes, with all the household goods and clothing and artifacts still inside. That's how it was after the first major exodus twenty years ago. I'm sure you heard about the glacier collapse and "first pulse," when the sea came miles inland and we lost all that land here in the north, and even more down south. West Los Angeles was the first to vacate. We stayed in the Bay Area then; we were on the eastern side of the bay at a higher elevation.

Thousands of homes were only partially flooded, but abandoned nonetheless. The scavenging then produced enormous amounts of goods for trade at markets, farther east, set up in parking lots all over the place. There was never a shortage of parking lots in the suburbs. I loved Joni Mitchell. She was my mother's favorite singer. Do you know who I'm talking about? California *California.* It can still bring on the tears.

"What?" I call when I hear Star calling out to me. She's motioning for me to move closer in to join the others. There's an impromptu meeting, it seems.

"Shanika says we've come about five miles from the shelter," she tells me. "We're at the halfway point, blessed be. It's 1:30 so we'll keep goin' 'til 3:00. Then we'll take a break and wait for a signal."

We'll have to be at a higher elevation then, I realize, and it will be slow going as we make the gradual climb. Even now as I look behind us and to the west, we are high enough that I can see all of New Bay. The headland hills rise beyond; and on this side there are miles of marshland and the occasional deteriorating highrise or utility tower sticking out of the water. I think of the underground streets that are rumored to exist in the Heartland, where blizzards can go on for weeks in the winter and rivers flood for miles in the spring. I will miss these shores.

"Yes, okay," I say to Star now who is getting annoyed with me, I can tell. I am not exhibiting the necessary focus and I am sorry for that. I suppose I still feel a bit out of balance, or it may be that I am indulging in recollections and musings. This is not the time for it. I look ahead up the old asphalt roadway. It veers fairly sharply to the right 100 yards ahead where it inclines farther inland. Shanika wants me to walk with Ariel, who is seven years old and getting tired, of course. Although surely the children are used to boredom or minimal stimulation. Long treks. Some deprivation. I'll try to engage her in whatever biodiversity there may be on this route. There were the songbirds a few miles back. Maybe something else will come along. I hope it's not a coyote! More likely a murder of crows. At least most of the invasive pampas grass was inundated years ago and there's very little of it left.

"Hi, Ariel." I smile at her as she joins me. She has a little pink backpack, god knows where she found it, it looks ancient. I reach my hand down and she slips hers into mine. Her long, black hair is shiny. We all were able to wash ourselves and our clothing at the shelter. We used the brackish water of the marsh, but collected enough rain water to lightly rinse ourselves. Our clothing is still damp, of course, though we hung it to dry for days.

"Mom," Ariel says, smiling at me shyly. Everyone calls me Mom, it's my name now. "Are we almost there?"

"Well," I say with a laugh. "Not really, honey. But we'll stop for a nice long break in a little while at the top of a hill." I look at the rivulet by the side of the roadway where dark water continues to run between grasses and mud. "Let's see if we can find any bugs."

"What kinda bugs?" she asks.

"Any kind! Crawling or flying or just sitting."

"I saw bugs in the shelter. A lot."

"Oh yes. I saw them, too. They're called cockroaches—have you heard of them?"

"No, they were really little. A lot of ants."

"Oh, of course, those." The fact is, since my glasses broke, I have a hard time seeing anything so small. I pray that there will be optometrists in the Heartland, not to mention dentists.

"Look at that!" I say with some excitement. It looks like there are blackberry bushes ahead. It's too early for the berries, but I think I see some blossoms. The tall barrier along the other side of the roadway was knocked down long ago and bramble and shrubbery have taken over the concrete there. Ariel and I cross to the left side of the roadway. Remnants of the white painted lines are still visible and the raised yellow reflector lights, though battered and broken, will probably remain even after this road, too, is underwater.

"Oh look!" Ariel cries. My heart stops. There are bees hovering among the white blossoms of the berry bushes. We stop and stare in awe. "JoJo! JoJo!" Ariel calls to her *tia* and she and the others look over to where we're standing. "Bees!" I call to them. A few come running over to look. For the amazing novelty. For the rush of hope. Even Shanika comes over and uses some precious battery power to take a picture of them with her device. Of course, it is important data. But she soon ushers us back to the group and we hurry to catch up. Ariel is buoyed by her discovery and the importance she sees it has and she is now seriously on the lookout for more creatures. And I decide I really must stop all the reverie and pay attention! There is new life. Life goes on. Revel in it! I tell myself. I remember a friend, years ago, saying that even if we humans are going extinct—this was after the influenza epidemic—as well as all the species we have destroyed; the Earth will go on. And I thought, yes, the cockroaches and kudzu and crows may replace all the lush, diverse beauty we knew, but they will still go on and new species will emerge, and new geological ages, until, perhaps, there is an interstellar collision and the Earth will fragment, but its fragments, then, will still orbit some star. Life goes on.

"Mom, what's that?" Ariel points to the marshland beyond the broken concrete on the west side of the road. Again my breath is taken away—the bright red flash of the wing. "A red-winged blackbird," I say. And then I hear their call as three more fly up from the grasses. I lean the walking stick against my side and reach in the cloth bag slung over my shoulder to pull out my pencil and a small notebook. "Let's write them down," I say. And Ariel solemnly nods. Somehow she understands why it is important. And as I begin to record her sighting I myself feel something so unfamiliar, but like a déjà vu. And as I write, I realize what it is. A sense of purpose. A sense that has hope as its underpinning. And I know then how sad I have been.

"Do you want to write the number?" I ask Ariel after I have written the name of the bird. I hand her the notebook and pencil, glancing ahead to see how far we are lagging behind.

Silently and seriously, Ariel takes the pencil and writes the number 4 by the bird's name. Then I take back the book and write, May, 2047. I smile at her. And her smile in return is so pure, I busy myself with putting the notebook away. "Let's catch up with the others!" I hold my walking stick aloft and make a game of hurrying back to the group. Nothing makes me sadder and more fearful than feeling that what I am doing is futile.

"Mom," Star says. She seems to still have rearguard duty. "You gotta keep up."

"I know." I decide to hustle Ariel and myself to the center of the group so we have a little lead time. Ariel is all in now, following me along. I know she must be starting to get blisters like I am with the damp shoes and now we're all perspiring. It must be in the nineties. Or more.

In fact, it takes all our energy to slog up the hill for the last hour to the signal point. Ariel holds my hand and I don't know who is pulling who along. She is such a dear. I love her. And all our group.

The grass is so green as we come up out of the brambles and occasional stands of trees to the higher hills. The same rolling, gentle slopes of all the centuries past. There were never many trees on these hillsides, in my memory. But at this time of year they would have been covered in poppies and lupine, when I was a girl.

We all straggle in and form a circular group as we sit in the grasses. There are groans and moans and some laughter. The earth is dry here and the only towel spread out is for our food. More of the same, of course. The dried fruit and fish. Kelly promised fresh vegetables and tofu, of all things, at the next shelter. The more inland we get, the more resources we will find, ze said.

Ariel sits close, leaning against me. We both look skyward, ready to find more living creatures. There are a few wisps of clouds, and the sky is a soft pale blue. It's been decades since I've seen that bold, bright blue of a glittering summer day. But even so, this pale clean sky feels like a bounteous gift. To my amazement, Ariel points off to the right and as I squint, Shanika, who sees it too, says: "hawk." I get out my notebook. Ariel writes it as I help her with the spelling.

"Is it a redtail?" I ask Shanika.

"Can't tell," she says and then looks down to her device. She's got to be alert for a signal and any word from Kelly, with minimal battery use.

I glance around our band of travelers and it looks almost like a group picnic on a late spring day, decades ago. Or is that a picture in a book, or a picture in my mind? Because really, everyone here has lumpy packs with all their belongings and is dressed only in their worn underwear. Their hair is in braids of some kind, or chopped off, probably with a knife, as my own is. Everyone is barefoot now with their shoes or sandals set out in the sun. For some reason I think of that ridiculous painting by Manet, two Frenchmen fully clothed and a nude woman, seated together in a glade in the woods. And the sadness returns. Or I suppose it's anger.

"Got it," I hear Shanika say. She's studying her device and then reading aloud. Tania is writing it down quickly in her notebook. I'm too far away to hear every word, but from the tone of her voice it sounds like everything is on track. Kelly is already there. The road is clear. Apparently there are some others at the shelter, but it's a huge place, another "box." They are a mixed group, gender-wise. Some children. Familial, cooperative. I find I sigh in relief. I don't know what I'd been expecting.

Star

The dogs start barkin' when we come up on the box. It's in a pasture we see ahead when we crest the last hill. They can smell new people. Little Dot runs out like crazy and then in circles. Ze's funny and we're laughin'. We're happy to get here, that's for sure. We were movin' so slow those last three miles after the signal, I thought the sun would set. But it's only dinner time. I can't wait to eat. Some of the kids start runnin' ahead.

"Hold up!" Tania calls out and they stop.

We gotta regroup and come in together. Kelly said the new people are a good group who call themselves the Potters. The word is they're ceramicists who made dishes and urns from clay soil on the creek bank where they had houses, 'til recently, up in the hills way south of us. There's a lot of mudslides there now. Someone said they used to sell their wares way inland at the markets before the passage flooded out. But Tania said ze heard they were called after Harry Potter, the magical kid from the old children's books. That would be funny. I can't wait to meet 'em!

We gather in a tight group together and remind ourselves of who we are. The Caretakers we call ourselves. We do healthcare and teaching, and care for old people and children, work that still mostly females do. Tania's armed tho as am I and Shanika—just knives. There weren't any guns to be had in New Bay, what's left of it, and those who had 'em couldn't get ammo. And some of us have the sticks—mainly to shove off coyotes or critters, like the snake.

So Tania's in front, and Shanika gathers people in the middle of our group, and I take up the position in back, always lookin' around, lookin' around, I feel like my neck is gonna twist off.

Then Tania shouts, "Kelly!"

I see zir up ahead wavin' at us to come on over and we start walkin' down the hillside toward the box.

Kelly hugs every single one of us as we come on in and ze is smilin' and tells us what a good meal the Potters are makin'. I guess we look more ragged than I thought. Some of us have bloody feet and scratches on our skin. One of the kids cries a little, with relief, I guess. I look at Mom. Ze's holdin' Ariel's hand and has that walking stick in zir other hand.

Kelly knocks a special code on the wood plank of a door at the box. It opens and a big person with a long beard shoves the door aside. Ze holds up a hand in greeting and we all nod and hold up a hand and smile.

It's pretty dark inside the box except in a corner in the back I see candlelight. There's still shelves in this box and people have set up some kinda beds and there's a big plank table. Tania's talkin' to Kelly but the rest of us head over to the lit corner, watchin' for rats and bugs. We don't have any kinda handheld lights. We had an oil lamp but ran out of oil awhile ago.

I'm feelin' so shy and it's pretty odd to have such a feeling, but I guess we haven't seen anyone but each other in so long. We were some of the last to leave as is the case with caretakers.

The person who opened the door picks up a candle and leads us to the back where the Potters and the beds and table are. Some people get up or stop what they're doin' and come over to greet us. I can see they're better off than us. They have some real clothes that look new or specially made. They're clean and none of 'em are too skinny or even all that tired. They smile and they have generous kinda smiles. I can feel us all relax like a collective sigh. Shanika and I move to the front of our group and start makin' introductions.

The Potters have set up a couple benches for us and we seat ourselves around their tables. I count twenty-two of them and we're twenty-five with the kids. Then I see the dishes and not only are they beautiful, they are full of food.

A few of the Potters at a smaller table have mortars and pestles and are grindin' something up. They work fast, like they're used to it. One of 'em might be closer to Mom's age but the others look really young.

Kelly and Tania come up to the tables now and Kelly starts talkin' in zir musical voice. "Welcome to you all! So grateful everyone got here safely. Since no one is badly injured and the Potters made us all this delicious food, we're gonna eat and rest up, and head out tomorrow morning after sunrise." Ze turns to Tania. "This is Tania with the Caretakers and ze says they have first aid for any Potters or Caretakers who need bandaging or medical attention. They're setting up over there." Kelly points about fifty feet away where there's another table with candles and, blessed be, a pump lantern. Two kids are workin' it and laugh a little but they get serious when Tania and JoJo show up. A couple Potters get up right away and head over there. I can see one of 'em has a gash in zir arm.

I sit down with Ariel and Mom and two Potters—they say their names are Catherine and Dix. Dix has boots on, leather boots. Or I think they're leather. And ze's wearin' cut-offs from some old jeans and a good-looking scraps shirt, hand sewn, like a lot of people have now if they can find one. Catherine has similar clothes but no boots, just old running shoes that look like they came from one of the first box lootings back when.

I get a whiff of a big platter of food someone brings to the table. It's hot food! and savory—I can't wait. More people greet us and bring dishes, terra cotta, looks like, very thin and not too heavy. Some are glazed pretty colors.

"Roasted seeds," someone says and I look. You can't believe how good everything smells. I see a bowl of cooked kale with wild onions.

"What's this?" I ask Dix with a smile and point to a plate someone just put down. I can't believe my eyes, it looks like a pancake.

"It's flat bread," Dix says, "from the grains of wild grasses. We collect them." Ze points to some urns back against a wall.

"How do you transport those urns?" I ask.

"Carefully." Ze laughs. "In backpacks packed with grass and blankets and on drays and wagons."

Someone passes a bowl our way, clams on what looks like dried seaweed. I help myself. "This is a feast," I say. Tho I know to be careful cuz I paid a price before for eatin' everything in sight after so little for so long.

"Have any of you been inland?" Mom asks all of a sudden. Ze has an intense look. I know ze's startin' to worry about what we're gonna find as we move on. It's part of why we were some of the last to leave, ze just didn't want to go. I understand. Mom has never lived anywhere else. Those hills in east New Bay were zir home since childhood. Back then, ze said, ze could see miles of land before the bay began and also that famous bridge, the golden bridge, they called it. You can still see the tops of the towers and span at low tide. They're not gold now.

"Dix was last year," Catherine says, cuz Dix's mouth is full. Ze chews a little and nods and we wait.

"Up north of Calistoga Springs," Dix says.

"There's a big need for urns there now," Catherine says. "They're making wine." Ze smiles.

"Their farms are really coming along with the new techniques," Dix says.

Mom's eyes get squinty and focus on Dix. "Like what?" ze asks. Mom was so involved in our garden back in the day. And when New Bay tides came higher and turned peoples' yards all marshy, ze tried to grow rice. Ze might have gotten a real crop growin' if we hadn't decided to leave.

"Trenches and stone terraces to stop erosion," Dix says, "and stop runoff so aquifers refill. They plant grasses like Vetiver that handle drought or floods and hold it all together."

"What crops do they grow?" Mom asks.

"They do intercropping like the Zapotecs in Oaxaca. Fruit trees make a canopy on top, coffee trees under that then small food plants on the ground. The tree leaves fall and make a compost that stops weeds and feeds the soil. They also do a "milpa" system with maize at the top, beans underneath, squash at the bottom."

"Oh, I read about that. Years ago," Mom says. "At Jack London's old estate in Glen Ellen. He learned the techniques when he was traveling in Mexico."

"The Zapotec farmed that way for centuries, but London was ahead of his time up here. The most important thing now, though, is saving seeds."

"We're trading for seeds" Catherine says.

Mom looks so happy. "I've got some!" ze says.

Dix and Catherine look pretty interested. "What kind?"

"Rice, green beans, sunflowers—I'll show you. But I can't carry any pottery, too heavy."

"We have candles," Catherine says.

Both Mom and I are surprised.

"Some of our group are Candlers, too. They use the oil from wax myrtle that grows in the clay soil where we lived."

"The oil?" I ask.

"Yes, they boil the berries and the oil rises."

Another Potter comes up then, or maybe a Candler, and looks right at me and smiles. Really white teeth in a brown face. Ze stands next to Dix and extends zir hand to me and Mom. "Riga," ze says and ze sits down with us. Ze is wiry and strong with skin like maybe from Mexico plus a lotta sun, and black hair with a sheen down to zir shoulders, a little wavy. I guess I'm starin'. I stop. But not before I notice ze's got river green, squinty eyes and is wearin' a deerskin jacket, and that takes me by surprise.

Mom and Dix have regrouped and got Riga into the conversation. Mom starts talkin' about seeds and candles. Ze's makin' a deal. Riga looks interested but then turns to me.

"You're with the Caretakers?" ze asks. I nod.

"I guess we're in the Last Wave," I say. That's what they're callin' people who stayed on the coastal edge all this time 'til we finally became official climate refugees.

"There are a lot of people in the Last Wave, no?" ze says. "I work as a guide for them for three years."

"How far inland have you been?" I ask.

"To Heartland, but not for a few years. Now I only go over the Sierra."

"Like Kit Carson, 200 years later," I say.

"Yes, and in reverse." Ze smiles.

"If there's one thing we've learned," Mom says, ze's been listening to us. "Time really does go backwards. Einstein was right."

Riga laughs and nods zir head. But, like me, ze's too young to have any idea what Mom's talkin' about and I like it that ze's kind.

"Oh, they hated the concept of relativity, in every way," Catherine says and I look at zir. Ze's on Mom's wavelength, I see.

"Well, it is a reverse migration," Dix says.

"And retrieving our natural selves," Catherine says. "RIP, *homo electronicus.*"

"I think not totally," Riga says. "There is tech in Heartland. It's a mix now."

"That's probably good," Catherine says in a friendly way.

"You've been to the Heartland?!" Mom asks. Ze didn't hear that part, I guess, and ze's excited again, zir eyes are squinty and focused on Riga now.

Riga nods. "Three years ago. But even at that time they had all the electricity going again."

"How?" Mom looks doubtful.

"There were prairie fires in Heartland for centuries, no? But with the changes extreme fires came. Maybe you remember the first in 2017?" Riga gives Mom a kinda sharp look, but friendly, too. "Three thousand miles of Oklahoma burned. After many years like that all the ranches were lost. Finally came the end of the cattle industry. Then the children of the ranchers built windfarms. You should see it!" Riga says. Zir eyes get wide and sparkly and ze spreads zir arms way out like ze's gonna give us all a big hug. "It goes on forever. Hundreds and hundreds of miles. All windmills."

Mom and Catherine glance at each other kinda instinctively and I know what they're thinkin'. The birds.

"So sad about the birds, though," Riga says.

"I heard some species are adapting and changing their migration routes," Catherine says.

"And there is something good in Heartland for birds because there is cleaner air," Riga says. "There are only electric cars now and also electric trains. Some day one will go over the mountains. Now we have to burn slash for the locomotives in Mountains and it makes filthy air."

"Every single thing has its pros and cons, it seems," Mom says.

Dix reaches a long arm down the table and brings a plate over. "Amaranth," ze says. "Best protein we've got tonight. If you eat it with the beans together, it's as good as meat."

"Thanks." Riga takes the plate Dix offers. I'm thinkin' these Potters must not be vegans cuz they miss their meat, and then I realize, no, Dix is talkin' to Riga, who is not a Potter.

"I have amaranth seeds, too," Mom says. "And quinoa." Ze turns to look at the back of the box where we have our gear. I can see the woven satchel where ze keeps seeds there on one of the shelves. I'm so glad ze's gonna trade some cuz I couldn't see us startin' a farm in the mountains. I want to go all the way to the Heartland.

I look back at Riga. "Tell me more about the Heartland," I say.

Mom

I wake suddenly and open my eyes to a dusky light and my heart pounding. My eyes close again and the image reappears, tall trees and that howling sound. The boughs of the trees—firs or redwoods—flail wildly like screaming women waving their arms, frantic, and I am terrified. I open my eyes again. The dull gray light is quiet but not reassuring. I try to imagine where I might be. Or recall. I take a deep breath, two or three, and my heart slows and I turn my head and see shapes emerge in the gray. Shelves, like a library with bodies instead of books. And I hear muffled voices and movement and of course I know now, we are in another box on the way inland. I lie still awhile, deciding if I want to rise yet. The bleak inertia I often wake with has settled over me after the shock of the dream image. I try to recall more of the dream but there is only the freakish wind in the forest, and a sense of fear. Then a sharp yipping noise, high pitched—rrak rrak rrak—and a scuffle. I know without looking it is Dot catching a rat. Or maybe barking at one of the Potters. I put my fingers in my ears, but it is a sound not easily blocked out. There is some grring and gruffing and I can tell Dot has sunk her teeth into something. Then I hear Millie's voice and more scruffing and growls. Then it's over.

This scene, which I see clearly in my mind although not in actuality, depresses me. I should be glad if Dot killed a rat, especially if it was eating our limited food supply or was crawling on anyone in their sleep. I should feel heartened so why don't I? And I realize I'm thinking of Callie, our little dog years ago, and when we had to put her down. It was a terribly hard choice because Callie did not have a terminal illness. She was old and could no longer run, nor play fetch, nor see much. She was confused and had arthritis. The list goes on and in the end Dale and I decided the level of care she needed along with the decrease in her quality of life did not "add up".

When I think of it now, euthanizing Callie when the burden of her existence seemed greater than any pleasure she got out of life—well I can almost say the same of myself. I reach down to the floor to feel for my walking stick. It is still there. Although I shouldn't worry; the dizziness has not returned yet. One vet said Callie's illness could primarily be described as neurological. The confusion, the degenerating coordination, even the vision impairment.

Almost everyone is rising now, shuffling about in the near-dark. Voices are getting louder, not bothering with whispers. I see at the other end of the box where the food tables are set up there are candles glowing. It's a beautiful sight, their soft glow. I'm so pleased with the thick, beautiful candles I got from Catherine and Dix in exchange for a portion of seeds. This lifts my spirits. Something of light, not darkness.

Riga, that was the name of the person who joined us toward the end of the evening meal. Star seemed somewhat taken with zir. Can't say I'm sure of Riga's gender, ze is exceptionally androgynous.

It's been quite a while since Star has had an intimate, as far as I know. She takes too much responsibility for me. We are so attuned. We weren't always; her teen years were a nightmare. After Dale died, she and I became very close, like survivors in a life boat. It could have gone either way but, thankfully, we chose to unite. Early on, it seemed miraculous after the problems and estrangements when she was younger. Everything was so chaotic then in the world, though Dale and I clung to our home through all those years; and when he died, Star returned and, I guess I would have to say, replaced him in keeping the home going. The garden, the filtered water from the creek, the exchanges at the transformed farmer's markets—that especially was her job as it had been Dale's. Extroverts excel at bartering, I've found. I suppose Star and I are in the Last Wave because we lived in one of the most temperate climates in this hemisphere. We never needed heating or air-conditioning in order to survive. The winter nights were long without light. I wish I'd known how to make wax myrtle candles. Such a simple thing and wax myrtle is abundant on the coast, still now. We made do with wood fires. There was a bounty of wood from abandoned flooded homes and furniture we hauled out and dried. I hate to think how toxic some of it might have been. When the water table rose—the groundwater in aquifers miles inland from the sea, and welled up through the earth, leaching through basement walls, flooding out of backed up toilets; then the toxins really poured in. Sewage pipes became corroded from salt water rising beneath water tables, creating an ungodly sludge that gushed up through manholes. But the worst were the chemical toxins, benzine and chloride and all kinds of lethal substances buried in the soil that surged in with the groundwater. That's when people gave up. They left in droves.

This Riga, I gather ze is a Guide and has even been to the Heartland, although ze mostly takes people over the mountains, the Sierras and then, I guess, the Rockies. But if there are trains, why are ground guides needed? I wonder how reliable these trains are. The flailing trees appear in my mind. I try to grasp the image, the inevitable broken branches—on the tracks?

"Mom?" Star is standing above me and I open my eyes and smile at her. "Don't you want something to eat before we leave?"

"Oh," I say and nod as I turn and lift myself a bit stiffly to get off the makeshift bunk bed.

"Better hurry," she says. "It's almost gone."

Hurry, I laugh. Impossible. She's headed back toward the tables now. I find my walking stick and am happy to realize that bending over to pick it up and standing up quickly has no ill effect. The dizziness is gone. I even wonder if I imagined it. Nonetheless I pick up the stick and lay it on the shelf-bed, then take a minute to run my hands along my toga to smooth it out and find my shoes. I take a cloth from my kit and wipe my face and hands a bit roughly to clean them and run my fingers through my hair. Hopefully there will be time for more grooming later. I make my way across the immense concrete slab that is the foundation of the box.

I see Star coming back my way and she has something, one of the pretty Potter bowls of a remarkable greenish glaze. I wonder if she's bartered for it, but no, it has some red berries—wild strawberries—and grains and seeds. There is a plastic spoon from days gone by and she hands all this to me for which I feel immeasurably grateful.

"Thank you, Star." I put the waking stick under my arm and enjoy this wonderful feast standing where I am as she returns to the food area and joins the others in cleaning and packing up. I see Riga at her side briefly and some words and even laughter pass between them. This also makes me immeasurably happy. Kindness and laughter, the greatest gifts in these times, or perhaps, at my age.

My guess is that Riga was in the war. The deerskin jacket, or something in zir manner. And I saw Riga showing Kelly what looked like a very detailed map, far better than the one our group has been using. Probably an old military map. If so, ze must be over thirty. I will ask Star. I look at

Riga a moment. Ze is neither handsome nor pretty, but intensely attractive. Sexy, I suppose.

I'm quick to return the bowl and get back to my gear to get ready for the trek. Today we are headed due east along another old highway to a town that is mostly underwater but we are hoping for an abandoned box store up on the highway as we approach. I hope it's half as good as this one we are leaving now with its particle board tables and beds made from the original shelves by previous refugees.

Kelly and Riga are pulling open the huge doors and light floods in. It must be well after sunrise. There is dust in the shafts of light and I see how pitted and stained the concrete floor is as it becomes brightly illuminated. Perhaps salt water reached here too some winters in the storm surges. Yes. It's time to leave, to go inland. Past time many would say.

After our seed and candles exchange last night, Catherine told me she'd heard rumors that inland people thought we refugees in the Last Wave were fringe lefties, vegans, "hippies". I was surprised to hear these words from the past. My mother was something of a hippie, or so she said. And I saw pictures—one comes to my mind so vividly, and I laugh. She was wearing a deerskin jacket! Fringed, and a leather Crocodile Dundee hat with feathers and bells, a long purple skirt and waist-long blonde hair. Pretty. Laughing.

"Mom!" Star is calling me from the doorway. People are checking and hoisting gear and packs onto their backs. And I see Riga and Kelly already outside, far up on the highway embankment, looking around. Suddenly I realize Riga probably has a gun. And I'm relieved.

Star is making a face at me as I nod and grin at her— yes I'm alert and ready to roll. I bend to my gear. Her face said so much—worry, exasperation, incredulity. Honestly, I owe it to her to cut out the reveries and project more competence. I double check my pack and put it on, take up my walking stick and move purposefully ahead to join the other stragglers falling into place. Shanika and Tania, I see, have also scrambled up the highway embankment, taking the short cut. The rest of us head to the onramp we came down last night 100 yards to the south. I see Star lope ahead to climb the embankment with the others as well as two of the Potters I have not yet met.

As I come out into the sunlight I realize I need my hat and will grab it from my pack the minute I have a chance. I peer into the glare and see Catherine not too far ahead walking with Dix. She turns and is scanning behind her when she spots me and beckons for me to come and join them. She puts her hand on Dix's arm and they wait a moment for me to power walk toward them, clacking my walking stick along the rubbled asphalt parking lot, careful not to stumble on the many protrusions of tufted and bushy grasses. I am so grateful for this warm, sunny day, not too hot yet. The little blue and purple buds of the wildflowers in the grasses are just starting to open and I see bright orange poppies on the green hillside beyond the highway. A beautiful day for a hike. Again I feel so grateful for the protection of Kelly, Shanika, Tania and Riga.

Dix and Catherine separate as I approach and make room for me between them, which touches me. All this protection. Such a new and blessed feeling after so many years on our own. Well not really on our own, the few neighbors who stayed—we did many things together. We were a small community until the very last days. Until Star insisted we join this exodus.

Catherine, Dix and I are silent as we hike up the onramp with our heavy packs. I wonder now, about the older couple down our street who chose to stay on even though almost everyone else has migrated east by now. My guess is that they have chosen to die there. I'm comforted to think they will have an enormous supply of food from our community gardens, now abandoned but sure to produce until next winter.

"Riga seems quite taken with your daughter. Star, is it?" Dix says to me. We are on the flat of the highway for a stretch. He takes me by surprise. Perhaps he is concerned for her and, in fact, he's giving voice to my own observation, which he probably knows.

But even so, I say, "Do you think so?" and look up at him trying to read the expression on his face. He is wearing a hat, like a Fedora only with a broader brim and made of dense woven straw. I wonder if he got it from the Weavers. He remains silent and I can't see his eyes in the shade of the broad brim but his thin lips have a neutral, relaxed composure. I suppose he's just curious. "You're probably right," I add.

"Riga has quite a reputation," Catherine says. I startle at this and look at her. I assume Dix and Catherine are husband and wife, long-term spouses. I would say they are in their 50s. Closer to my generation than Star's.

"Good or bad?" I laugh.

Catherine laughs, too. "Just interesting. Brave and competent. Ze was in the war."

"I thought so."

We're trudging along at a decent pace. My walking stick goes click...click...on the hard asphalt as we pick our way through the cracks and weeds. Our shadows are long. Dix so tall, Catherine also tall but rounded, like an hourglass, and me, the shortest and thinnest by far.

"So ze was with the Reformers?" I realize I'm holding my breath, praying ze wasn't on the other side.

"Yes, ze must have been. Leaders in the Guardians were generally white."

"Ze must have been so young at the time, too. There were so many young people." My eyes fill with tears. I haven't thought of the war, intentionally, in so long.

"Late teens, probably," Dix says.

"You didn't..." I begin.

"No, no," Catherine answers. "We're pacifists."

I nod. "I suppose I am, too, although I was too old, in any case, and Star was too young; though she wanted to join."

"So many were lost I still can hardly fathom, but..." Catherine looks around as if to say, who expected any of this.

I nod as does Dix, but I also think—didn't we? I suppose only the worst-case-scenario types; but then, I am one of those. And of course, by the time of the war, the cascading disaster had become obvious.

"Where did you hear about Riga before?" I ask them

"At a market up north. We had our wares and were trading with some Weavers," Catherine says. Ah, I think—Dix's hat. "We started talking about emigrating. This was about a year ago."

"One of the Weaver's showed us a map," Dix says. "It was incredibly detailed and appeared to have the most recent flood boundaries and tide lines of the entire western coast. It had the new Capitol, and the outlines of New Bay and the Delta Lakes...anyway, I asked where she got it. She said a Guide had allowed her to copy it for a large trade of baskets and clothing just a week earlier. She assumed the Guide was going on an expedition, and the Guide's name was Riga."

"Then one of the Orchardists from the hills selling fruit next to us—he was probably in his '80s—said, 'Riga?' He'd been listening to us," Catherine says. "And we all looked at him. He said he knew a young Guide named Riga who was a war hero."

I think of the old Orchardists in the hills and how I'd believed they were Guardians during the war. Though he may have been a small organic farmer, not one of the large landowners. I look at the ground as I plonk my stick down step by step.

"Did he say more?" I ask.

"He himself had fought in the Gulf War. Or was it the Iraq War?" Catherine turns to Dix.

"The Gulf War, I think."

"Was he the person who told you people still on the coast were lunatic fringe and hippies?" I ask Catherine.

She nods. "In fact, I think he was."

Again I watch my stick hit the ground, plonk, plonk, plonk.

"You know veterans like a war hero no matter what side they're on," Dix says.

"Really?"

"I suppose he's not such a reliable source," Catherine says now. "But I was so surprised to actually meet a Guide named Riga last night and I remembered that day at the market. I think the Orchardist said Riga had saved a large party of people on a trek through the mountains. They had come down from the Sierra into the Valley the first winter of the war. I think we were even still calling it the Central Valley then. It was 2029, right after the Wall came down."

"They must have been coastal refugees coming up from Mexico and then north through the Sierra," Dix says.

"That would certainly be Reformists then," I say.

I'm so caught up in this discussion and watching the ground and my walking stick that I come up short when the whole group slows and then halts. Then there is some back-stepping and as a mass we all walk backwards a few steps, and for a moment I wonder if we are all going to turn and run but we stop again. I hear some loud voices toward the front of the group fifty yards ahead. And now everyone is drawing in closer to the center as Kelly and Shanika walk quickly along each side of the group to the back, herding us closer in while scanning the hills on each side of the highway. I look at the hills to the east. Green, bare, orange poppies and an occasional spot of blue—lupine? I wonder. I've seen so little of it in recent years. Then I quickly look to the west but there are only more empty rolling hills.

"People on horseback," Dix says. He's tall enough to see over the group ahead. We are about fifty with the Potters.

I can only think we truly are walking through the last frontier, our fringe of still habitable coastal land. Horses can ford streams that electric cars cannot. Gas cars haven't existed here for years, of course. And electricity is scarce. And so. Are these riders predatory? My heart is beating double-time but that is not reliable evidence. I put a hand up to cup my ear to try hard to hear as Dix raises his chin and peers ahead. Now that I know they're there, I can hear the snorting and hoof scrapes of a skittish horse. The human voices seem to be calmer.

"Rangers," Dix says. Catherine and I look up at him, alarmed. There are a variety of Rangers, some helpful and some predatory.

"What color clothes?" Catherine asks.

"Dark blue tabards, I think. I can't see much."

"Are they Fire Rangers," Catherine asks.

"Maybe." Dix nods.

I pray that it's true and the calm that seems to come over our group is a possible confirmation. The Fire Rangers ride up and down the West, examining new plant growth, wild grasses, brush and shrubs, to make predictions for the fire season. It makes sense that in May they are here near the coast, surveying spring growth and who still lives here. In the month before the long fire season they evacuate people living in harm's way. Those that are willing to leave, that is. No agency or forces have tried to extinguish western wildfires since the war.

"How many are there?" I ask. I hear more voices join the talk and horse hooves clopping and then going still.

"Seven or eight," Dix says. "They're dismounting."

"Mom!" I see Star power-walking toward me along the ruined asphalt. "We're takin' a break here. Tell the people around you we can sit down right here and get some nutrition, too."

"Okay."

Dix and Catherine hear her and move to talk with other Potters as I look around for the women and children in our group. I walk among the clusters of people as Millie and Dot, Chela and her little child Taddie join me along with a few others. We set up a picnic of sorts with Catherine, Dix and some of the Potters. As people sit and find the old military canteens of mint tea and the fried wild grain bread in their kits, I stay standing and see that Star is power-walking back to the front where she joins Tania, Shanika, the Rangers, and most particularly, Riga. Kelly stays in the rear scanning, scanning, scanning. The hills, the highway, the ravine down the highway embankment. After a moment, Dix joins zir. His height certainly suits him to the job. My guess is he will be joining Kelly from now on to assist on this trek. I suppose Dix is nearly a foot taller than most of us.

I turn back and watch Star. I'm envious of all the news she will hear and hope to pry it out of her once we reach the next shelter, wherever it may be. I see something glinting in the sun as one of the Rangers takes an object from a backpack and hands it to Tania. Something metal, but it looks too small to be a gun. Tania gives zir a woven tule basket. Oh dear. I feel a little sad. I loved that basket. Star traded it to Tania for a sleeveless tunic just days ago, no doubt a wise move, but... I wonder what the shiny object possibly could be. And then I'm caught by a movement between Star and Riga, some private exchange—a look and a hand on an arm. I look at the ground and seat myself with the aid of my walking stick.

Our break turns out to be brief. Twenty minutes? I look at my watch. It's been losing time, but I would still guess it's near midday. Possibly 11:30 PST? I laugh at trying to be so precise.

"What's funny?" Catherine asks as we gather our gear.

"Oh." I shrug. "My watch." She looks perplexed and I hold my forearm up. "Checking the time," I say. She laughs. Then she glances over to Kelly and Dix standing several yards away, their backs to us, scanning.

"I think I'll see what's up," she says to me and heads over to join Dix. For the second time I feel some envy for those "in the know." They're all getting the scoop while I'm plodding along with this stick. I see Millie at the edge of the road, waiting for Dot to finish her rituals.

Plonk, plonk, plonk. I watch my stick, as I avoid the clumps of weeds and rubbled cracks. My mind can't help but go to Star and Riga. A development I did not foresee, but then—foresight ...come on. I laugh. As if anyone can predict anything now. Telling time is far less an absurd idea. But this Riga. Who is he? Okay, I guess I think he's male. But I could be so wrong. He's not very tall, but then—if he is from the southern hemisphere, or indigenous to here, he would be of average height. He is wiry and I cannot make out any breasts. But in a tunic, and his body type, he could well be female. Long or short hair has no connotation whatsoever. If anything it's more an indicator of what people find more onerous—washing long hair or finding a way to regularly cut it off. And of course, there's an element of vanity to that choice. But these are Westland choices. I've heard there are plenty of hair salons in the Heartland and even the Mountains, and probably the Capitol. I hope so. Though Star has done a good job cutting my hair, as far as I can tell. What my mother would call a pixie cut. A gray-blonde that I would never bother to dye as my mother did hers.

Well, Riga, whoever ze is. Perhaps a good match for Star. She was so unpredictable as a teenager. Determined to join the Reformers in the war. It was Tania who finally persuaded her to stay in school, convincing her she would be of more value to society as a bioeconomist. Climate scientists were in such high demand then. Predicting what would be underwater could be very lucrative. There were so many start-ups modeling flood zones. People were always looking to turn a profit back then. Even on "black swan" disasters—catastrophes so rare they were totally unforeseen. But Star was not yet born in 2014, the beginning of the "unforeseen" increase in natural disasters, double what they'd been in past centuries and each one more devastating than the last. The wildfires in the west. Hurricanes in the east. Billions of dollars in damage, growing so exponentially that when Star was in school everyone was studying bioeconomics. She chose an emphasis in botany, and Tania somehow convinced her that was more important. How I don't know. There were plenty of degrowth activists in the Reformers. And The Fail proved them right.

I tip a bit when my stick catches on a bright green clump of weeds coming through the asphalt. I catch myself and realize my balance has been fine since that strange dream of an electrical outage in my brain the other night. Oh well. My imagination playing tricks, although I need this walking stick and I'm glad I found it. It's surprising how hard it is to navigate a ruined highway.

I've wondered if Star blames me as the real culprit who kept her from fighting in the war. Had the Reformers won, I doubt it would have prevented The Fail. Most people I knew at the time believed the war contributed to The Fail. Star and I don't discuss it.

Riga must have a tremendous appeal to her. If it's true that ze was protecting bands of refugees, bringing them through the Sierra. I've heard the Mountains region has the largest population of people from the southern countries. The Weavers are in the Mountains now, and so are the Glendors. But the Glendors were Reformers in the war. Some of those very same degrowth activists. They had even started a school teaching bioeconomics with a focus on Georgescu-Roegen, and Star planned to study there. I don't think it still exists.

It's like we entered a Dark Age after the war. Yes, I do hear news on what remains of the internet on the rare occasion there is a signal, and people pass along the stories. But who can believe any of it! We couldn't even believe it when Star was a baby. And now, thirty years later, it's all "fake news" I assume. Anyway, I prefer first-hand, or second-hand or even third-hand eyewitness reports. I imagine Riga has a lot to tell.

Star

"Did you see Riga's map?" Tania's standin' right next to me all of a sudden. Ze's run up from the back of the group.

"Yeah," I say. I know people are thinkin' the map is wrong. It shows the town we're comin' up on completely underwater which would be very bad news. No one wants to believe it cuz then whatta we do? Tho I'm thinkin' maybe there's a box outside of town here up at a higher elevation, somewhere along this hiway. That used to be how it was, you'd see the box stores at the offramp so people could drive right into the parking lot from the freeway. Except this isn't a freeway we're walkin' on, exactly. I look out to the west and it's all water and some rubble and dirt along the edge tryin' to become wetlands. There's some vernal pool grasses like hairgrass and foxtail. The old wetlands are sixty feet under. Or forty or a hundred, nobody knows, but Riga's map is supposed to be the most recent and I believe it.

Riga has a telescope and ze's lookin' thru it to the northwest. The sun is still high and I'd say it's probably about five o'clock, maybe six. My watch stopped again. I look around behind me. Tania's lookin' at zir phone but I can see ze can't find a signal. Mom is way in the back with Catherine and Dix, looks like.

Riga looks at me all of a sudden and flashes a big grin. I can't help but kinda light up and I walk toward zir. "What's up?"

"A house," ze says.

Ze holds out the telescope as I come up and I take it and point it in the direction ze was and focus it. I scan around and just see a kinda knoll and some trees…and then I see it! Under a few very tall coast redwoods—a gray, square shape.

I give back the telescope and look at Riga, I know ze can see the question in my eyes. Who knows who's in there.

"I'm going up there to see what is the story. Can you ask people to go down there and rest and eat some food." Ze points eastward down the embankment of the hiway and I see ze wants us to be out of sight and protected, in case.

"Okay." I, for one, totally believe in Riga, and Tania seems okay with zir. But Millie said Riga looks like a gypsy and I don't know if that's good or bad in zir eyes. There's always problems when someone new comes in and takes charge. But Kelly and Tania and Shanika and I want to let Riga lead. Ze has the map and compared to ours it's like a GPS. And Riga's a good person, I really feel that. Tho Tania says that's cuz I'm in love. Tania's crazy. I laugh.

"What's funny?" Riga's watchin' me while I'm lookin' at the side of the road and around at the group, thinkin' of how to get everyone down the embankment, and also thinkin' about zir.

I shake it off and smile. "Tania!" I yell out and wave for zir to join us. "Bring Shanika!" Kelly's still doin' rear guard duty and ze'll go along with whatever we decide. I feel like Kelly is so happy to pass on the job of leadin' us all with that crazy map we had.

We all get on the same page and Riga heads up the hill. Tania, Shanika and I spread out and start gettin' people to slow down and head down the embankment to a grassy area below. There's some slippin' and slidin' but everybody gets down there. People are too tired to get worked up about anything, and they see Riga head off like ze knows what's up, so they feel secure something's gettin' done about the situation. The situation bein' that we're in the middle of nowhere on a new coastline that's uncharted, more or less, with nowhere to go and not a lot of food and no idea of who will come along, "friend or foe" as Millie keeps sayin'.

Tania and I sit up on the incline where we can keep an eye on Riga to the northwest and the group behind us down the slope. Some people are layin' down and some get out some food.

Tania reaches in zir pack and takes out the compass ze got from the Fire Rangers. It's a good looking thing. "I love it!" I say and reach for it. Ze lets me take it and play around with it. It's like something from a museum and it probably is. A lot of stuff from museums is more useful to us now cuz it isn't electric and doesn't need a signal.

I find due North, then northwest ahead of us, and see Riga's a tiny figure now on the hillside. Ze seems kinda vulnerable. And then I hear a shot. Riga dives down for cover. Everybody panics and Shanika and Tania and I all shout—"Stay down. Stay down"—and people lay flat against the grass. The kids are cryin' and the little dog, Dot, is yappin' out of zir mind. I see Riga doin' a belly crawl toward some bushes, then a couple seconds later ze's got a white cloth and is wavin' it up high.

"Where'd that come from?" Tania says to me and I shrug. I have no idea what kinda weapons they have, museum rifles or crazy state-of-the art grenade launchers. I'm sweatin' and prayin' for Riga, and I pray that whoever fired that shot doesn't have a lot of military stuff to spot us down here and start a massacre. You just don't know. Maybe it's just one lone scared soul up there.

Then we see Riga stand up still wavin' the white cloth as ze heads up the hill. Everyone's gone silent in the group. A few of the curious edge their way up to where Tania and I are to see what's goin' on.

And then someone starts down the hill toward Riga. I can't see if ze has a gun raised or not. And then they're both standin' there talkin'. I admit it, I start to cry. Tania gives me a funny look, sympathetic and you're crazy at the same time. After another minute or two, Riga waves both arms at me, or us I guess, a big beckoning motion. Everyone up here on the high part of the embankment sees it and they cheer. We all turn around and start gettin' our stuff. But some are reluctant, cuz they just don't want to follow Riga. I hear someone say, "What if it's a trap," and stuff like that. At this point I'm feelin', then just stay here and take your chances, but I can't really say that. I see Mom lookin' at me with a kinda question in zir eyes.

"Tania," I say. "Can you and Shanika get everybody to come on? I'm goin' up now." And I turn to head across the road and up the hill. We both know someone's got to get up there right now or things could reach a stupid impasse. I glance back again and see Mom clompin' along with zir stick as fast as ze can. Ze's gonna come with me. I slow down a little so ze can catch up. And then Dix and Catherine are comin' along with Mom. And Millie and Dot. And the momentum shifts a little, so I hurry on ahead.

I'm the first to reach Riga and the person ze's talkin' to, but most of the Caretakers are right behind me and the Potters too. Kelly is still in the far back, bless zir.

It's a tall person with a beard by Riga and ze has a rifle, pointin' at the ground now. Ze nods at us as we approach.

Riga gives me a knock-out smile as I come up and stand beside zir. "Star, this is O'Leary," Riga says. We shake hands. O'Leary looks over my shoulder and ze is truly leery. Ze doesn't like the look of fifty people comin' up the hill, I can tell.

"O'Leary and some other Tinkers are living there in the Muir House," Riga says. "Ze says we can shelter there until the ferry comes to take us across Valley Sea." I can actually hear some relief in Riga's voice, tough as ze is.

"The Muir House," Mom says. Ze's next to me now. "John Muir's House?"

O'Leary nods yes. Ze is probably only a little younger than Mom. I've heard of the Tinkers, they're from up north near what's left of the redwoods up there.

"What're you all doin' down this way?" I ask O'Leary.

Riga shoots me a warning look and answers instead, "The Fire Rangers evacuated them and a few decided to come this way, no?" O'Leary nods zir head again. Ze is not a happy person.

We've started the trudge up the hill. People are quiet cuz it takes all our breath to get up the incline, tho Mom says to me, "I've always wanted to see the Muir House." I look at zir to see if ze's jokin' around and ze is not.

"What is it? What does it have to do with John Muir?" I ask.

"It was his house. I'm sorry I never took you there. It was built in the 1880s. They made it a National Monument; that's probably why it's still here."

"The feds maintained it until The Fail," O'Leary says to our surprise. "Then the Muiristas took it over."

Muiristas? Mom and I look at each other. Does ze mean old-style environmentalists? Or what? I'll ask Riga. I'm startin' to get how out of touch we've been in New Bay.

"Where are the Muiristas now?" Mom asks.

Riga's up ahead, movin' faster than us, lookin' all around.

"They probably left after the third sea pulse—maybe thought they'd be the next to go under. But this place is pretty high. I reckon it'll be here a while longer." O'Leary shrugs.

I'm startin' to like O'Leary. Ze seems friendly even, to Mom anyway. Maybe ze's glad for a new face. I sure am— new people, news—Hallelujah! I feel kinda happy.

We can see the house now and, I gotta say, it's beautiful, even with the old palm trees. It's big with two stories, tho nothing like a box and I look behind at our crowd of people comin' up the hill. We'll just have to pack in if the Tinkers'll let us. Three of 'em are standin' on the porch starin' at us as we get near. They're all younger than O'Leary and none too friendly at all. They all have rifles. I don't see any rocket launchers tho, just some tough, tired people, probably really mad about gettin' evacuated. We all stand back and let O'Leary go on ahead and up the wooden steps to the porch.

"These folks are passing thru," ze tells 'em. "They're gonna stay here until the next boat." They don't say a thing. That's when I realize O'Leary is their father or something like that. They're a family, anyway, and ze is the oldest and in charge, that's what's clear.

So I relax a little and look around. It's gorgeous. The sky is blue and the grass very green, ryegrass, looks like, and there's orchards south of the house with fruit on the trees. I see Mom lookin' at it like ze's seen an angel, and our group of travelers starts talkin' among ourselves, real quiet and respectful.

Riga climbs up the porch to where O'Leary is and calls out to our crowd, "These kind people will share this house while we wait for the ferry. Let's find a place for our gear and where we will sleep tonight. We can camp there in the meadow." Ze points to the grassy slope between the house and the orchards and ze glances at O'Leary, like, "Okay?" and O'Leary nods. And the fact is, these Tinkers don't own this place. They just got here first, like probably yesterday, since the Fire Rangers just came thru here. Riga's good. Ze knows how to play it.

So the Tinkers go about their business and we all start millin' around. The mood is a whole lot lighter. One of the Tinkers who O'Leary called Alice has a towel in zir hand and goes back in the house. I climb the porch stairs and follow zir. Ze's one of O'Leary's kids, I figure, probably assigned to kitchen duty. Yep. There ze is in the kitchen. It's like a museum with an old iron stove they got workin' again. Tinkers are great at fixin' things, of course. Alice takes a steaming brass kettle off the stovetop, and then ze turns to me. "Want some tea?" Ze smiles. Blessed be. I smile back. "Sure. Please." I continue lookin' around and see there's big wooden crates of apricots, oranges, lemons and bunches of grapes, and some nuts and seeds in bowls.

Alice hands me a cup of mint tea. "When did you get here?" I ask.

"Two days ago," ze answers. "The Rangers said the fires have already started in the hills up north."

"How'd you find this place?"

"They had a map and they led us here. They just left this morning going on down south."

"Yeah, we ran into them on the roadway."

"Are you waiting for the boat?" ze asks me.

"Yeah. You heard anything about it?"

"The Rangers said it'll probably be here the day after tomorrow. That's when it's due. But we're staying here." Ze looks at me, kinda defiant, seems like.

"Okay," I say. "Where's the rest of your group? Did most the Tinkers stay north?"

"Some of them did but our family decided to head south for the boat, but...." ze looks around, "we like this place. We're going to fix it up some more and make it a hotel, for people coming for the boat. We can trade for coin if people are coming from the east."

"What?" I'm kinda amazed at their plans. New Bay is less than a mile west and it's comin' this way, no doubt about it. At least we believe that and that's why we left our home. We've watched it rise and rise and rise for twenty-five years.

"What do you mean 'coin'?" I ask.

"The Heartland Coin. Dad said it's good in Mountains now, too. Haven't you seen it?"

I shake my head. "What's it look like?"

Ze makes a circle with zir fingers about the size of a walnut. "Some are gold and they're stamped with the shape of Heartland. I've seen more that are silver, though. Those have a wind turbine on the front and a picture of the Earth on the back."

I feel a kind of wonder. "Is it some kind of international currency?" I ask.

Alice shrugs and then admits ze's only seen a couple silvers and not the gold coin, ze just heard about that. Zir dad's a famous Tinker, sounds like, and people from the north bring all kindsa stuff to get fixed. Ze says zir dad showed zir the silver coins once. They're not much good here in the Westlands. I guess, cuz we barter mostly.

"How're you all going to pay for the ferry?" ze asks me.

"Oh." I gotta say I've just been goin' day to day, tryin' to get this far. I don't know. "We have some wares and…what do they want?" Was I thinkin' it would be free? Yeah, I guess so, cuz where I come from, in our community everybody shared things, and only special things got traded. There weren't that many of us the last years.

"Dad said we'll charge in silver coin when we run this hotel. Maybe the ferry's the same."

I look at zir. Is ze just braggin' to me? I can see now ze's young, maybe twenty? Ze's friendly, tho, and seems sweet.

"There you are." Riga comes in the kitchen. "Hello," ze says to Alice, and Alice smiles. Ze's pretty.

"I'm Riga."

"Alice."

"I'm Star." I smile at Alice.

Riga looks at me. "I want to show you something."

I set my teacup in the sink. "Thanks for this!" I tell Alice. Ze seems sad we're gonna leave. But we've got days to talk more, seems like, if the boat's not comin' soon.

Riga goes to the front of the house and up some steep wood stairs. I look in the old rooms as we go by, they're full of antique furniture that still seems in pretty good shape. I guess the Muiristas kept it all up. I heard of them, I remember, years ago, they're like descendants from the old Earth First militants.

"Look at this," Riga says and takes my hand. We go up lots more stairs and then we're high up in a little room on the roof, like a cupola.

"It's a widow's walk, I think," Riga says.

I look around, there's windows on all sides. We can see forever. I look at Riga, our eyes lit up, this is glorious! Blessed be.

Riga points to the northwest. "That's where New Bay meets the Delta Lakes now. It seems about a quarter mile away, no?"

I'm lookin' west at New Bay where diamonds glitter on the water in a path to the sun and I turn a little to see what Riga sees. There's a narrow strait that goes into the lakes. Ze takes my hand and we turn and walk to the opposite side of the cupola.

"Ooh!"

"The Valley Sea," Riga says.

There it is, beyond a ridge of green hills, maybe a mile east. Blue water as far as I can see. And blue sky above— something flyin'…a thousand birds.

I look at Riga and then we kiss with a kinda crazy joy, and my head is full of light. I don't know this feeling, like I'm breakin' apart and we're on fire.

Mom

I haven't seen Star since we got here. I think she's off with Riga somewhere. That didn't take long. They seem so in love already, like there's no tomorrow. I laugh. Well.

This house is wonderful. Once everyone tramped around looking at everything they all went outside to see the orchards and gardens and what's available for dinner, except I think the girl, Alice, is still in the kitchen. She's the only girl with the three brothers and their father, the patriarch. They're an old school bunch, it seems, and I imagine the oldest brother was a Guardian in the war. And maybe the father, Sean O'Leary. They've gone out hunting, two of the brothers.

I wander alone upstairs in the dusky rooms and find a lovely antique chair by a window and sit with a great sigh of relief. I didn't realize how much I've been missing solitude. To be in a room, in a house, totally alone. What a gift. I part the lace curtain to look at the grounds below, people are wandering far and wide, feeling the safety of having armed men in charge. Temporarily in charge, I hope. There will be a meeting tonight after sunset to discuss and plan. I'm hoping the O'Learys have more information about the boat. Someone said Riga saw a dock out in the Valley Sea with a telescope from the roof here. And that the Sea is only a bit more than a mile from this house! And since New Bay must be less than a half mile to the west, we are on a very narrow peninsula of land indeed. I want to get a look at this mysterious map that is supposed to be in Riga's possession. Maybe at the meeting tonight.

A friend of Catherine's told me this afternoon on our trek that San Diego is under water, and that on the east coast, Florida and the Carolinas are completely gone! Can that be true? She heard it at the same market, a year ago, where Catherine and Dix heard about Riga. Three or four Category Six hurricanes in one season, she said; I don't know what year. And where did all those people go?

I heard one of the O'Leary brothers talking to Dix when we first arrived with some kind of bravado, I hope, about a Rancher from Montana who had paid for him to come and fix one of his tractors, convert it to solar or I don't know. He said he took the train there and they paid him in gold! A gold coin of some kind. And from the train he saw signs along the tracks in Montana, saying, "Refugees will be killed" with a picture of a noose. The reason I believe him is because it seemed to frighten him. Anyone can be mistaken for a refugee. Who is a refugee now?

But Dix had already told me, just before Riga spotted this house, that the Potters have a reputation at the inland markets for being a "left coast" fringe group and "hippies." So those old labels really are still around, and still pejorative to some. Dix said some of the old codgers at the inland markets say the Heartlanders miss their cattle and burgers and resent all the wind farms on the ridgeline there, and the underground vertical hydroponic farms using LED lights to grow food; which is the very source of their power and wealth now. So many of our old solar farms in Westlands are underwater now. Geography as destiny.

I don't know what to believe. But when I told some of the young Potters that, when I was young, we drove gas cars to restaurants with special windows where we ordered food while we sat in our cars with the motor running; and the food—beef burgers mostly—came in Styrofoam boxes in plastic bags, with plastic utensils, paper napkins and carbonated sodas in wax-coated cups with plastic lids and straws; and that as soon as we ate we threw all that packaging in the trash for landfill, or simply threw it on the street; and that this happened over 85 million times per day in the United States thirty years ago; I couldn't help but laugh when I saw their faces because they were trying to be polite but they did not believe me for a second. Now they really think I'm crazy. They cannot conceive of an entire nation of people being so insane. I start to wonder myself, even, about how things really were. But about fast food culture and its trash, I do know the facts, because Dale and I wrote about it in our blog when we were campaigning for the Green New Deal. We were activists. The Resistance. The movement that would become the Reformers. We sheltered refugees. Until they all left in the endless emigrations.

What a different time. We were worried, and alarmed—that's why I wrote the article! But we had no idea. No idea.

I look at my forearm, refraining from scratching it. There are red and gray patches of skin. Well. The young people aren't used to permanent rashes, and aches and pains that don't go away, and cuts and bruises that take forever to heal. Not now in the Last Wave, in any case; others left with their elders years ago. I realize as I stretch out my legs, that I have not sat in a chair in many days. But the discomforts of this trek, the blisters and rashes and aches and pains, seem nothing to the young. They were born when things were already falling apart. They know hardship.

I suppose they know little else, except self-reliance, adventure and what it is to create your own life without aid. I think of Star and Tania. They were nearly twenty at the time of The Fail and quickly learned to live without their "devices" for weeks at a time. No invisible engineers doing their thinking for them. I have to believe these young people are far healthier than my generation. Well, those of us who have survived. I think of Millie, with Dot trotting beside her all along the way. She and I are the only hold-outs, the only people long past their fifties that I have met so far on this trek. Millie is one of those women, you've met them, thin and savvy and full of energy. Nothing gets her down. She reminds me of women I met in my grandmother's circle of friends. They, too, lived without the invisible hand of engineers. The Depression and World War II shaped them. Grandma told me stories of her childhood, the milkman and the ragman and other venders in their horse-drawn carts. And I think of the Rangers this morning. Horses are in again, Grandma, I want to tell her. I can't shake this strange sensation of going backwards in time. It's this house, probably. As I sit here looking at the tall sash-windows I feel it could be 1890. The same sky, the stately trees outside. So peaceful. I used to envy Grandma's childhood, without television or cars, even. Or airplanes. The silence. The blessed sounds of nature. But then, after The Fail, all the human noise fell off dramatically. But not completely. It was more random and unexpected, a jet shrieking overhead, a truck growling up a hill. Oh, and the "beeps." I'd almost forgotten. Hahaha. How everything beeped, every single thing. That stopped. I thank The Fail for that. At some point we'd all been hallucinating them, a fork clink on a plate and someone jumps from their chair, is my child in trouble, did my sister post a photo, is that item on sale? And later, should we evacuate, shelter in place, run for cover? And then the Silence.

The last years at home were in some ways one of the happier periods of my life. Because I'm seventy I don't feel cheated; I've had a long life. Longer than my father's and most of my ancestors. The simple, quiet life has felt right to me. I, and the land around me, being reclaimed by the Earth is the natural cycle of things. But what was more surprising to me was how the silence changed the young people. The ones who stayed, until now. There were no tattoos and piercings for them. Everything has been about the basics. Food, shelter, clothing. And stylistic flourishes have followed suit. Embroidery on one's tunic. Unusual plant dyes for your tabard. Fanciful ways to braid hair. Shaved heads are no more, although shaved faces are more common than one might think possible—it's a priority for many men. Beards are hot and messy. And as you know, testosterone levels in American men have been decreasing for years and facial hair is more manageable. I wonder if human hormones are permanently altered by our chemical consumption history, or if they will return to some historic baseline, or what.

I've heard in the Heartland, there are still barber shops—did I mention that? We haven't heard much in the way of rumors over the last few years, until now, since the internet mostly disappeared and because no one comes west. Pirate bands on looting missions were frequent after the war, but we still had police forces then. Since the Thwaites—the ice cliff collapse in Antarctica ten years ago, and the formation of the Valley Sea, no one has been able to get here. Not at all easily. So our peninsulas and islands have been left to those of us who were already here.

I heard in the north there is a band of people who wear sky blue tunics, pants and head caps, not turbans, but something like what we used to call bathing caps, I suppose, only cloth. They are very regimented. I don't know if they are friend or foe, as Millie says. Perhaps a cult of some kind. Or did I dream that? There are so many tribes now, at least in the west, I frankly don't know about the rest of the world. And haven't for a very long time. Only rumors. For example, I heard that in Russia fossil fuel oligarchs were drilling for oil all over Siberia as the permafrost melted, and when local people revolted they were crushed by mercenary paramilitary groups. And that bands of white supremacists had spread from the Caucasus on an "ethnic cleansing" mission through Russia and Ukraine and the population, depleted from the loss of St. Petersburg and other cataclysmic flooding, was further culled. This was years ago. I think the sea level rise was only half what it is now. The Great Melt, as some called it, was minor then, relatively. No one—really no one except the most pessimistic—understood how quickly the rate of melting would accelerate and the ice feed on itself as it heated. Nor that the moisture held in the warming atmosphere would increase so much that torrential rains and inland floods would be frequent and catastrophic.

Riga's map, the one ze let the Weavers copy last year—the one Catherine told me about; I believe that is the map we are using and I have heard mutterings among the Potters that it is badly outdated. There was the Yuba fire recently and mudslides last winter, and that's probably the least of it. The Valley Sea may be higher by many feet, someone said. It formed after the Benicia Bridge collapsed and debris amassed creating the Benicia Dam, flooding the Delta Lakes there and eventually some of the Central Valley. But tidal flows are encroaching, overflowing the dam and the sea has risen, some say.

I do know for a fact the coastline everywhere is in constant flux. Storm surges, slides, fires, these have always historically changed the topography; and now there is zero effort to restore or shore up the coast's previous contours, not since The Fail. So the changes, too, feed on themselves. There's no keeping up with it. There are no cartographers. There are no Lewis and Clark expeditions heading west that I'm aware of.

It's amazing how long people can carry on day after day as if nothing is changing. Certainly that's what I did until now. It's hard to fathom that I could watch New Bay form and rise gradually—and then the year of the Thwaites so dramatically—from my big picture window in my living room high in the east hills and just carry on week after week, month after month. As I said, we who remained had our gardens and this is still the temperate zone despite all the extreme weather. If anything, the growing season here is longer. Why else would we have apricots and pears in May.

What a joy to have them; I miss our fruit trees at home. And to tell the truth, I balk at the thought of the winters in the Heartland. If you wonder why I stayed after so many left, I am not a fan of snow, blizzards, and underground cities. I shudder thinking of it. I'm simply following Star. The one being I cannot let go of yet.

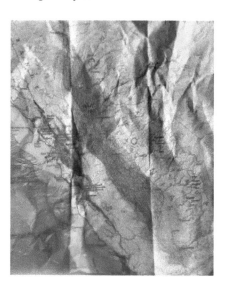

As terrified as I feel of the unknown, and as numb as I have become to that terror, I am still inordinately grateful for the disappearance of the electronic world. It is almost entirely gone here and the Earth is still total and alive. I think of ruined cities from ancient civilizations, the stone walls crumbling and fallen and lush green jungle overrunning them, burying them in new growth. The Earth goes on. The "will to live" as Jane Goodall described the unfathomable resilience of flora and fauna.

Do you remember, leading up to the war, and especially during the war and The Fail—before the great silence descended on the digital world—the social trash heap of human communication online? The snark and gotcha and hatred on every channel of online messaging. And the news was full of scandal and disaster. To read online news was to drench yourself in numbing sorrow. Unless one gave way to spectators' bloodlust, watching lions eating gladiators in the Roman Coliseum. Gawker and the National Enquirer were cesspools, of course, but even CNN was full of trash and the New York Times had its share of sensationalist drivel—though somewhere in the dung heaps, if one was willing to paw around, there might be a thoughtful essay or reflective, insightful commentary.

I supposed I could blame myself. I was a news junkie; I needed my daily fix and would sometimes wallow in it for hours. So much was happening, things changing so fast, I felt there was something vital, something I absolutely needed to know. But there wasn't, nothing that filtered through the garbage. You had to work hard, perhaps be a scholar, to find out anything useful. And even scholarly works were being faked to a greater and greater degree.

Now, there is only a very rare paper periodical expressing human thought that makes its way this far west. For the most part, there is the blissful silence, and the rhythms of nature again. The body and mind, rather than in a perpetual state of outrage, despair, distraction and stimulation, is rather...still. Listening. Resonant with the immediate environment. We experience the creation we are part of, unmediated. Without the media. I find it to be a profound blessing.

That's not to say rumors, gossip and stories flowing along human channels don't still exist, or that humans aren't still perpetually hungry for news. It's to say that the vast excess has contracted to a tiny fraction of its former self. At least here, in the far west hinterlands. Until now— on this journey. I suppose in some ways this was how the prehistoric tribes lived, or indigenous peoples in the

Americas and Africa before the Europeans arrived. Is it regression to live as ancient peoples did? Or is it progress to get rid of all the useless, destructive noise that was our cultural output, until the silence that followed The Fail? Are we looping back around to the beginning? Being given the chance to try again? Those of us who still live.

When Star was a baby, the elected president of the United States told us climate change was a hoax and he boosted coal and oil. Then years later the Green New Deal saved us for awhile, until the war. The infrastructure built during those years is why we have any electricity at all, they say. "They say." The omniscient they.

At least, with the great digital silence we are spared the insanity of scandalous "dick pics". Remember those? You may not if you're under thirty. Even the richest and most powerful men could not resist the impulse to send photos of their genitals to unsuspecting females. What possessed them?! Although phallus worship is not dead. I hear there are plenty of pistols, rifles and rockets in the Heartland. Guns are something there will never be a shortage of here. Remember penis envy? Freud's theory? Men are still on the downslide though. That is, they are not in total control of the world as they were. What's left of the human world. When I looked out my plate glass living room window, taped up to protect it from the gale force winds, up on Skyline Road where I lived for so many decades, until now; among the towers still sticking up, visible, in New Bay, the tallest was a phallus to end all phalli. So representative of our age then. Exhibitionist, arrogant, sinking.

Was it the less conventionally handsome men who were especially compelled to display their genitals? Possibly, in the same way some less than beautiful women compensated by showing their breasts. We are all animals, it's true. Whatever it takes to find a mate... But really, how widespread was this overt behavior? Who knows.

"Mom!"

I start at the sound of Tania's voice shouting up the stairs and jump to my feet. "Yes?"

"Come and have something to eat!"

"Okay, thanks!" I call back to her. All those people. I hate to have to go downstairs. I'm blistering hot! I realize, it must be over one hundred degrees up here and I'm perspiring. No wonder my rashy arms itch. My gear is downstairs so I'll just have to re-enter the fray. I use a corner of my cotton t-shirt to pat away the moisture on my face and ruffle my short hair with both hands. There is a small mirror on the wall, old, discolored and cracked. Perfect! I see my face reflected and the mirror is wonderfully flattering. Just an idea of my face without the worn and wizened details. Cheered, I head for the staircase. Any delusion in a storm. Really, what's the point.

No one is downstairs and I walk out to the porch. Everyone is out on the grassy slope and there are clusters of people seated here and there. At a far edge of the field there is a small makeshift canopy formed by a piece of fabric draped between tree branches. JoJo, Shanika and Liddy have brought a table from the house and have their medical supplies spread out and seem to be running a clinic. There's a line of about ten people. I should probably get some aloe for this rash.

"Mom!" I turn my head sharply and see Star waving me over. She's sitting with Riga, Kelly and a couple of the Tinkers and a few others. Well. I wave and smile and head their way. Tania has joined them. I glance around for Catherine and Dix and see Dix walking toward the orchards.

There is another table from the house, a larger one, set in the shade at the side of the porch. There are plates piled high with sliced fruit and some kind of fry bread, made from wild buckwheat, someone says. Something the Tinkers brought? And then I smell the meat. Farther along the side of the house is a fire pit and what appears to be a large goose turning on a spit tended by the Tinker girl, Alice. I thought I heard shots when I was upstairs but assumed if there was anything to do about it someone would tell me. Two of the Potter boys are standing nearby, helping I suppose. Allice is very pretty, and young, I see now, despite the perspiration glistening on her face and her uncombed hair. She looks tired. A few of our group—it looks like Chela, Sky and Laila are at the food table cutting fruit and bringing out cooked peas and bush beans they must have picked in the vegetable garden and prepared in the kitchen. Bless those Muir loyalists who tended and protected this place so well all these years. But why is it all women making the food tonight? There are only a handful of Tinkers, their patriarchal influence can't be that pervasive! Oh well, our group is called the Caretakers. I suppose it creates a certain expectation.

I fill a dish with some scarlet beans and oranges and a piece of the delicious smelling bread and dodge smoke from the cook fire as I walk to the other side of the grassy slope to Star. She pats a spot beside her on the grass and reaches up to take my bowl while I lower myself to the ground. Oh oh, I have no idea where I left my walking stick.

"It's been this hot up north for a month or more. Hotter," Sean O'Leary says to Kelly. "Trees are dyin' and dry as tinder, that's why they got us outta there. Though some stayed."

"A lotta people stayed, Dad," one of his sons says with what sounds like resentment.

"Just a matter a time," Sean says without looking at his son.

"The Rangers said fires will come as far as the Valley Sea this season," Riga says. "How many still live in the Coastal Range by you?"

"No idea," Sean says as his son says, "A couple thousand."

Riga looks surprised. "Is there still a train from Shasta?"

"Oh yeah. We get some people comin' from up there and there's business. See, we got farms and horses and lots a grass now, it never snows anymore where we are."

"Mitch is mad we left," Sean says.

"She said you're gonna take the ferry and get a train east. Is that right?" Mitch says to Riga as he gestures at Kelly. I catch my breath, slightly horrified, as Tania and Star look at each other and, to my surprise, seem to want to burst out laughing. They turn away from each other and study the grass as Kelly eyes the man serenely.

"Ze's right," Riga answers. "That's the plan."

"Zezezeze. What's all this ze stuff," Mitch says to Riga, taking his mood out on zir or maybe Mitch is genuinely outraged by unisex pronouns.

Riga smiles, says nothing.

"I mean you're a guy, right?" There is definite tension now but again Tania and Star glance at each other and then away, trying hard not to laugh.

"What's it to you?" I ask Mitch. This startles everyone, as I'd hoped, just as JoJo joins us with Ariel. JoJo plops down in the space between Tania and Mitch and Ariel sits in her lap.

"A lot of bug bites," JoJo says. "Do you still have that book on insects?" she asks Tania.

"Yeah, in my pack. Is it my shift?" Tania looks over at the make-shift clinic and stands up and leaves the group.

She gives Star an amused smile as she goes but I feel very tense. This Mitch feels like a loose cannon.

"How're you gonna pay for it?" Mitch asks Riga now. "I heard it's a silver for every five passengers, somethin' like that."

"Kelly already booked our passage with the Captain," Riga says. "We traded wares and they want a clinic in the foothills. No problem. How about you? Are you coming too?" ze asks Mitch. Zir voice is friendly, unfazed. I see Star watching Riga with something like affectionate awe. She is in deep, I see.

Mitch looks surprised, taken off guard for a second and he glances furtively at Sean. Then he lifts his chin. "Yeah. I might."

Sean turns to Mitch, narrows his eyes.

"What about the hotel?" Star asks Mitch.

"Now, who told you that?" Mitch asks.

"No secrets around here," Star says, imitating Riga's friendly tone.

Riga glances at Kelly, who says, "Do you all have a map of this area? A recent one?"

"You wanna buy one?"

"I just want to tell you the last map I saw shows this peninsula is a lot narrower than it was. I doubt many people are going to be heading this way once the Last Wave has left New Bay."

Sean frowns, looks around to the cookfire to see if the goose is ready. Then turns back.

"You gotta map?" he asks Kelly.

"We can look at it later," Riga says.

"What do you know about these coins," Star asks, "silver and gold? Is that what people use east of here for trade?"

"Where you been!" Mitch hoots.

"New Bay," Star says. "All of us, and no one new has come by in five years. That's the truth."

"That's about when we started to see 'em," Sean says, "Four, five years ago—just one or two. Now more lately with people comin' from the northeast."

"They're from the Heartland," Mitch says.

"Or could be the Mountains," Sean says.

"Or Latin America. The silvers," Riga says. Star looks at zir. I guess they haven't gotten around to discussing new currencies.

"I heard they use blockchain," JoJo says. I look at her surprised. Ariel is humming a little tune and playing with JoJo's long braid twined with a bright red yarn.

"You've been usin' that phone for more than communication!" Star says, scolding but not seriously.

"I haven't got a signal in days. But yeah, I did read it on the internet. A lot of places have been rebuilding their grids in the last few years, in Heartland especially, but Latin America, too," she looks at Riga. "And Asia, Europe, Africa. Blockchain is what they're using now wherever they can."

"They have Earth coins, too, no?" Riga says. "What you call silvers," ze looks at Mitch. "But blockchain is in all the cities where there is internet again."

Blockchain, blockchain, I'm thinking. Yes, I've heard of it and cryptocurrency and if I had the internet right now I'd look it up and try to figure out what the hell it is. But since we don't have internet, I don't need to know. The Tinkers don't seem to know what it is either.

"Did they use blockchain when you were in the Heartland?" I ask Riga.

"When were you there!?" Mitch demands.

"A few years ago. Yes, they were starting." Riga looks at me. "There are new types of banks with no coin, only blockchain. The coins were everywhere, though, changing hands. I heard they came from Latin America. But I can't say for sure."

The motto of our times, I think. What can be said for sure. About human society. Or about nature itself.

"I hope you have good weather for the crossing," Sean says, sincerely. I don't want to think it's because he wants us out of here, although I know he does, but I hope it's also a generous thought. He seems kinder than his angry son. I wonder where the other Tinker boys are and look around. I see one of them is helping Alice carve the goose.

"This heat." Sean looks at the clear blue sky above, still full of light although it's late evening. "One of those atmospheric rivers can blow in outta nowhere."

"Right," Riga says, also looking at the sky and then we all look up, gazing at the blue expanse, and then, as if as one, we look west to the sun lowering in the sky. It looks like there will be about an hour of light left.

"I'm going to see if Tania has something for a rash," I announce, as a way of politely departing, and lean on Star's shoulder as I right myself to a standing position.

"Where's your stick, Mom?" Star asks.

"Oh," I look toward the house. For some reason I don't want to admit I've lost it.

"I saw it in the front room, near the staircase," Sean says, to my surprise.

"Oh thank you!" I reply. "I'll get it when I go in." We exchange a kind smile.

As I walk toward the clinic, I think—there are so few of us left. Old people. Elders, as they like to call us. I hear the words "blockchain" and "storm clouds" as I walk away from our little group. I realize I left my dish and hope Star finishes the food. It's too hot to eat. No wonder everyone has bug bites, so much exposed skin. I think it was the "elders" who "died off" first. That's how we have to think of it; we are animals, after all. The elders, small children, the ill and infirm, the usual casualties in a natural disaster or a severe deviance from the norm of social stability. The birth rate had already begun to decline thirty years ago, after peaking sometime around 1970. The "lost generation," that's what they call the people born after 2035, because there are so very few. Ariel is one of them. Although I heard, from JoJo probably, that more children are being born now in cities where the grid is being re-established and some are calling this new generation of humans, New Worlders. I'll have to ask Riga if that's so. Oh that zezeze comment from the Tinker. And this is probably just the beginning. A lot of people died in the war, including a lot of Guardians but they are still around and Mitch is old enough to have been one. Riga handled it with such aplomb. Ze seems to have learned how to navigate this New World in more ways than one. Some say well over half the human population is gone. That there are less than three billion people living now on Earth. Or possibly far less. No one knows. Did they ever? I always believed those population figures like gospel. Three billion in 1960 and 4 ½ billion in 1980 and 6 billion in 2000 and 8 billion in 2020. And then the war, the sea rise, The Fail and people dying by the millions from dengue fever and viral pandemics, swept away in floods, mudslides, starvation, heat waves and fires and everything else that our human society did nothing to prepare for.

"Hi. Are you ill?" Catherine has come up to the clinic line that I'm shuffling along in, thinking my thoughts. I must look glum. I laugh.

"No. no. Just a rash. How are you? I didn't see you at dinner." I look back at the food tables and see the goose has been served. The Tinkers and several Potters are putting morsels on their plate and so is Riga, I see. Catherine is following my gaze and then turns back. "It's a

Canada Goose," she says. Then, "Just a splitting headache. Am I delusional to think they'll have ibuprofen."

"I'm afraid so. But they will have lavender, basil, maybe some peppermint oil."

"You know when we'd all go through the abandoned houses for food and clothes and whatever, I always headed straight for the medicine chest. I had an enormous horde of ibuprofen and a few other things. But I shared." She smiles.

"It's all gone?"

"Sadly, yes. Except a few magic pills I'm keeping to the bitter end."

I must look shocked or concerned because she laughs. "For pain, like broken bones, or extreme cases," she explains.

I nod. "We still have an ample stash of medical supplies. So much was abandoned when people left, although hospital staff were some of the last to leave."

"What do you know about this boat ride? I saw you sitting over there with those in the know."

"It's all arranged and paid for, by Kelly."

"Oh yes. Kelly collected pottery from us and some baskets we had from the Weavers, and candles."

"We provided seeds, and we'll be doing a clinic in the foothills before taking the train east."

"I just hope the boat comes soon," Catherine says, looking east. "And the weather holds."

Star

I get up to go when Chela comes over and asks JoJo to come back to the clinic. JoJo went to medical school in Canada during the war, so somebody always needs zir. JoJo asked me to see what herbs are in the garden here and if any are growin' wild. I can see what looks like English lavender by the orchards and head that way, as far as I can get. That Mitch is such an ass.

I told Riga what Alice said about their hotel idea and we talked about it last night. Riga and Kelly want to use this place as a transit shelter for refugees until the Last Wave is gone. Those Tinkers just showed up here yesterday or the day before and it was the Rangers who brought them here. Riga knows the Rangers wouldn't want these Tinkers to decide they own the place now and start runnin' people off with their rifles. Or makin' them pay "silvers" to stay here, gettin' rich off of poor people, desperate people and whoever they can. What for? This place has everything you could need for a farm plus fish and game for hunters, which they clearly are. The way now is to share and cooperate with everyone that's left cuz the old way of suckin' people dry for personal gain did not work. How stupid are they? I am so mad I feel like my eyes are gonna burn right outta my head. I can hardly see any herbs. I know Mom would tell me to get off this kinda thinkin' right now and Riga told me we're gonna meet all kindsa people and it is more important than anything else not to hate them, cuz that's what the war was. Ze and Kelly are gonna go over the map, the sacred "map," with Sean and Mitch and their whole family, I guess, and try to convince them this little finger of land is gonna disappear and they should move on. Maybe Sean'll listen. I don't think this hotel idea is Sean's and I don't think ze's the one who shot at Riga. Ze's just the one who was brave enough to go out and meet Riga after Riga waved the truce flag. Sean looks too tired to want to start up a business and scare people off who can't pay. It must be Mitch's idea, or maybe the other brothers. Tho did Alice say it was her dad who said it? Anyway. Anyway. We'll be gone from here soon enough. I stop and stand still a minute in the pear orchard. The trees aren't ready, only just startin' to set fruit. Then I see Dix a ways up ahead sittin' with his back against a tree, readin' a book, looks like. Another introvert, I guess. I think of Mom. Ze's holdin' up pretty well. I'm afraid ze has cataracts. I asked Riga if there are ophthalmologists in the Heartland, if Mom could get surgery there. Ze said there aren't a lot of people who need cataract surgery anymore cuz so many elders are gone. I think I should go get Mom and see if ze wants to walk with me and I turn around to go back. Riga said there's some big hospitals in the Heartland and ze's sure some kept open thru the war and The Fail, and they have the old equipment they can use again with the new grid. The best place to look is the Heartland Capitol ze said. We'll see.

When I come out of the orchard I see Mom is over by the clinic talkin' to Catherine and I feel so glad. Catherine is funny and interesting and closer to Mom's age than anyone here except Millie. I don't know how ze's able to carry zir extra pounds, not that many but a nice rounded shape, cuz the rest of us are so skinny. We need more food, especially protein, and I thought maybe I'd eat my very first bite of animal flesh when I saw Riga eatin' the goose meat. I wasn't shocked. Of course Riga's an omnivore, ze's an omni-everything. I can't wait to talk to Tania about that ass Mitch. I don't want to get worked up about the Tinkers again, tho, so I look around for the lavender and I see Ariel there talkin' to it. I walk over quietly. Is ze singin'? No, ze's tellin' the lavender bush something, or askin' it something?

But when I get near enough to hear, ze looks up and sees me. I smile at zir.

"Want to walk with me?" I ask. Ze comes over to me and we hold hands. Ze is so sweet, quiet now.

"Can you smell this lavender?" I ask when we come to another large old plant that must be as old as me at least. Ariel nods her head. I feel my heart get warm and open up with zir hand in mine and wonder why I let myself get so angry sometimes. It's just not healthy unless there's something I can do about it. We see some yerba buena and I squat down next to it and take a leaf in my hand. Ariel's eyes are level with mine, big and liquidy brown with long dark lashes.

"Do you know what this is?" I ask. Ze shakes zir head. "It's yerba buena," I say. "We use it to make the mint tea we drink." Zir eyes light up just a little and then ze reaches out a hand to touch it. "We can pick some leaves," I say and carefully tear off a few. I crumble one between my fingers and hold it out to Ariel. Ze leans in and smells the fragrance then stands up and looks at me with the sweetest smile and it heals my heart. I remember this instant cuz I will need to stay calm as a sunlit pond when I run into all the Mitches and everybody and anybody else out there. Ariel and I pick a few leaves from this plant and the one next to it and I put them in my satchel. Mom got this satchel from Catherine. It's woven from plastic bags and I love it, it has so many colors and a weave that's kinda loose so air gets in.

I stand up and take Ariel's hand and we walk on. Ze's sayin' something and I bend my head to hear. Is ze talkin' to the plants or to me? Ze's not lookin' at me but I lean down and say, "What do you think, Ariel?"

In a small voice ze says, "There's some more over there," and ze points a little behind us to the left. Blessed be. It's an herb garden.

"You're right!" I grin at zir and we pick up the pace to get over there. I hand zir my other small bag, the cloth one I used before for gathering. "You can put some in here."

I tell Ariel the name of each herb and show zir how to collect and put 'em in the bag. Ze is so focused and even happy, it looks like, I start to feel kinda excited, or maybe relief cuz I'm thinkin' maybe Ariel could be my helper, or more important—maybe ze is gonna find a purpose for life.

We work pretty hard cuz the sun is about to set. I'm hopin' we can treat the herbs by candlelight tonight for the ones that need to dry. Tania told me JoJo said they still have a lot of pharmaceuticals from the hospital, or at least it isn't zero, but they can only use 'em for severe problems and we need a lot more herbs. This garden is a blessing.

I guess the pills are a secret. And I remember I told Mitch, there are no secrets here. But we will probably trade pills if we need to tho we don't want to. We just want to do the clinics as our trade. I miss it already, how simple life was with Mom and our community in New Bay. I wish we could of still sustained it and stayed there. I laugh. I guess I have that in common with Mitch too.

"We better go." I smile at Ariel and stand up. I know ze doesn't want to stop but there's a lot to do before dark. The moon is still gibbous but won't give much light here with all the trees. They broke down the clinic, I see, cuz Tania and Liddy and Shanika are carryin' the table and supplies to the house. People are settin' up their camping spots. It's so hot, I don't think we'll make any fires, except for light. I saw Dix a minute ago walkin' back from the orchards with zir arms full of wood.

"You want to sleep in the house with me and Mom?" I ask Ariel. Ze nods yes and zir hand is sweaty in mine. I feel like ze might be gettin' scared. I'll hang on to zir and I squeeze zir hand a little. JoJo usually watches after Ariel but JoJo's so busy now.

We find Mom in the house. Ze's waitin' for me cuz we agreed we'd sleep in here. Good thing the Tinkers are too hot to stay inside and they made up their beds of old sleeping bags outside on the porch. They're still proprietary, looks like, cuz their rifles are all leanin' against the porch rail ready to shoot. I felt Ariel kinda shrink when we walked on thru their scene there and into the house. Mom's sittin' on the bottom step and has her walking stick again.

"There's a bed upstairs," ze says. "Can you stand it? I think we could get the window open."

"A bed? Sounds like it's worth it." Tho I'm thinkin' it's probably a lumpy old thing. But at least Mom won't have to get up and down off the floor. I get a candle out of my pack and light it. It's still dusk outside but it's dark in here. The three of us climb the stairs.

There's a bathroom up here and I see a commode that can be emptied outside. Everybody's been goin' down the hill toward New Bay it seems to me, stayin' out of the gardens and orchards I hope. I guess there would have to be some kinda rules about how to use everything here if it becomes a transit shelter. Maybe they'll get the Muiristas' compost toilets cleaned up and workin' again. But I'd sure rather see Kelly in charge than the Tinkers.

Mom is sitting on the bed, kinda bouncin' on it a little. "Come on up," ze says to Ariel and gives zir a hand up. Ariel kinda smiles now and sits up next to Mom and bounces a little too. I put the candle on the antique nightstand. It's a pretty thing made of parquet wood. Mom had a little desk kinda like it at home.

"Where's Riga?" Mom asks me then.

I shrug. "Talkin' to the Tinkers, I guess. Ze and Kelly were gonna have a kinda meeting with them."

"I thought all the Tinkers were setting up camp on the veranda now. You don't have to stay with me, honey. Ariel and I are fine here. Sean said no one would come upstairs, there's just the one bed."

I squint at zir. "You sure?"

Ze nods zir head, and I think ze's probably gonna be more comfortable with just Ariel in the bed with zir. I go over to the window and tug and tap on it 'til I get it open a few inches, it's not that hard. Somebody probably lived in here not long ago.

"Okay, Mom," I say. I give zir a kiss and Ariel too. "See you in the morning."

I know where I'm gonna find Riga. Ze told me to look for zir there after dark if I had a chance. I take another candle out of my pack in the hallway and then I find the stairs to the cupola.

Ze smiles at me and holds zir arms out in that welcoming, big hearted way when I come up into the little room. Ze's got all the windows open and the sky's kinda indigo with the first stars lightin' up. But really my eyes are on Riga's and we get lost in a kiss.

It's close to dawn when I wake up but still so dark, I see the Milky Way. I guess we slept a few hours. I feel Riga's warm body by me and I can hardly believe it, that we found each other in this world, the miracle of it.

Riga told me about the war last night, and I still feel heavy with it. I didn't realize it started when the Wall got bulldozed by the Reformers. Riga joined the Reformers before the war when ze was sixteen. Ze was already a runaway and an outcast by then. Zir parents were immigrants from somewhere, I'm not sure where, ze didn't want to talk about 'em and I don't really care cuz they weren't very good to Riga. Ze lived in Seattle with a lot of other runaway kids before the Great Melt. Then ze joined a militant group of Reformers when Seattle started to flood. Ze was a really good scavenger, ze said all the kids were and there were even still some freegans then. The Reformers loved Riga and sent zir to the southern border right away. The Wall had been up for years from at least San Diego to El Paso, or that's what they said, nobody really knew. Mom told me back then ze didn't believe it was as big or as long as they said. But there was something there, cuz Reformers came from all over the country, even I heard about it, and they dynamited the wall and bulldozed it and tore down miles of the thing. Riga was there. Ze was nineteen by that time and the Reformers put zir in charge of bringin' refugees across. There'd been some bomb cyclones in the Pacific that hit Mexico hard with storm surges floodin' out their western cities and people were on the move everywhere, a lot of 'em goin' to the Sonoran desert. They needed to get north for fresh water and they wanted to get to the Sierra Nevada. Riga was bringin' refugees from Baja up the Colorado River. They had rafts, I guess like the ones we used in the wetlands Kelly gave us, and they could only cross the border maybe ten at a time. The Wall was makin' people die. It already had caused so many to die, not just people but a lot of wildlife too. I knew that much cuz we learned about it in school. Mom and I cheered when we heard the Wall got blown up. But when Riga tells it, it's different. It took a long time to plan it and get the supplies and when it happened a lot of people got hurt and killed by the Guardians who'd figured out something was goin' on and amassed a lot of their militants. They already had armed vigilante groups at the border for years. It was ugly, just a chaotic deadly scene for maybe three days and then big groups of refugees arrived thru the desert and came stormin' across cuz they'd heard about it. Hundreds of people got shot, families and all kindsa people from everywhere. I just cry when I think about it. Riga didn't cry when ze told me but ze said that was the day the war started for them. And the next week the Reformers were makin' regiments and they made Riga a Major at age nineteen. But that's how it was, ze said. They weren't the military cuz the military people mostly joined the Guardians. Riga led a band of Reformers who were in charge of bringin' big groups of refugees to shelters that Reformers set up on the hiways goin' north.

Mom and Dad were Reformers. We had refugees stayin' with us for years, 'til about five years ago. We heard some awful stories, tho Mom tried to keep me away when the talk was bad, when I was a kid. And usually anyone who made it all the way to our house was one of the lucky people cuz they were healthy and strong enough to get that far. Riga has seen so much worse. I hear zir breathin' beside me so regular, calm as always. I turn and wrap my arms around zir and ze stirs a little. It's hot already and I'm sweatin' even tho we don't have clothes on. The sky turns cream pink then pale blue. Riga opens zir eyes. I look into the green and see so much gold at the centers and light in the dark.

Mom

I wake to a sense of déjà vu and the dream comes to me immediately. I'm seeing patients again. Star is an infant in her bassinet in the hall so I can hear her if she wakes. I'm in the sunroom, my office. I can see the door to the garden where patients enter from a stone path by the side of the house. The tall French windows on the other wall look onto the creek. Lucia is sitting across from me, her hands clenched in her lap. She is in a serious depression. It started after the election, she says. Of course! I remember now, it is February 2017. And all the rest of what has happened is not true. As if to prove it, I see Dale in the garden. He's holding Star in his arms and showing her the freesia blooms. I can smell how fragrant they are. I tell Lucia, it will be all right. I know I'm not supposed to say things like that. But still I tell her that, not right away, but eventually, it will be all right. It's what she needs to hear. And I have the feeling—a knowing. Her little hand holds mine and I look to see, what? I open my eyes. It is Ariel. She has put her small hand in mine. Oh. I see her face, she is watching me. I smile at her.

"Good morning."

She gives me the smallest smile. Like a flower beginning to bloom. I feel suffused with light, a well-being so rare, and so unfamiliar these past years.

"Shall we get some breakfast?" I ask her.

She nods her head.

As we come down the stairs we hear women's voices, exclaiming, then quiet murmuring and then an "Ooh! Look at this one!" I can't tell if they are happy or sad.

We walk toward the sounds. They are in the sunroom. As I step in I see the morning light flooding through the windows and feel as if I have walked back into my dream.

"Mom, you've gotta see these!" Chela waves me over. Ariel and I walk to the windows where five or six Caretakers are gathered around an antique table with a vase and a wooden box. There is a drawing or etching on the cover of the box. Kamala opens it and pulls out a photo. There are several already spread on the table—printed photographs. Beautiful scenery.

"What is this?" Kamala asks. "A snow field?" She hands the photograph to me.

"A glacier," I say. The others crowd around to look at it and I put it on the table in the light. There is the feeling of a wake with mourners gathering to look in the open casket.

"Where did these come from?" I ask.

"Laila found them in this box," Chela says. "We think it must have belonged to the Muiristas. Look at this one. It seems pretty recent." She holds up a photo of a bird.

I take it and study it a moment. "Beautiful."

"We don't know when they're from or who put them here. Maybe they were left by passing travelers."

"A record of natural beauty, I suppose," I say, looking at a photo of a redwood tree.

"Before it's gone," Liddy says.

"Or maybe it already is," Kamala says. "Some of these look pretty old."

There is silence as the women pass the photos around among themselves and I realize that their generation has seen so little, other than what was on their devices when they were children before The Fail, because travel for pleasure is a thing of the past.

"Oh my god." Kamala hands a photo to Chela and they look stunned, awed that such beauty and variety existed.

Liddy and Elena are poring over photos of creatures that I know are now extinct. Birds and butterflies and mammals and reptiles.

"Is this a Monarch?" Sky asks and holds up a photo. "I had a t-shirt with this butterfly on the front when I was a kid."

"Me too!" Kamala says.

"Are they gone?" She turns to me.

"Probably." I remember around the time Star was born, there was a tremendous effort to save them. In the Sierra Madre, in Mexico, where hundreds of millions of them overwintered, the indigenous Purepecha people believed they were the souls of children who had died. They arrived on the first day of November, All Souls Day, year after year for centuries. Until they didn't.

The women are silent again, murmuring, as they study photo after photo. I wonder if they feel cheated. But they seem only to be curious and awed. This is not a resentful generation, which I consider a miracle in its own right. If any generation has a right to resent its ancestors, it is theirs. Or perhaps, Ariel's. I look at her and she has gotten down from her chair and now stands at the edge of the table on tiptoes to see all the photos laid out here. She is so small for her age. It's not malnutrition, exactly, JoJo told me, but. close.

"Let's get some breakfast," I say to Ariel and take her hand.

We walk to the porch and down the stairs to the campers' grassy slope. The food table has baskets of fruit and seeds and grains. Someone has made some of the fry bread again. Oh! I see someone has gathered quail eggs. I try not to rush to take some for Ariel. I hope she will eat them. She stands by shyly not wanting to take anything until it is offered. I don't know where she lived before JoJo brought her to us and she joined our group. She came with JoJo to all our meetings in the months of planning before we set out on this journey.

"Hi Mom," Shanika says as she appears from behind us. "Hey Ariel," she says and squats down to be at eye level with her. "Let's have some breakfast and then can you come and help me at the clinic?" Shanika looks up at me and smiles, then stands. "JoJo wants Ariel to help with cleaning herbs. And ze wants to keep an eye on that tick bite." She nods at the back of Ariel's thin neck where I see a small mark. I hadn't realized. It must have happened yesterday.

I hand Shanika two small boiled quail's eggs. "I hope she'll eat these."

"Thanks. I'm sure ze will."

"I think I'll take a walk," I say and take an orange and an apricot from the bowl. "See you later." I smile at Ariel and pat her arm. She smiles at me, her hand in Shanika's.

I feel so grateful to the Caretakers, as I turn and head in the direction of the orchards, down the grassy slope. The shadows are still long from the grand, old trees. Everyone takes good care of Ariel. Somehow she especially breaks my heart. As if she has suffered more than anyone for all the greed and irresponsibility of the generations before her.

Yet, she is so fortunate, thanks to JoJo especially. What a saint JoJo is and with boundless energy.

I am tired. I forgot my walking stick again. What is wrong with me. The very least I can do is take care of myself. I look around for something else I can use. Surely there will be something with all these trees. I scan the ground and see a fallen branch just twenty feet to my left that looks promising. I go and pick it up and it's a better height than the stick I found the other day, and it's a hardwood and quite straight. I feel inordinately pleased and I hear a phrase from my childhood in my mind, "The Lord provides," or something like that. A religious person's saying. "Seek and you shall find." Where do these words come from?

I set off again, toward the woods beyond the orchard. The truth is, I'm not exactly hearing voices, but random phrases announce themselves in my mind now and then. Perhaps they always did, but now it seems more frequent. Words I have heard somewhere over the course of my seven decades. Memory fragments. And I think of my dream, the sunroom. Was I in the sunroom here at this house before this morning? I think hard, trying to retrieve any memory of it; but all I recall is sitting in the room upstairs in the chair by the window. And last night the bedroom upstairs with Ariel. It was so hot. But did Lucia look like Ariel? I try to remember her, it was so long ago. She was deeply depressed but then eventually she joined the Resistance and, I believe, the Reformers after that.

But the feeling of wellness. The knowing, in the dream. What would I have thought then, thirty years ago, about...Today, for example. I look around and laugh out loud. I would have been thrilled! All the doom and the foreboding of those many years is over now. It happened. The worst, or what seemed the worst, happened. The war. The Fail. But the joy I feel now is that we're nearly gone!

The scourge of human greed on the planet has been defeated. I look up at the sky, so blue again. And the warm breeze ruffling the spring-green leaves of the trees is luscious. I don't hear a single sound other than birdsong and the humming of insects in the woods. It could be 200 years ago. Before even John Muir himself lived.

I stop a moment and allow myself to absorb this living woods and air and earth. Deeply calm at the moment. No threats at the moment, of storms or pumas or ticks or Tinkers. I continue walking. I've heard there's a wide creek on the south side of these woods.

I used to believe, and I suppose I still do, that each organism, including the human, is a cell in the great mind of creation. That we contain all of it within our unconscious and Creation contains us. A sort of Gaia or pantheistic belief. But now I see, perhaps, I am an amalgam of experiences and memories, a manifestation of a certain time and place, in the way that a wave of pure energy becomes a particle only when it is observed. When I observe myself I exist as a being, but in my decline I begin to dissolve back into the energy field. I feel it with my fragmented thoughts. The voices and phrases that come through my mind out of nowhere. Or images. Fleeting memories and words. There are so so many stored in my mind now after all these years. My hard-drive is fragmenting, as Dale used to say. I laugh. He was a bit of a materialist. No Gaia for him. Except, perhaps, at the very end.

I peer ahead through the trees. I hope I'm not lost for god's sake. I look up to see the sun is still shining from the east, yes I'm going north. I wonder if, as my mind becomes more forgetful, less focused and more receptive to random thoughts and memories—if this isn't what dreams are. An assembling of all manner of images and thoughts and metaphors and entities—the great soup of our unconscious; and I am re-entering the unconscious from which I came, becoming ever more in a dream-like state. This makes me unaccountably happy. I hope it's true. Although I know Dale found the "fragmenting hard-drive" terrifying in some ways. He did make his peace with it. Beautiful Dale. I can feel his presence for a moment. Strongly. His love. I stand still. The woods are so alive. A bird, a finch? sings a pretty, flutey song. I lift my head and look up to see a flash of red. A house finch.

I should eat something. I take an apricot from the pocket of my tunic. It's wonderfully sweet and quenches my thirst. I hope to help with the water filtration if I ever find the creek. I look ahead. Honestly, where am I? It was only supposed to be a mile or so north from the house. I wish I'd asked Tania to borrow her beautiful compass. I check the sun again, slightly higher in the sky now. It's going to be very warm today—hot.

I quicken my pace. Though I'm reluctant to leave these woods where I feel so whole. This was the feeling in my dream this morning. Perhaps it's what I meant when I told Lucia "It will be all right." We are no longer in the age of *Homo Electronicus*. At its core was a great hollowness. On the outside everything was polished, glistening, purring, scented, fake. At least in the wealthy world. People in extreme poverty lived not much differently than we are now, scavenging, foraging, near-starving. But we once-wealthy climate refugees have some pretty fancy gear. State-of-the-art at one time— backpacks, camping equipment, filtration systems.

I stop and look around again. It can't be this far. Am I going in circles? I hesitate and my mind quiets. I have no idea. Why do I find this funny? Oh oh. I think of Star and the others. The woods are so dense here and in full leaf.

"Lovely, dark and deep." There is a quickening in the breeze and the leaves rustle. And something else. The sound of voices? I walk ahead and no, it's laughter. Or no, the sound of water, rushing over rocks? I continue toward it, attuning my mind to the sound. It becomes clearer as I come out of the thicket of trees. I head toward it. There is a clearing and then a glade and beyond a slight downward slope.

Catherine. I see her through the scattered trees as the woods opens up, she is in the distance at the creek's edge. And there are a few of her friends. I don't see Dix's tall figure among them.

"Hello," I call as I approach the group, plonking along quickly with my stick.

They look up. "Hi!" they call to me. Catherine waves me over.

There are five people working with baskets and tubing and filtration equipment and they are filling ceramic urns of the finest craftsmanship—thin clay sides, remarkably lightweight—aligned in an old wood wagon with cattails stuffed between so they won't break when wheeled to the house. Dix told me some Potters learned to make the urns from a Cahuilla elder before the war, when they visited the Coachella Valley.

"Just in time." Catherine laughs and hands me a basket. "We need one more person. These filters work best with two people. Do you mind?"

"That's what I'm here for." I smile at them, Potters all. Catherine introduces me and I try to remember their names. Two other women and two men. One of them is using a solar pump.

The baskets are tightly woven and Catherine tells me to fill one with water from the creek to pour into a plastic jug attached to her filter while she operates the mechanism and keeps the tubes directed into an urn.

We work quietly for a few minutes. The others are talking among themselves several feet away. They seem to be discussing the boat—the ferry—we are all waiting for. I hear the words "solar" and "storm" and I stop listening.

"Where's Dix?" I ask Catherine.

She glances at me and her face is suddenly sad. I turn and dip the basket into the creek and fill it with water, then carefully balance it as I turn back to the jug and Catherine.

"I'm worried about him," she says quietly, with her eyes trained on the filter and her work.

I wait a moment.

"You know he's struggled with depression in the past."

"Oh." My heart goes out to him, and to Catherine.

"It's been coming on since before we left. He needs to work the clay, but of course he had to leave his wheel and kilns behind."

I murmur sympathy, continue to work.

"It's getting darker and darker for him."

"Does he have any medication? Has that worked for him in the past?"

"It's been gone for years, but he seemed not to need it anymore. We spent so much time with the clay and at the markets and he loved that."

I say nothing. Should I offer to speak with him? He knows that I and Rosa are therapists and available, or I think he does. There are signs at the clinics.

"We're hoping he can find medication in the Capitol, or in the Mountains, or at the very least in the Heartland."

I nod my head. I have no idea if that's possible. I suppose we could ask Riga.

"If he makes it that far." Her voice is very low and I thought I may not have heard her correctly, but I have. I stop and look at her.

"Where is he now?" I ask.

"I don't know. He can't stand me hovering over him asking how he is."

"Would he speak to someone? One of the Caretakers? We have therapists, doctors."

She looks up at me, as if this is a new thought, or one she has already dismissed, but could reconsider.

"I haven't asked him." She goes back to her work. Then says, "I may be overreacting. He had such a bad episode ten years ago after The Fail. I just feel like I'm starting to see the signs again."

"It's important to be aware," I say. "Perhaps you could suggest he speak with one of us. I'll ask JoJo what we have in the way of herbs or pharmaceuticals."

"Who are the therapists?" she asks.

"Rosa is a holistic therapist who trained at the Consciousness and Healing Center in New Bay. And I was a clinical psychologist."

She looks at me sharply. We've abandoned the filter and walked down the creek a way. "Was?" she asks.

It is odd that I said "was," I realize. "I haven't practiced in years, since the '30s. Except informally, occasionally. And to be honest, my mind is not what it was."

"Maybe you're exactly who he needs to talk to then." She laughs, which surprises me. But then I laugh, too. I know what she means.

"I might mention it to him." She looks at me. "Would that be okay? He knows you a little, and he doesn't know the others."

"Of course." Although I feel some self-doubt and at the same time a surprising eagerness to be useful in some way. I'll discuss it with JoJo, I decide. And do what I can. Dix seems like such a kind man, sensitive, alone in a certain way. In the way of an introvert.

"We should get to work." Catherine seems a bit lighter as we walk back up the creek to her filter and the urns.

Star

Riga says we're gonna meet with the Tinkers this morning. It'll be me, Riga, Kelly, JoJo, and Sean, Mitch, Alice and their brothers, Kevin and Rob—the whole O'Leary family. Tania and Shanika are gonna run the clinic and it's all supposed to happen before the noon meal.

I take a basket Riga hands me full of nuts and apricots and put it on the ground where we're gonna sit while ze goes to get the tea. There's mint tea and sun tea. Alice has that brass kettle goin' on the stove all day seems like, tho it's so hot in there I don't know how ze stands it. Shanika made sun tea yesterday with chamomile from the herb garden. This place is so beautiful. I look around at the house, the green field I'm in, the orchards and gardens and woods to the south, then east at the ridge of hills we're gonna hike over to the Valley Sea when the boat comes. I have a strange feeling and I realize it's that I'm gonna miss this place. I've been so worked up to go east, but...I don't know.

Riga comes back with the tea and sits down with me. Ze's got a rolled up paper under zir arm and I know it's the famous map and ze's gonna finally show it to me. Ze's gonna show it to all of us at the meeting, ze said. And now ze unrolls it and spreads it on the ground. It's kinda crumpled but I can see what's what, or I think I can. Riga says it's not really finished and it maybe never will be. It's like a work in progress and ze's always changin' it based on what ze observes, or what people report if ze believes it to be true, which is hard to know.

Ze points at all the dark blue areas and tells me that's where there's water now for sure, tho it changes levels sometimes cuz of storms, tides, and the state of the Melt. Basically, tho, dark blue is all water and that includes where the town down the hill is under the Strait now, near a new beach a short walk from here. Some high buildings from the town still stick up above the water, Tania said. She saw them when she walked down there and all the windows are blown out and birds live inside. But the few buildings due east, higher up on the ridge, lookin' white now in the sun, are houses and maybe horse stables from before this area was abandoned. Only this house, the Muir house, was still lived in and kept up by the Muiristas, as far as anyone knows. Kelly and Riga went up in those hills and everything they saw up there was empty, falling down or blown down.

Then Riga points to where the dark blue of the Strait widens past a collapsed bridge and debris dam near here, and how it spreads north and a lot farther south and east. Miles and miles of dark blue—the Valley Sea.

Then ze traces a light blue color around New Bay and the Strait and the Valley Sea, which includes this patch of land we're sittin' on right now. Riga says light blue represents what's expected to be underwater like flood plains and lower elevations, but it's a prediction not a fact. Maybe the water will flow where this map says dry, or some light blue will never flood, or the climate could change and stop the Melt and there'd be a kinda stasis. And this is obvious to me cuz I've been here for the changes and I remember all the predictions of this and that and how some were right and some were dead wrong.

"What's that?"

We look up. It's Mitch. Zir shadow is long and falls across the map. Riga stands up but I stay sittin' with one hand on the map and my other hand on my cup of tea. Sean, Alice, Kevin and Rob come up behind Mitch. I turn to look where the clinic has started down the green slope. I'm feelin' kinda scared all of a sudden but I see JoJo grinnin' at us and walkin' fast our way with Kelly behind zir. Mitch looks to see what I'm starin' at and squints zir eyes at JoJo and Kelly and then, I swear, ze kinda smirks. But I don't know. I just don't like Mitch.

Riga spreads zir arm out to me and the map and says, "Let's all sit down and have a look." There's some shufflin' and then each one sits on the ground to make a half circle with JoJo and Kelly next to us.

Riga puts the basket of fruit and nuts in the middle. And then ze takes the map and spreads it out and looks at the Tinkers. Ze's put one corner of the map under the basket and holds the other end with zir hand, tight, I notice. Ze isn't gonna let anybody touch that map probably. But ze starts talkin' and pointin' at stuff and explains to them what ze explained to me. When ze's done there's quiet for a second.

"I don't see anything says this house'll be underwater any time soon. If ever." Mitch looks at Riga.

Riga explains again with different words. "This map shows what travelers observed and sometimes also measured. We don't have satellite images now, only what travelers saw most recently, no? When we learned the Muiristas moved from here, we knew they had good reasons. Something has changed."

"Yeah," Kelly speaks up now. "When I came up this way in early spring I heard the Muiristas were leaving the west coast everywhere. Fort Ord, The Lost Coast, Point Arena, Piedras Blancas—" Ze's pointin' at spots on the map. "They left every single National Park and Monument lower than 100 feet elevation on the old maps from 2015."

"Muiristas?" Sean says. Ze's lookin' at Riga.

"I know them," Mitch says. "Tough bastards. Even the girls. We fought 'em up near Yosemite in the war."

"They've been guarding all the national parks and monuments in the country since before the war started," Kelly says to Sean. Then ze looks at Mitch. "Yeah, and they're tough. The Muiristas were some of the fiercest fighters there were in the war. But they weren't with the Guardians or the Reformers, they had their own organization. Though it's true if battles got too close to them, they fought with the Reformers. So maybe that's how you ran into them, Mitch."

"So you know what tough bastards they are." Riga jumps in before the old Guardian vs Reformer issues start up. "They don't get scared. They don't run. If they left here it is because they know something. They know what's coming and it can't be stopped."

Mitch shrugs and looks off, out toward New Bay, then ze looks back at Riga. "So where'd they go?"

"Yellowstone, Glacier, the big parks."

"Fighting off refugees probably," Mitch says.

"Maybe," Riga agrees.

"I heard they were sending some of their people to Mountain Capitol," JoJo says. "And Heartland Capitol. They're trying to get representation in the regional governments that are just starting to form there."

"They just have the one issue," Kelly says.

"It's a pretty big one," JoJo says.

"Defending parks?" Sean says. "Who needs government for that?"

"No, the issue is the U.N. declaration in 2032, the same year they banned fossil fuel world-wide."

"The U.N. That's funny." Mitch laughs.

"What's the one issue?" I ask. I don't tell Mitch how the U.N. is rebuilt and is called Earth Corps now. Riga told me, and ze said its main headquarters are in Turkey and the world representatives come from all over on solar trains, and boats of all kinds, and even a solar airplane. Mitch wouldn't believe it anyhow.

"There was a Swiss billionaire thirty years ago," Kelly says. "Ze donated eleven billion dollars to buy up fifty percent of all the land on Earth—"

Mitch laughs hard. "Eleven billion must have bought a little tiny island."

"—an idea proposed first in the book *Half Earth* by E.O. Wilson," Kelly finishes as if Mitch hadn't spoken.

"There was a lot more land back then," Sean says. "Sounds crazy."

"Not to the Muiristas," Kelly says. "If fifty percent of the land on Earth is in a public trust, like National Parks, it would preserve clean water and clean air and forests to sequester carbon and sustain life."

"Didn't happen though and now all the numbers are different anyway," Mitch says.

Kelly shrugs. "The Muiristas are conservationists. They're preserving the idea and they're fighting for it."

"They never give up on any parkland," Riga says. "That is how we know their leaving this coast is serious."

"Dead serious," Kelly says. "We already found out this map needs to be updated for New Bay here at the Strait. We paced it off yesterday."

"You just said," Mitch looks at JoJo, "the Muiristas left here to go push their agenda in the Mountains and the Heartland. It's political. It doesn't mean anything about this place."

I can see Kelly feels like ze and JoJo said too much. Ze's quiet. But JoJo says, "If they thought there was a future here they'd still be here, Mitch. This is John Muir's house! Come on, it's like a temple for them. Have you seen their website?"

I can't believe how much battery ze must use surfin' the internet.

"Of course not," Mitch says.

JoJo shrugs, like, 'nuff said.

"The land changes we saw this year in north and east New Bay and the Delta Lakes show erosion is constant. The mud cliffs at the western wetlands here are collapsing," Riga looks at Kelly, "six inches a month?"

Kelly nods in a kinda sad agreement and I don't know if this is bullshit or not.

"One mid-size earthquake, or a big one like during The Fail..." Riga shrugs. "The Muiristas were here then, so they know."

"I don't know." Mitch stands up all of a sudden and walks away.

Sean hasn't said much tho ze's listenin'. Alice looks scared and sad and zir brothers Kevin and Rob don't look happy either.

Riga says, "Kelly is bringing another group of refugees here next week. They are from the Santa Cruz mountains and they will take the ferry east. We need to know they are welcome here."

The Tinkers all look at Riga and it's not very friendly.

"No shooting people or charging rent," Riga says to Sean.

"Who made you the boss?" Mitch's voice is a threat. We all look up. Ze's standin' behind Alice, outside the circle, across from Riga.

"Who made you the owners here?" I stand up and stare at Mitch. I'm gettin' mad and Riga's eyes catch mine, too late, cuz I say, "JoJo can get the Fire Rangers back here. They'll sort it out."

JoJo sucks in zir cheeks but stays quiet and nobody says anything.

Then Sean says, "Well... Kelly." Ze looks at zir. "Why don't you and I have a talk about how we're going to share this place. No shooting."

Kelly says. "Sure. And fair trade." Ze stands up and extends zir hand to Sean who slowly stands up and they shake hands. Riga's on zir feet and shakin' all the Tinkers' hands, and then JoJo and I join in for handshakes all around. JoJo gets Mitch to shake so then Mitch's gotta shake hands with everybody. I keep my face still as a stone for the whole thing. I have a feeling Mitch won't be stickin' around here very long. I just pray he doesn't get on the boat with us.

"Let's find Mom," Riga says. I know ze just wants to go somewhere and talk. I hope I'm not in trouble cuz bein' a tattle-tale and makin' threats isn't Riga's way.

So I guess I'm kinda defensive when we're away from the others and I say, "Was that a lotta fake news about the six inches a month?" I give zir a "you can't be serious" look.

"It's true enough," Riga says, real calm. "There is a geologist who believes it who I met last month." Ze grins at me. Then ze stops walkin' and squints zir eyes at me. "You've got a temper," ze says.

I tense up, but then, "I do," I admit.

Ze doesn't say anything.

I let out a long breath. We start walkin' again.

"Let's find some food," Riga says.

"We could pick some apricots."

We can't get to the orchards fast enough and we run down the hill and find some trees far from everyone and we lean up against a tree kissin', then we're on the ground. The sun is so hot overhead, I'm on fire. In the back of my mind I'm prayin' no one comes by, I wouldn't hear them if they did. We're crazy. This is probably not okay.

Later, Tania tells me ze saw us run off into the orchard and ze knew but everyone was at the midday meal by then and not payin' any attention to us or anything but food. The Tinkers shot another goose this morning and were cookin' it. "Poor Riga missed out," ze says to me. This is around two o'clock. Riga and Kelly are helpin' everybody organize their gear for the boat cuz it's not that big and we've gotta get all our stuff compact, especially the wares for trading. Tania and I are takin' a break, tho. We've got cups of sun tea and are upstairs in Mom's room sittin' on the lumpy bed. It's crazy hot. Tania has on a t-shirt and cotton shorts and I have a tunic with no sleeves. Tania got the shorts and a woven fan from Catherine for an ibuprofen pill. I don't say anything to zir about it but I know JoJo would be furious, except JoJo's usin' up our battery and only Shanika's phone got a signal yesterday.

"Did JoJo get a new phone battery from the Potters?" I ask cuz it just occurs to me. The Potters traded inland and stuff comes there from the east, like maybe batteries from the Heartland.

"Yeah, I think ze did," Tania says.

I don't ask what ze traded for it. I just know we Caretakers need another meeting. And I know now why JoJo went off with Kelly after the meeting, they're probably climbin' hills in search of a signal.

"How'd the clinic go this morning?" I ask.

"One of the Potter kids, about Taddie's age, got bit by Dot. It wasn't too bad but I don't know if Millie should bring that dog at this point."

"Ze can't live without Dot," I say.

"Ze felt so bad and I had to tell zir it was fine, fine, no problem. And it was, the kid's fine, just a scare."

"I doubt if Dot ever had any shots, ze's not that old."

"It didn't even break the skin."

"That's good."

"But Millie said something about both zir and Dot staying here."

"Here!? With the Tinkers?"

"I guess."

"What if they leave?"

"Ze can get the boat then, I guess. If it keeps showing up once a week."

"It's supposed to all summer." But I think of Mom, not that ze and Millie are best friends, but Mom'd be the only elder then.

"Mom would miss Millie," Tania says. I know what ze means.

"Mom's tired," I say.

"I know."

We're quiet.

"It might get better on the other side of the Sea. There are farms there, and we'll do clinics," Tania says.

"I know."

"And ze seemed happier today. This morning ze walked to the creek beyond the orchards, once the hunters got out of the way."

"Yeah, that was early. I heard the shots."

"I'll be glad to get away from these Tinkers."

We start laughin'.

"God, that Mitch," ze says.

We laugh some more.

Then we're quiet.

"There's gonna be a lot of Mitches out there," I say.

"I don't know," Tania says. "It's not like the Guardians won the war."

"It's not like they lost it either."

"They sort of did."

I shrug. "The Reformers didn't win it, tho, it's The Fail that stopped the Guardians and brought them down. That's what Mom says."

"So we don't really know. We have no idea who's out there, or what the Heartland's like." Tania bites on zir bottom lip, maybe tryin' to imagine it. "What did Riga say?" Ze looks at me and starts fannin' zir face with the fan.

"Oh," I say, thinkin'. I lean back against the wall and fan my face with my hand. "Ze was there once about three or four years ago, and not for all that long, but ze said it's a totally different world. It's like the way things used to be, and also not. There's power outages all the time, but they're scheduled. There's a lot of people cuz so many emigrated there and they're from all over. You hear lotsa different languages. There's electric cars, but not a whole lot. The power is mostly wind but also solar and hydraulic. They comply with the ban on burning fossil fuels, as far as ze could tell. But ze said the ban's been enforced a lot more since The Fail anyway, cuz any oil fields that weren't sabotaged during the war are abandoned now, or under water. I mean, basically, there's no oil anymore anywhere, ze said, and coal's been gone since the war.

"But ze said it seemed like white people were still in charge, tho maybe not as much, and that could be changin' too."

"What about the Guardians?"

"Ze said ze didn't see a single red uniform, not even the red hats, and no blue either, not a single sign of Reformer gear. People wear all kinds of things, ze said, tunics and tabards and clothes from the last century and from other countries, and plastic coats and big wool hats. It sounds wild." I start feelin' excited again to go there and I see that Tania does too.

"We should go help," ze says and gets up. "Kelly said the boat could come any time." Ze folds up zir fan and sticks it in zir shorts like it's the most precious thing ze has right now.

We run down the stairs. I'm thinkin' about what Riga said about our deal with the Tinkers, how it never would've happened like that during the war, or right after either. There would've been guns or some kinda violence.

"There ze is," Tania nods zir head at the parlor and I see thru the door that Mom is with Catherine and it looks like they're packin' some of the Potters' wares usin' cattails. Somebody must've picked 'em down by the wetland. They're probably *Typha latifilia* that are native here.

Mom sees me and turns around. "Remember Styrofoam?" ze asks us.

We laugh. "Kinda. The white stuff?" Tania says.

We all look at the door when we hear someone running up the wooden porch stairs and into the house, breathin' hard.

It's Kelly and ze's got the telescope in zir hand, and JoJo and Riga are comin' up behind. "The ferry's coming," Kelly says. "We saw it from up on the ridge. We found a signal too and saw a message from the Captain. They expect to arrive at the high tide in a few hours."

We all kinda take a breath and look at each other and around the room and out the windows. Are we ready? Not really.

"The Captain said we'll leave at the high tide tomorrow morning. So we've got all night to finish packing and get all the food we can together and maybe get some sleep."

I can feel the relief in everybody and excitement, too. We're all revved up now like we weren't a minute ago.

"Shanika, Tania, can you go break down the clinic and start packing up? I'll be there in a minute," JoJo says. Ze looks at me, "Can you go and gather as many herbs as you can?"

"Sure." I look around for Ariel. I see zir over in a corner of the room lookin' at Kelly, then JoJo, then me. I wave at zir to come with me and zir eyes light up, and ze looks less scared.

Riga and Kelly are talkin', figurin' something out. I squeeze Riga's arm as I walk by with Ariel and ze turns and grins at me. I can see ze's excited, like ze's charged with new energy.

I have one of the Potter's baskets that Catherine handed me as we left and Ariel and I run down the stairs and head to the herb garden.

"What's the rush?" Mitch is coming across the field from the orchard and stands in front of me and Ariel.

"What are the Busy Bees up to now?" ze says.

"Keepin' busy." I smile at zir, Riga style. Mom told me how Mitch started callin' us the Busy Bees cuz of our pronouns, and clinics, and food-gathering and childcare. I'm thinkin' all ze needs to do is walk out the door and shoot a bird and then hand it off to Alice. But I just keep smilin' as Ariel and I kinda skirt around zir and keep on goin'. I'm not gonna get into the nickname game with Mitch. Tho yeah it's tempting, but that craze went out when twitter died in The Fail. Blessed Be.

Mom

The ferry is not as large as I expected it to be. I can see now why everyone was calling it "the boat." It's like a long room with benches set on top of catamaran hulls. Once painted dark green and faded now, very weathered looking. The solar panels are smaller than the ones produced in New Bay before The Fail. This ferry must be over twenty years old. Then I realize it's one of the original solar ferries San Francisco imported from Kochi, India in the late '20s! I confess I never rode on one but I saw the news coverage. This one must have been docked at the port, now underwater, on the east side of the Benicia Bridge, now the Benicia Dam.

I'm glad it's a catamaran, anyway. Star said a deep hulled boat could crash into barely submerged buildings all over the floor of the Valley Sea.

"Do you think we'll fit?" Catherine says quietly to me and I can tell she's only half-joking.

We've brought all our gear and the new supplies, hiking over a mile to this wetland dock. It's high tide and we have to load the boat and get out before the water recedes and we're grounded. The Valley Sea still has tidal flows from New Bay that regularly surge over the Benicia Dam. I'm feeling anxious and I think some of the others are also. Though not Riga, nor Kelly, Tania, JoJo and their group. They're on the decks, stowing wooden crates of baskets, pottery, urns, backpacks and tents, solar-powered water filtration systems and the drays the Potters use to haul their wares. We have our extra packs of medical supplies. It's an amazing amount of stuff and seems to have grown exponentially since we left East New Bay, but I don't know how. Is it the human way to accumulate stuff everywhere?

"We're going to need more people to carry all this," Catherine says. Dix is out on the dock heaving bundles up to the young people. I've told Catherine I will ask Dix if he'd like to talk while we're on the boat, if possible. Although now that I look at it, I'm afraid it will be too jam packed for any privacy.

I feel anxious but also I'm treasuring that moment of exhilaration when we reached the top of the ridge an hour ago and saw the sun rising above the Valley Sea. It was extraordinary, even in these extraordinary times. A red-orange, glowing path extended toward us, a divine invitation, I felt. And the water is such a deep blue, beginning to absorb the light now. The hills are profoundly green all around us, and they are purple in the far distance to the north. I would think this were something only the indigenous people had seen before, but this sea was not here during the human epoch, so perhaps the dinosaurs.

Star told me Riga had talked with a geologist last month from this area. I wonder if ze will be on the boat. I feel an ache to know. To know more of what is happening and I quell the longing as always. There is no access to factual information anymore.

I turn to Catherine and see she has her eyes on Dix, and she seems...what? Hopeful? Curious? Wary? I look around for Star and see she is in the cabin of the boat—I think that's her I see through a window. Ariel is with her and has climbed onto a bench to shove things into overhead compartments. The crates of pottery and baskets are stowed on the stern deck under benches. It won't matter if they're splashed or even drenched as long as they don't go overboard.

"Why don't you sit?" Catherine suggests to me, gesturing at my pack. It's true, I could plop down on it and not really squish anything beyond repair, and so I do. I must look as tired as I feel. I have my new walking stick but leaning on it is not the same as getting off my feet. I think of Millie. Unaccountably she decided to stay at Muir House with Dot and the Tinkers. I heard about Dot nipping the Potter toddler but I can't imagine that is her whole reason. Millie is tough, she can take care of herself more than others her age and Dot will defend her. And she's in good health, as far as I know. But to stay on with those Tinkers? Or possibly alone if they decide to move on? For a second I wonder if she fancies Sean. And who knows. Maybe something has passed between them. Didn't I say, people are joining up these days like there's no tomorrow. It's less funny every time I say it.

Anyway, Kelly assured me when ze and Star and I were talking about it before dawn this morning, over our last cup of tea before leaving Muir House; ze said ze would check on her later today and also ze would be up this way with the refugees from the Santa Cruz mountains in a week or so. Millie would have another chance to leave then if she chose. And chances are we Caretakers will still be doing clinics near the Capitol a week from now. I wonder what we'll find there.

Catherine plops down on her own pack beside me. "I guess they're not going to call on us to help."

"I sincerely doubt it."

"Lucky us."

Then she asks, "Did you see those photographs in the box in the sunroom?"

"Yes! Such an interesting find."

"It must have been a Muirista who drew the Muir house on the wooden box. I don't think it was from the last century."

"No, I don't either. It was a pine box. One of them made it, possibly."

"Or it was made in China back in the day. But it was almost as if it were a coffin. Do you know what I mean?"

"I do. Saving photographs of the beauties of nature when they can't save the living thing itself."

"Wasn't the Valley Sea stunning at sunrise, though?"

"It did give me hope."

We're quiet a moment.

"Dix smiled," she says, "when he saw it. I'm not sure when I last saw him smile."

"He seems fully engaged now, too." I glance at him heaving up another heavy pack and stretching skyward with it until Riga and Shanika grab the straps and haul it up to the deck. The blue water of the sea glistens beyond the dock.

"When we traveled to the inland markets, before the Valley Sea expansion cut us off, he loved to set up our wares and even talk to other traders sometimes. Although he generally left the trading to me while he sat and read his book, he wasn't withdrawn or shut down."

"Maybe this part of the journey—finally heading east—will revive him. I hope so. Finding somewhere to work with clay again would probably be especially helpful."

"I've wondered if we should just stay in the foothills somewhere near the Capitol. Although it used to be Guardian territory there."

"I know. I don't know what to expect."

"They may not want refugees, even white ones."

"I know." I didn't want to say that could be true everywhere we go. For some reason there was a rumor or myth here in the west that the Heartland was some kind of haven for immigrants, but how could that be possible, I've often wondered. People don't remember, as I do, that the Midwest of the United States was more hostile to immigrants than almost anywhere in the world, except the Deep South, which is now underwater, rumors have it.

"Things turn into their opposites," Catherine says, surprising me. She often surprises me.

"I remember some of the young Orchardists we met at the markets a few years ago. We'd heard the Orchardists were all Guardians, but some of them were taking in refugees and helping them set up homesteads and small farms on their land. The Orchardists had acres and acres of fallow land since their trees died in the droughts, so, why not? If someone could work that soil, let them."

"It's true. Anything is possible now. Who said that, by the way? 'Things turn into their opposites.' Marx or Hegel? Or Mao?"

"I don't know. Ask one of the young people. That's where I heard it." Catherine laughs.

"Mom!" Star is calling to me, waving at us to get up.

PART II

Star

I can't believe Mom sittin' there chattin', tho I guess it's good if ze's feelin' okay. I just wish ze'd focus a little.

I look ahead across the water and I can't see a thing but blue. Nothing on the other side, just a blurry horizon between the sea and sky. It is so pretty.

Riga says it's gonna take 'til tomorrow to get to New Rose, which is the town we're headed for northeast of here, and longer if bad weather comes up. It's over a hundred miles cuz we have to skirt around the old Capitol. Ze said we'll see a lotta tall buildings stickin' up outta the water there.

It looks like Dix and Catherine are with Mom so I look around for Riga or Tania to see what needs to be done. Riga's up front with the Captain and ze has zir map spread out. The Captain looks interested like maybe ze doesn't have a map of zir own, if that's even possible. Then I see ze has some old instruments—museum stuff again. There's no GPS anywhere cuz the navigation satellites don't work. They're all just space junk now, Riga said, and the Earth's magnetic pole has shifted anyway. The old satellites never got recalibrated for it so it wouldn't matter if they did work cuz they'd be wrong.

I remember in school they said the magnetic pole was movin' way faster and farther than it had the past 100 years so the government had to recalibrate their equipment more often. Then with The Fail, they stopped and that was why the GPS didn't work. Who knows how far it's shifted by now, or if it's reversed completely and turned into its opposite. It happens every two or three hundred thousand years. North becomes South.

But Riga said ze heard that in the Heartland they were gonna launch a new satellite with a rocket powered by fusion. I forgot to tell Tania that! I look around and see

Tania's blonde hair blowin' in the sea breeze where ze's standin' with Ariel in the back of the boat. I feel so sad all of a sudden how I hardly see Tania now. All we knew and did together is back there, invisible. She's talkin' to Shanika. I look where they're movin' something. Looks like all our gear's been stowed. Everybody's sittin' on the benches in the big cabin with tall windows or else outside on the decks. Riga, JoJo and Kamala all went up to the wheelhouse with the Captain and are wearin' hats with big brims and dark shades for the glare from the solar panels on the cabin roof, I guess, or from the water.

"Tania!" I call out. Ze looks around and waves at me. Ze looks so happy. Ariel waves too and Shanika's holdin' Taddie now. I run over. The boat's still goin' slow as we leave the shallows and it's ridin' up on the hulls like a hydrofoil. The water is so clear past the white foam from the wake, you could see if anything is stickin' up from whatever towns or fields were here before, at least at this speed.

Tania and Shanika and the kids are lookin' over the back rail. The kids are laughin' at the white, foamy water pushed out from under the boat. It's exciting. Tho I feel sad. I look up at the horizon, at the higher hills of the Westlands, as we leave this land for good.

Shanika turns to me. "How long's it take to cross?" Zir dark brown eyes look sad too.

"It depends on what we have to skirt around and the currents today" I say. "The Captain says it's 100 miles and this boat does six knots at full speed, which means twenty hours goin' full out. But we've got a big load and if we gotta go farther around or slow way down...I don't know. I guess we'll get there tomorrow sometime. Riga says the solar panels are so old it's not sure they'll store enough power to go thru the night." I look back out at the hills we're leavin'.

"Well at least there's enough room," Tania says. "I didn't think we'd all fit with all our cargo."

Ze looks around the boat, keepin' a tight hold of Ariel's hand. We're pickin' up speed and Ariel's mesmerized by the white water wake.

I look around too and see what Tania sees, a colorful scene of all kindsa people and lotsa stuff and the dark green and glass walls of the big cabin and wheel house above. Then blue. Blue as far as the eye can see.

"Crazy how silent it is," Shanika says, holdin' Taddie close. Taddie seems to be fallin' asleep, probably too much excitement. I'm glad ze isn't startin' up a wail and chooses to zone out instead, but ze's a child of these times.

"Yeah, remember the old ferries in the Bay we rode on as kids? Couldn't hear yourself think," Shanika says.

"And those big clouds of black diesel smoke," I say. We're quiet a minute. Fossil fuels then, and now we have the Valley Sea.

"I'm gonna look around. You good with the kids?" I ask Tania and Shanika.

"Sure," Tania says and gives Ariel a little squeeze. Ze giggles. I haven't seen zir this happy since...ever. For some reason ze seems to feel safe on this boat, or maybe ze thinks we're goin' somewhere safe.

Ariel might be the only person on board who's purely happy right now. I scan the scene as I squeeze between benches where people are huddled in little groups talkin' in quiet voices. They look tired. It's been a crazy effort to get here and no one knows what's next. Just gettin' across the

Valley Sea's an unknown, tho the Captain tried to reassure us all and ze's come from the other side so ze knows what's what. The problem is the uncertainty of the weather cuz we need sun to power the boat. And then also the stuff shiftin' under the water, like debris that might be somewhere it wasn't yesterday, and the currents.

I go to the bow and lean over the rail. There's no foamy wake here in front and I see deep into the water between the hulls. Then just out front I see something—maybe a seal. It's sleek with a round head and it's bobbin' up and down. I crane my neck back to look up at the wheelhouse and wave and point but no one sees me. But then the boat turns a little so I can tell they're veerin' off. I go to the side where the animal's swimmin' and grab my phone out of my bag and turn it on. There's a drop of battery, blessed be. I take three photos keepin' up with the animal by huggin' the rail, walkin' back along the deck. Then it's gone. We've passed it.

I go inside the cabin, makin' my way between stuff and people, smilin' and sayin' hi, and get back in the darkest corner where I pull up the photos and zoom in. I can't believe it. It isn't a seal and it isn't a sea lion or an otter. It has a more pointed face, but not like a porpoise, blunter than that. Its eyes are huge and seem to have double lids. At one point, those eyes looked right at me. And I mean, it's like ze was lookin' thru me. I guess if anything I'd say it has the head of a yellow lab. Its fur is that color and its eyes are like a soulful dog, but the body, as much as I saw, is a sea mammal, looks like. It could be a very large harbor seal except it has ears, I see them in the photo and they are big, like a terrier's. I'm tellin' you, it's like a dog. There it is, clear as day on this phone. What kind of species? I need to show JoJo and have zir help me research it. I head toward the wheelhouse.

When I climb the metal ladder to the top, I see Riga and Kamala are gone but JoJo's still here, and ze's chargin' zir phone! There's three phones plugged in. I guess there's hydraulic power from the boat gettin' some juice for the phones.

"Hi," I say quietly. I don't want to interrupt, but they turn and look at me.

"Did you see that sea dog swimmin' out there about ten minutes ago?" I ask.

"Sea dog?" JoJo says.

"Yeah," the Captain says. "I've seen him before around here."

"What is it?" I ask.

"You called it. Looks like a dog to me. I have no idea."

JoJo laughs. "Are you discovering new species again, Star?"

This kinda annoys me but I let it slide. It's true I often think I'm seein' a zebra instead of a horse, but sometimes I'm right.

"I got some photos," I say and hold up my phone. "Hey, can I charge this here?"

"Help yourself," the Captain says. Ze unplugs one of the phones and I plug mine in.

Then I look around. You can see for miles and miles. There's not a cloud in the sky, tho that doesn't mean much cuz a band of moisture can come outta nowhere, suckin' up all the air and dump an inch of rain in an hour, especially when it's hot like it is right now. And it's hot up in this wheelhouse even with the open windows. I can feel myself startin' to sweat.

"I'm gonna check on Mom," I tell JoJo.

I find zir in the front of the cabin in a shady spot. Ze's talkin' to Dix and Catherine and Riga. I squeeze in next to them, sittin' on a box of stuff. "Hi."

They all smile and welcome me. It feels good, like family all of a sudden. Then they go back to what they're talkin' about—the war, sounds like. And I remember how that meeting with the Tinkers and Mitch yesterday kinda triggered stuff about the war for Riga. I think for a minute about our conversation, Riga and me, right after that meeting and about how I was with Mitch. And then I get it! The test with Riga—it's not that I have to be perfect. It's that I admit it that I'm not.

Dix is talkin', kinda like a professor, "...the Guardians were afraid of socialism. They were afraid that if workers took over the economy they would have to give up their own possessions and be forced to cooperate and share with people who aren't like them. The irony is that, instead, capitalist greed devoured all our resources and destroyed the economy, when socialism would have saved it. The Fail didn't have to happen."

"The Reformers weren't only socialists, though," Mom says. "Many were humanitarians and religious people helping refugees. But the Guardians believed the far-right propaganda about us and the sanctuary movement. I think 8-Chan inspired the racist mass shootings that were a precursor to the war."

"And its spawn, QAnon," Catherine says. "But there were so many issues and factions leading to the war. The Muiristas could be as brutal as the Guardians. A one-issue fighting machine."

"They were tough," Riga agrees. "But you know...." Ze hesitates and I look at zir.

"Everyone is brutal in war, right?" Catherine finishes for Riga.

Ze nods. "It was ugly on all sides."

"Did you know anyone who fought?" Mom asks Dix and Catherine.

"We—all the Potters—gave material support to the Reformers, but no battles were fought near the coast where we were," Catherine says.

"I met some people inland," Dix says. "There were bands of white nationalists all through the foothills."

Mom and I look at each other. Are they still there? we're thinkin'. "When was that?" I ask.

"Oh, maybe six or seven years ago. It was after The Fail and there wasn't much left of their organizations. Some were followers of Renaud Camus." Dix looks at me and Riga. "Maybe you're too young to remember."

"He was a French philosopher who wrote *The Great Replacement*," Dix says. "His idea was that white male patriarchy was being replaced by foreign cultures and nonwhite people. His book helped to spark an international movement of white male supremacists and attacks on immigrants." Ze looks at Mom. "I agree those attacks were precursors to the war."

Riga nods. "Yes. That is how I think the war started. The white nationalist groups were the first Guardians. Then many nonviolent people who weren't so racist before, they became caught in a web of fear and propaganda. And they became violent too."

"We all know who spun that web," Mom says. Ze and Dix and Catherine look at each other. Mom told me once ze still won't say the name.

"But people were already leaving the coasts before the war because of the changes," I say "And a lot of refugees were white."

"That's right," Dix says, "but by then the interior regions were like a tinder box waiting to explode. You had to choose sides. So it's probably true," Dix looks at Riga, "the seeds of the war started with white nationalists and then got conflated with socialism vs capitalism, and environmentalism vs consumerism, so that even white male liberals got targeted by white male nationalists."

"Are they still around? Inland? The nationalists, or Guardians?" Mom asks.

Dix shrugs. "Hard to know, you hear so many rumors. I've only been as far as the foothills and it was years ago when the central pass was still open."

"Maybe it's like the Civil War 200 years ago," Catherine says. "The grievances and ideologies are still around but they've gone dormant again."

Riga says, "That could be so. But I saw in Heartland many people are like a different species than we were before the war. There isn't anyone still alive who remembers the times you are talking about because they were small children or not born then. And after The Fail, everything is gone, so people care more now. I'm not sure how to say it, they care about surviving, like before, but now they care about context. They can see they aren't separate from context—nature and other people and animals. I would say...people are more humble now."

Dix nods zir head. "Yes. That's it. That's the difference I saw in the Guardian veterans I met after The Fail, their righteousness was gone."

"Not only Guardians," Riga says. "Humans in general."

"But what about those signs in Montana the Tinkers talked about?" Mom asks. "Refugees will be hanged."

"Well," Dix shrugs. "Rumors. But it's true, Mitch seems like a real throwback."

"He's been isolated, though," Catherine says, "up there in what's left of the redwoods. True, he fought in the war over a decade ago, but since then he's been living in the Coastal Range. He hasn't been part of....part of the New World. That's how I think of it, I guess." Ze looks away and ze seems kinda embarrassed by how hopeful that sounds—a new world.

"Like after Noah's Ark," Mom says.

Catherine says, "Right!" Ze looks at Mom. "A new covenant. We have a new understanding of our place, here, with each other, animals, the Earth."

"I want to let myself hope," Mom's says. "I want to believe *homo electronicus* has evolved, and the world according to engineers and all its hubris has been left behind. And a *homo spiritus* will emerge." Ze and Catherine share a look. They must've come up with these ideas in all their talks. I gotta wonder. Dix is looking at them kinda funny.

But for a second I feel a flash of joy and the fear is gone again. The future could be something great.

Mom

We've been gliding over this sea for much of the day although the sun is still high. I left the cabin to stand here near the back of the boat on my own for a bit. I feel uneasy and want to clear my mind. I gaze out across the flat blue sea, to its distant, vague horizon. It is empty and vast, inhuman, in the best sense. Inviolate.

But I know there is human civilization on the other side. Supposedly, there is a new world there with remnants of the past and a sci-fi future. I feel suddenly swallowed by grief, physically stricken. Involuntarily I look back at the distant shore we have come from. The Muir house is no longer visible, of course, and the coast is a blur to my failing vision. The Westlands. California. The most beautiful land of mountains and deserts and redwood forest and white sand beaches. How much of it is left now no one knows, despite Riga's maps. The day is brilliantly blue and still. As pristine as a newly born world. Would that it were. I turn back to look east across the water but I cannot discern a single thing that lay before us, just a fuzzy line where the blue sea meets the blue sky.

And then I see a white, flat mass ahead, to the northeast. Like a layer of rocks or perhaps rooftops of submerged buildings and my heart jumps in my chest, pounding, when at the same moment the white mass lifts, and becomes white wings. Hundreds of thousands of birds rise, flying. "Snow Geese," someone yells from the front of the boat. Enormous flocks of migrating birds. I watch them, transfixed, as they disappear in the distance. I feel a blessed peace fill me. The creative Earth continues, without us, regenerating. Its myriad creatures and magnificent beauty. At least here, in the Westlands, where the seas have reclaimed the land and the humans are gone.

After lunch I spoke with Dix privately for a bit, as I'd promised Catherine I would. Although he has seemed much better since we left Muir House, and the Westlands in general. Perhaps he is glad to be leaving the ruins behind. He said as much. There were so many reminders for him of all that he's lost. And he's struggled to know his purpose since leaving their home and their small cottage industry there. The trading suited him, the difficult traveling and the encounters with other "survivors," as he called them, at the inland markets. He really does not want to identify as a refugee, I gather. He had already lost so much in The Fail. I hadn't realized he and Catherine had been quite wealthy, even during the war they managed to hold on to their large home in the Carmel area. They had electric cars, of course, Teslas probably. Dix had made a fortune with a start-up when he was in his early twenties. I hadn't known that and I had better watch what I say around him about the "world of engineers" and all my opinions in that vein. Although I get the feeling he agrees with me about *homo electronicus* and the excess and hubris of the tech age at its peak. His start-up was focused on renewable energy, fuel cell technology. Although, without a means to produce and transport hydrogen, that is all defunct now. Only solar and wind power have survived and flourished. Because the sun still shines and the wind still blows. I think I remember an ad saying that back in the day. And hydraulic! There has been a resurgence in hydraulic power, all the flowing water from melting glaciers, and pouring rain. Although it's primitive as of yet. Not exactly wooden water wheels, but burst dams have not been reconstructed nor any new dams built.

Dix said The Fail was mostly, but not totally, about the "carbon bubble" exploding. By that he meant the hydrocarbon world economy falling apart after the shale fields and refineries were inundated. And then the ban on fossil fuels. An enormous amount of wealth evaporated—that kind of wealth on paper that somehow becomes real in a crash. Credit dried up. And people stopped producing. In the Westlands so many businesses had already failed from sea level rise. There was no money and people were not building. The coastal power grids failed. Dix lost his company first, and then his home became a shell without power to run its many electronic systems. Catherine told me she felt like she was living in Miss Havisham's dusty, cluttered rooms. And that Dix's first depressive episode occurred soon after those losses. It wasn't so much the loss of things, objects, Dix said, as the loss of identity and purpose. He didn't know what to do with himself. And he had never before felt any doubt or hesitation about his purpose and goals. Even during the war, he believed he was part of the solution.

It was Catherine, who had studied ceramics in college, who had the odd notion to dig up the clay along creeks in their area, as she had seen some others doing, and begin to make pots. She enlisted Dix who was finally persuaded to leave the dark rooms of the house and follow her to the areas where clay soil was in abundance and that is where they first met the Potters. The Potters had not been tech millionaires. They had been students and artists, local organic farmers and crafts people. They knew how to create wares and take them to market. Catherine and Dix joined them. And for Dix, it was a reincarnation. He loved working with his hands and he loved traveling to the markets.

Catherine told me they could have escaped during The Fail, by which she meant Dix knew other rich tech entrepreneurs who had planned for just such a moment. They had Pinkerton guards, helicopters and private jets, large plots of land and homes in the highlands of New Zealand. Some had built "safe houses" in silos in the Heartland. And that is where they had lived during the war. And the war segued into The Fail. Business, financial markets, the global economy were only somewhat affected by the U.S.-based war between the Guardians and the Reformers and similar, smaller scale conflicts in the UK, Australia and parts of Europe. Asia initially was able to carry the economy and was instrumental in causing the Saudi-Iran war and Mideast conflagrations to be contained. The "space war" Russia had instigated against NATO fizzled with so many demands on tech. But ultimately the interruption of oil production and the destabilizing of society caused by the wars led to the collapse of the global economy. If it hadn't been for the wars, the ongoing shift away from fossil fuels and toward renewable energy might have kept things propped up and the world economy might have stumbled along, despite the great losses caused by sea level rise. At that time, the Thwaite ice cliff had not yet collapsed. The flooding seemed dire but manageable.

Then it all seemed to happen at once, Dix said—the sea rise, like a feedback loop of melting ice, water in the atmosphere, more rain, bigger storms, waves of refugees, the wars, the scarcity of energy, the halting of oil production, the mass failure of power grids worldwide. Only pockets of intact communities remained. How many are still out there—functioning communities with food supplies, medical services, transportation, anything resembling what once was? Not many, is Dix's guess. Though as he said, all we hear are rumors. But one thing we do know, there is still a skeletal internet. We wondered if somewhere in the world, people are still producing batteries, fiber optic cables, even launching satellites, perhaps with fusion. All unknowns for those of us long stranded in the Westlands. Finally making our move east.

Dix said the decline of the Potters' trade routes started with the expansion of the Valley Sea—the super storms of the last several winters that collapsed the few crude levees which had been keeping the sea from inundating the central pass. And as the routes closed, and the Potters industry began to decline, he felt the depression come over him again. He described it to me in detail.

First the shock when his primary route inland was closed during a particularly violent winter storm. He heard of it from other Potters but took a two-day trek to see for himself. The sight of the flooded pass, the crumbled bluff to the north, struck through him like a knife, he said. He knew what it meant. And he felt as if a dark hood were being pulled over his head. He had to fight the image and the only relief from it was a burst of his own tears, prolonged sobbing. He frightened himself with how extreme his response to the sight was. And he recollected a time as a boy, when his grandmother died, that he'd forgotten until then. He'd been only four, an age—I mentioned to him later—when one first realizes that death exists, and a young child can become preoccupied with it. His grandmother had been a source of joy and creativity for him. She was very imaginative, Dix remembered. She'd taken care of him while his parents worked. But then, he had to go to a preschool, after her death, which overwhelmed and depressed him.

I suppose it's always hard to resist the accumulated sense of loss over the decades, how one loss can trigger all those before, until it seems that all is lost. I told him this and he understood.

But now he is feeling a renewed sense of purpose, he told me. Something about loading the boat, getting underway. The uncertainty doesn't frighten him, I see. He is not risk averse. If anything it enlivens him, now that he has left the scene of his losses. The travel cure, I think. So popular for the wealthy in the 19th and 20th centuries, but not just the wealthy. Many people hit the road when everything goes to hell.

Now as I look out to where the snow geese were, I see a few small puffs of cloud have appeared in what had been such a clear blue sky.

I'm feeling a little stiff, of course. We sat like sardines at lunch in the cabin, crushed up against one another and all our stuff. With all that's happened and, still, we're lugging around "stuff." Humans and their "stuff." But I don't want to get negative now. I'd love to feel a renewed sense of purpose and vitality like Dix. I study the blue water running beneath the boat below the rail, wondering how I possibly might generate some optimism. The water is beautiful. And it is clean. Let that be my comfort because that is indeed a marvel.

And the birds. Life returns. I feel a glimmer of curiosity. What does lie ahead? Certainly there will be natural beauty. This makes me smile. I take a deep breath. The boat is a bit claustrophobic but we've had smooth sailing since dawn and for that I'm very grateful. There are "spotters" standing at strategic locations around the deck looking for floating debris, sea junk, anything out there that could snag the boat or cause a collision. They all have binoculars or telescopes, one of which definitely looks like a museum piece. I saw Star take up a station about an hour ago. She seems quite happy now. I know she has inherited, or somehow picked up, some of my anxiety but she is so much more resilient. I don't think it's just her youth. Dale was an optimist. I wonder what Dale would have thought of Riga. Ze is charismatic in zir quiet way. I have to admit I quite like zir, but, oh I don't know. How ridiculous to hope for anything conventional for one's child in this age! If anyone can survive, it will be this new kind of person—Riga. Certainly, if anyone is to create a new future, a sustainable human society, it is not the conventional humbug. I laugh. They don't even know that word. Remember Words with Friends? It's the only thing I miss about the internet.

Star said everyone is charging their phones up in the wheelhouse. That Captain has the patience of a saint. Thank god. She can't be much over thirty. She seems to know this sea, though. She has the eyes of a hawk, Star said. Star claims she saw some kind of golden dog creature swimming off the side of the boat early this morning. I hope she hasn't been influenced by those rumors, of the new species. Not exactly Big Foot or the Loch Ness Monster, but there are tales—more modest—of day-glo frogs and foot-long dragon flies. Though of course, who knows. All the chemicals that have leached out of everything not to mention bubbling up from the soil everywhere. All kinds of mutations could have happened. But so quickly? I wish Dale were here. He could make sense of so much of this, or at the least, he could talk me down. Dear Dale. I dreamt of him the night before we left New Bay. He was a kind, reassuring presence. I believe he was really there, helping me. An image comes to mind, something about trees blowing in the wind, branches flailing. I remember that dream, some days ago. But people are murmuring and then I hear a sound of alarm. I look around and am shocked to see so many people have moved toward the other side of the boat to look out to the southwest, toward the Westlands and then the Captain suddenly speaks loudly through some kind of bullhorn. "Move away from the rail. Move to the center of the boat." And it's true the sudden shift of weight to the left side of the boat, the port side, is seeming to tip us. Everyone redistributes themselves immediately, obediently. Gone are the days of pig-headed individuals flouting the common good. But I gasp when I realize what we are seeing. Far, far in the distance, fifty miles? the hills of the Westlands beneath a huge mass of white and gray clouds and shafts of rain in the late afternoon sky. It's magnificent. But it's headed our way. How fast could such a rain cell be traveling, and might it be spent before it gets this far?

I stay at the railing since I'm ballast for the starboard side, but now that the boat has righted, I look about for Catherine. I know Star will still be at work. I see Dix's blonde head, tall above the others, going into the cabin and I head his way. I assume he, too, is looking for Catherine.

They're sitting on the front corner bench where we were in the morning and I join them. The mood in the cabin is somber but not morose. I'm surprised how quick the Captain was to pick up that bullhorn. Can a two-hulled ship really tip over? But of course, any boat can capsize, I suppose.

"Now we wait," Dix says.

"What do you mean?"

"We can hope to outrun that rainstorm, but if the sky clouds over we may lose some power. We'll have to conserve what's stored in the battery to keep forward momentum and not go adrift. I suppose there's an anchor somewhere, but...." Dix looks a little confused and that alarms me. He's the engineer. But of course he's not a sailor, per se. I have the terrible thought that maybe he's making things up to reassure us; it's been well over a decade since he was involved in technology.

"How far are we from the other side?" Catherine asks. "We don't even know the name of where we're going."

"I think it's somewhere near Roseville," Dix answers.

"That's what I heard," I agree.

"That would be less than sixty miles as the crow flies from Muir House. But we have to circumvent Sacramento. I think I heard Star say the course is 100 miles," Dix says.

"We've been going more north than east," Catherine says. "I had a look at Tania's compass. We're not far from the western shore, really."

"Once we pass Sacramento it's about fifteen miles due east, three or four hours," Dix says.

"We should be able to see buildings rising out of the water if Sacramento is anywhere near," I say.

"Let's go see," Catherine says. We all get up and leave the cabin, heading for the bow.

There, on the starboard side, we can see to the northeast. The sky is clear blue and there are shapes in the distance, not a skyline, but yes, buildings. They look, to my eye, as if they begin at least ten miles away.

"I think it'll be another twenty miles before we can safely head east," Dix says.

"So we've come about two thirds of the way," I say.

"If we left at dawn and it's a couple hours until sunset...." Catherine says.

"Fourteen hours," Dix says. "About seven or eight to go."

We all instinctively look to our left, out to the west, to the storm.

Star

It's so dark I can't see a thing, not even Riga's face tho I can hear zir breathin' right next to me. We're packed in here so tight, all of us inside the cabin with all the stuff, like refugees, Riga says, only luxury style. Ze's seen so much worse, I know.

I hear the rain fallin' steady on the solar panels on the roof. Sometimes it's soft like pitter patter and then it drums down like crazy for maybe ten minutes and then it's soft again. I don't know how long I've been awake. It must be close to dawn. The storm caught up with us finally about an hour ago. It woke me up and I don't know how many others in here are layin' awake like me listenin' to it. The boat's still glidin' smooth as a canoe, but slower than before. Riga's asleep. I turn my head to Mom and her silhouette appears cut from some kinda low light comin' thru the windows to the south. Zir head's propped on her duffle bag and turned away from me. Ze's awake I'd guess, lookin' out those windows. There's some kinda glow comin' off the water, like a flat layer of light way below the storm clouds. I don't know if it's the full moon or a sunrise makin' that silvery glow. It's just a skinny strip of non-black comin' thru the bottom of the window panes. I hold my watch right up to my face and try hard to read it and I still can't see a thing.

And then my hand smacks into my face when a big thud tips the boat like a violent hand came and lifted it up. I jump up to a squat but can't stand cuz the boat's tippin', and the bullhorn comes on, "Everyone to starboard, everyone to starboard" and people start scramblin' and crawlin' to the right side of the boat. The back doors of the cabin swing open and there's a howlin' wind we couldn't hear before. I'm helpin' Mom get to a crawling position. Something hit her arm, some crate slidin' across the floor. I get her to the side bench where Dix and Catherine are hangin' on for dear life and Catherine holds Mom to her side. I get up then and slide and snake to the back of the cabin to help close the door that's swingin' open to the port side and I see stuff tumblin' out the door to the deck and break thru the rail, fallin' in the water. Emergency lights are on everywhere and I scream when I see Ariel hangin' onto a big backpack that's slidin' fast out the cabin door headed for the broken rail. I'm twenty feet away and run over the fallin' stuff and get slammed into the wooden rail when I see a streak of orange fly in over all the crap and fling out an arm and grab Ariel, hurlin' the two of them toward the stern where another arm grabs on and holds on like a crab claw, and then Riga and I finally get there. A black braid swings as the boat careens like a seesaw. It's JoJo. I knew it. Riga and I hold on to them and make a human chain with a couple Potters and get them pulled back to the cabin somehow. Some other Potters are on the deck tryin' to save the stuff. One of em jumps in the water like a crazy person. Ze's got a line of rope and looks like ze's tryin' to lasso stuff. I don't see what happens cuz we get back in the cabin and shut and tie the door. The boat's stopped buckin' but it lists about thirty degrees. Shanika and Tania and the Caretakers herd people to the safest corner of the cabin and everyone's linkin' arms and hangin' on. The first aid kits are out. There's blood. I hear people talkin'. "Tree branches, big log, debris, cracked hull, lodged underneath. Shifting. Engine disabled." I look out the starboard windows and see the oblique light on the water again. It's moonlight. The moon is nearly set and there's a refracted glow beneath the cloud layer thru the rain. I can see the shore, or maybe an island and tall, tall trees and branches blowin', they swing like crazy like they're screamin' and wavin' their arms. Some branches must of broken and got blown across the water, you can hear the wind outside. But the boat only rocks a little now at its tilted angle. You can't really walk anywhere tho without holdin' on or usin' a kinda crab step not to slide. The decks are slick with rain. I see some Potters still out there on the port deck where the rail is dangerously close to the water line. I wish they'd stop tryin' to save their stuff and get back in here and hug the starboard side like the rest of us. If they start haulin' their stuff up over the side there it's gonna tip the boat more, maybe right over. I look for Riga to ask zir if we should do something, but then I don't need to cuz the Captain gets the bullhorn goin' again. I don't know where ze's gettin' power to amplify that thing cuz the lights are gettin' dim and the battery must be close to dead. "Everyone to starboard, everyone to starboard. Get off the port deck. NOW!" All but one or two do as ze says and they get themselves back in the cabin when some of us untie the door. That's when we find out the two still out there are tryin' to save whoever went in the water with the ropes. They can't find 'em. Two Potters are out there somewhere.

Everyone's crammed in the cabin again except the Potters still searchin' for the two in the water. With our backs against the starboard wall we can see thru the port windows that the water's almost lappin' at the deck out there. It's still rainin' and the wind is loud. The boat rocks bow to stern as it still jimmies with the logs rammed under the starboard hull. It's a miracle we're all here, teeterin' on oblivion, that's all I can think.

"What's that," someone near the bow says, lookin' east out a little porthole window of the cabin. A couple others crowd in next to zir to peer out. "It's a light and it's moving," one of 'em calls out. Ze sounds either excited or scared, like is it a Martian or an ambulance?

I can't help laughin'. Riga takes my hand and squeezes it. Like, "ssshh." We all wait to hear more. All we can hear is the rain, steady and soft now. And I swear I can hear the water lap at the port deck even with all the doors and windows closed. I look back out to the south thru the windows we're backed up against on the starboard side and see in the silvery light that the water's not too rough, just spattered with rain drops. The wind must've died down cuz I don't hear it now. I can't see the island like I could, we must have veered off course. I don't know where due east is now.

"It's getting bigger, coming this way," the Potter at the porthole window says.

The Captain's on the bullhorn again. "Prepare children and the injured to disembark. A rescue boat is approaching. Capacity for fifteen passengers. Prepare children and the injured to disembark. Do not inflate life vests until outside the cabin. Prepare fifteen passengers to disembark. Do not take any belongings. Passengers only."

There's a lot of talkin' and shufflin'. There are six kids, Taddie, Ariel, Jasmine, Lee and Mikey and a Potter child. We decide to send JoJo with the kids even tho zir injury is minor, just some big bruises where ze slammed into the rail grabbin' Ariel. Mom's gonna go. Zir arm might be broken. Ze's holdin' up but ze's not sayin' a thing. Everybody barely moves, like we're on tiptoes so as not to "rock the boat." No kiddin'. Shanika and Tania are gettin' the kids and Mom and—it looks like Catherine, I see blood all over zir face now. There's two Potters, one limpin' and one with a bloody gash near zir eye. They all line up in the center of the cabin and four more people get selected. No one argues or cries or screams. Not all the injured are gonna get to go, just the most serious ones. Mom turns to find me. There's still the low light from the east. We look at each other for a long time, that's all. I send zir all my love and faith that's ze'll be okay and ze's sendin' me the same. Then ze gets jostled as the boat starts rockin' a little more and shifts when the broken hull settles again on the floating logs and branches. I don't know that we'll stay upright much longer. Or maybe we'll just plop back down flat and straight again, tho that hull would fill with water then I guess. Is it hollow? I don't know. I look at my watch. It's only been fifteen minutes since we got hit or maybe twenty.

"Prepare to deboard at the stern," the Captain announces. The line of kids and injured passengers all have inflatable life vests now that were in a ceiling rack. They turn and kinda shuffle toward the rear of the cabin lookin' pretty grim. I watch Mom and, yeah, I'm cryin' cuz I don't know if I'll ever see zir again. I feel so grateful JoJo's with them. Blessed be.

Mom

JoJo showed me how to keep my arm bent and pressed against my chest and I am focusing on that and nothing else, other than shuffling along in line with the others, the children and disabled. I cannot allow myself to be any more of a burden than I already am. I have no idea where my walking stick is. I take baby steps in the near dark. All but one emergency light is off. We're holding hands now but the poor young man behind me, a Potter with a gaping gash and a tourniquet above his elbow is forced to cling to the back of my tunic because I can't extend my right hand. We're just clinging onto each other so as not to fall and make things worse as the boat continues to rock gently like a cradle stern to bow and we must negotiate our way through bodies and cargo to the stern deck railing and gate. Word has passed back through our line that we will use an emergency slide to descend ten feet down into the rescue boat which is little more than a thirty-foot yawl with a large battery and electric motor. The winds are too high to sail but if the battery dies we will anchor and wait until sailing is possible. We are only three miles from our destination. I don't know where this information is coming from. Someone must be getting a signal or have talked to the Captain. Anyway, I choose to believe it. I focus again on my arm as I see the bright white light of the yawl reflected on the water to port as it comes around to the stern and prepares to tie up there. It's mesmerizing to see the bright light, the white shine on the rippled water spattered with rain; you can almost see the drops pinging off the black surface. I am trying to block the image of Star, of course, her face watching me and tears seeping from her eyes which I'm sure she thinks I did not see. Her courage. All of them. That gives me heart. They have so much more courage than we did at that age. And I think of Dix, an image I also would like to block, his shattered expression as he helped Catherine to the center of the boat and watched as Shanika cleaned the blood from her broken nose and gashed cheek. A crate of urns had slammed against the wall and shattered, tripping her. I saw it happen somehow, in the strange shaft of silver light through the lower windows. It was an instant just before I too fell, hit by the shifting cargo, and broke my arm. JoJo didn't have time to set it or even splint it, but Shanika helped wrap it to my chest with strips of cloth. Dix is still behind us, watching us leave, as is Star. I caught Riga's glance just before I turned to go and I swear ze was sending me a message; I could hear the words as if ze'd spoken them in my ear, "We'll take care of them, we will be safe, we will see you soon." Did ze really think or say those words? Yes, I choose to believe so. The yawl has been secured to the stern of our boat and the slide set in place. We are told to pull the string on our inflatable life vests. They must have scavenged these off airplanes. This random thought comes to me as suddenly I and everyone else become several inches wider and shift and stumble against each other. There is some sense of urgency that we disembark before any major shift to the boat, which so precariously rests on its fractured hull and the floating raft of enormous tree branches with which we collided. The flailing branches. I shrug but *ouch* that hurts. Focus. My purpose right now—take care of myself. And in fact, I'm next up after JoJo who follows the children. I am the oldest, by decades. And Catherine is next. I watch JoJo gracefully descend and hop to her feet on the deck of the yawl. I wave away the hand that reaches to take my right arm and extend my left and the young Potter instinctively understands and gently helps position me in a seated position at the top of the slide, legs extended. I lean forward a bit and let go. I'm grateful for all those playgrounds that still existed when I was a child. A young woman in an emergency vest smiles at me and helps me stand, then points to a cabin door that I should enter across the deck. Now I do wish for my walking stick. It's raining steadily and the deck is slippery. I shuffle along as if I'm drugged and reach out my good arm toward the lighted cabin so I can grab anything that presents itself. A hand comes from nowhere and grips mine, a strong steadying grasp for which I am deeply grateful. I see a young muscular man in an emergency vest who with just his strong hand nearly lifts me from the deck to the cabin door and waits while I find the rail of the metal stairway. I see JoJo and the children below and she comes to the foot of the steep stairs to help me to a bench. An oil lamp on a wooden shelf lights the cabin. It's comforting, the soft light and glow on the warm wood, despite the rocking, rocking, motion. I sit. The children beside me are totally silent, even Taddie. I wonder if we're all in shock. I see Catherine coming down the metal steps now. She looks dazed. I hope she hasn't had a concussion. Two more, the young Potter men, make their way down the steps and there are ten of us crammed in the cabin. I suppose the others are less injured and stay on the deck above because soon I hear some commands and lines being whipped from moorings and we push off from the Sunstar, our disabled ferry, and glide through the sea. There is a light slapping of water at the sides of the yawl, we are low enough to the water to hear it. The cabin door is open and there are open portholes above us. The air might be stifling otherwise and I am grateful. It's very warm outside, over eighty degrees. Very humid with the rain. I shift on the bench, trying to relax as we get under way. I look across at the opposite bench and the children sitting rigidly still with JoJo who is ministering to them, murmuring soothing words, giving them some kind of snacks she managed to bring. It looks like the pastries the Potters make, fried buckwheat pancakes rolled with honey. A precious gift. They take them warily at first, and then with enthusiasm. Only Ariel is slow to respond. She looks terrified. I want to weep for her because she had been doing so well. But I see that JoJo has her eye on her.

I turn to Catherine who is looking straight ahead at nothing, it seems. We are rocking more now, side to side and I wonder if the wind is stirring up waves on the water. Then suddenly she turns to me. "I'm so worried about Dix," she says. I nod. As I said, he looked shattered. "Riga said ze will take care of Dix and not to worry," I tell her. Somehow I believe this. She narrows her eyes, confused, considering. And then I see her decide to believe it too. I'd told her about my dream, after all, the wind, the trees. Her shoulders drop a bit, she leans back. She puts a hand up to her face, her nose that must be throbbing and then the gash on her cheek.

"Don't touch it," I say. Meaning the gash. There's no bandage or antiseptic, although I'm sure JoJo will see to it eventually, just as she will splint my arm. I have enormous faith in JoJo, in all the young people.

The Potter boys are clearly in a lot of pain and yet they seem excited, to be underway again, to have escaped, to be heading into the unknown. Although one of them looks sad beneath his eager face, to leave his family behind, I imagine. And I too feel a sudden stabbing pain, survivor's guilt, and dread of it. Especially me. Honestly. The 70-year-old! Couldn't you have let me drown and let Star live!! I want to scream it. Catherine takes my hand. We sit silently in our grief.

The yawl clips along, it must have a lot of power stored, it's like a Tesla I think, sleek and strong. A kind of light seems to be seeping through the portholes. One of the sailors in an emergency vest, the young woman who helped us off the slide, comes quickly down the metal steps into the cabin and smiles at us, then extinguishes the oil lamp. I see the light in the portholes is orange. Dawn. I want to stand and look out to see the Sunstar, if it is still upright, but think better of it. It must be. And my job now is to take care of myself and present no problem to anyone, and to heal and help the Caretakers in their mission. How can I forget something so simple?

I think of Dix. Was all the cargo lost, I wonder? Will there be clay soil in the foothills to begin again? It's too devastating to think of. Our precarious hold on purpose and meaning, at the bottom of the sea. If that isn't the truth of our times.

The young sailor is speaking quietly to JoJo; I can hear some of her words.... "Dock....town...shelter...." And then she turns to us and says that we will be arriving in fifteen minutes. I hear JoJo say her name, "Sandia," and ask her something; could she have said the word "wheelchair"? I feel that must be wishful thinking, and then I feel an extreme wave of anxiety. I catch my breath and close my eyes, willing myself not to hyperventilate. Catherine continues to calmly hold my hand. I let all of my bodily sensation focus on her calm hand in mine and I begin to right myself. This moment. This moment.

And then we are there. The children go out first, climbing the stairs with the help of Sandia and JoJo. The boat is rocking less, moored tightly to a dock I assume. Then Sandia returns and motions to me and I follow her to mount the metal steps, squinting as I come into the morning light. It has stopped raining although the sky is overcast. I immediately peer out to what I think is due west but it is too far away to see the Sunstar, I tell myself, since I do not see it. Sandia is guiding me to the gate in the rail at the edge of the deck and instructs the young man on the other side not to touch my right arm. He leans out and takes my left hand and Sandia gives me a little guiding shove so I can jump over the gap between the boat deck and the dock. My arm screams, although I do not, when I land on both feet safely. And then, can I believe my eyes? It's a wheelchair. Someone is rolling it up the wooden dock which appears to be made of prefab siding. It is a floating dock I realize as I mindlessly gaze at it and feel its swaying. They must need to move it as the sea keeps rising. The pain is greater now that we've escaped the boat, like someone has plunged a knife into my upper arm. Catherine is staying by my side as she removes her life vest and Sandia removes mine and I get in the wheelchair and the three of us turn and head slowly along the swaying dock to the shore ahead, where two young people in bright emergency armbands lift me, chair and all, to solid ground. A stone path leads to a large shed, some kind of receiving building? We pause just outside.

"Look," Catherine gently touches my shoulder and I turn my head to follow her gaze, back to the dock and the sea. The yawl is turning and raising its sails, and just ahead are four large sloops fully rigged and heeling to port as they skim over the water gaining speed in the light northerly wind. The wind that must have finally blown the storm away. I look south and see distant dark clouds, but due west not too far from us a thick white mist rises from the sea. The heat is already more intense. Even the puddles on the path, where we wait for the rest of our refugee group from the yawl, have a light mist lifting as they evaporate. So quickly the moisture falls hard then rises gently back into the laden atmosphere. We were so lucky, I think, to have the four dry days on our trek and at the Muir House. I look west, peering hard into the mist as the sloops disappear one by one into the white cloud. The Sunstar must still be upright if they are sending rescue boats. I look at Catherine who rests her hand on my shoulder.

Our group of survivors gathers together as someone—the Mayor?—comes out of the shed and asks for our attention. He welcomes us in English and then in Spanish until Sandia tells him we are all English-speakers. He explains that we are in New Rose, established in 2028 as a transit hub and waystation for refugees from around the world. The train to the Capitol and farther east to Mountains and Heartland originates here. Although many in our group seem to know all of this, it is news to me. I'd thought we were going to Roseville, the old railroad town Dale and I visited once decades ago en route to Heavenly Valley for a ski trip. Did Star know this? We are being gently herded into the shed for some kind of screening. We see large windows on the eastern wall of the shed looking onto a paved road where a few electric carts stand; and up the hill is a cluster of structures—a small town. Catherine and I are guided to a table staffed by young people in lab coats. They have some kind of electronic wands they run over us, like the TSA of old, I think. And in fact our next stop is to go through metal detectors. Catherine has taken to pushing my wheelchair as Sandia is needed elsewhere. At the next station we get some kind of swab, like a TB test; I'm not sure. I feel my hope flagging a bit. If this is not Roseville...did I hear him or someone say, population just over 400? There will be no hospital here. As I'm waiting for the second swab to be prepared I glance around and, as my eyes adjust to the dim light, I see photographs on the wall. They look like historic photos, perhaps of the original Roseville? I ask the young woman with the swabs, "What happened to Roseville? The original city?"

"It was abandoned during the war," she says. "It's just a few miles from here, down the hill. It flooded the last several winters and sometimes in summer, too." She gently takes my good arm and scrapes some skin.

"But it was such a big city," I say. "I mean, for this area."

"Some people still live there in the abandoned buildings on higher ground. They're people from all over the world."

I'm stunned and say nothing. An international squatters' zone? Or can you really say "squatters" now.... I don't understand. I feel thoroughly exhausted and would fall asleep this instant if it weren't for the stabbing pain in my arm. If "shock" had been protecting me from the pain two hours ago, it's worn off.

We are shunted to the next table near the east wall of windows. There is light here and a young man sits at a table with an actual laptop in front of him. I look for the cord and see it is indeed plugged into the wall. He sees my gaze. "Hydraulic power." He cocks his head to the left toward something. "Rose creek, running strong right now." I look out the window he's indicated and see only dense foliage and trees. A riparian landscape, I suppose.

He looks at me more closely and his eyes soften. "Could you tell me your name, please? And age, and where you're coming from?"

I give him the information.

"What are you bringing with you?"

"Not much, I'm afraid." It all feels familiar now. We are in customs. "I have some clothing and personal effects but they're still on the ferry. I also have a mid-size pack of medical supplies I was carrying for our group. And a few hundred plant seeds."

He nods sympathetically, typing on the laptop.

"Where are you planning to go eventually? Your destination?"

I press my lips together. I have no idea now. He sees my hesitation. "I'll put destination status pending." He glances at the open door to his left.

Sandia is back. "Please follow me," she says to Catherine and me and we go out the door to a beautiful shaded patio. I feel quite alert because the pain is keeping my nerves zinging. I look around; the fabulous colors of the flowers in the wooden boxes look psychedelic to me.

"Beautiful," Catherine murmurs. So it must be real. But then I remember she's probably in a great deal of pain also.

There are scarlets, deep purples, lush greens of every hue and bright yellows. The pale stone of the patio is richly veined with golds and silvers. All is in dappled shade from the surrounding tall ferns and dogwood trees. There are comfortable chairs and benches along the sides and Catherine wheels me to the far edge and sits on a bench there as we wait for the others. Sandia stands nearby and I take the opportunity to ask her. "Did I understand correctly that the population of New Rose is about 400?"

She turns to me. "Yes, that's right, for our permanent residents. But there are over a hundred refugees in town at any given time and there are as many as a thousand others staying down in Old Town. The train only runs once a week," she finishes, as if this explains it all.

"Do the refugees all arrive by the ferry?" Catherine sounds bewildered.

"No, no. Most of the coastal population has already emigrated in the last decade. Many people are coming up through the southern deserts now."

JoJo and the kids come through the glass doors from the customs shed and the kids rush to sit with us, sticking close. JoJo holds Ariel's hand and may not have let go of it for the past three hours. They sit on the bench with Catherine and on the ground. JoJo looks exhausted but she smiles at me and then Catherine. "How are you?"

"We're fine," we lie and smile. Sandia goes to the door to see how the others are coming along and then disappears inside.

"Marcus said there's a clinic in the town and we'll go there as soon as possible."

"Marcus?" I ask. "The Mayor?"

JoJo actually laughs. "I don't know if ze's the mayor, but ze is in charge of refugee relocation here. Ze and Sandia."

Sandia comes back again and tells us she will be taking Catherine and me to the clinic as soon as the injured Potter boys come through. Someone named Mae will be arriving to take JoJo and the kids to the Mariposa House where we will all be staying temporarily.

I can't help it, I ask Sandia, "Is there any word about the Sunstar?"

"The rescue boats haven't arrived at the scene yet but they have sighted the ferry and it is still afloat."

"Are they in contact…." Catherine's voice trails.

"They're conserving power. The goal is to get everyone to safety and, also, to save the ferry itself."

I realize then that the ferry is the only remaining means of transporting people from the coast of Westlands.

Sandia offers me a gentle smile and asks, "Are you ready?"

"Yes, thank you." I return her smile and feel somehow restored in her presence, able to mirror her kindness. The five words "you reap what you sow" appear in my mind like ticker tape. I hope I'm not starting to hallucinate.

I feel my chair inch forward as Sandia pushes me into position and Catherine joins us on the winding path. The two Potter boys have limped up to join us. Sandia has given one of them a crutch, and I hear Catherine offering them words of comfort and reassurance. One has a blood-soaked bandage covering his forearm, though the blood looks dried.

We are taken to the road where we transfer into the electric carts—golf carts, we used to call them. I almost laugh. Sandia loads the wheelchair onto the back of ours.

As we wind up the steep incline and over a rise the whole town comes into view, nestled among blue and valley oaks and bright green leafy buckeyes with their white fragrant blossoms. The birdsong is music to my ears. And again, there is the brilliant color of flowers in window boxes and fenced squares like miniature parks along the roadway. It's confounding. Who has time for this?

"Here we are." Sandia stops and gestures at a structure to our right beyond a stand of willows, and as we approach I see it is a large adobe building with a colorful mural painted on one side. I gaze at it, a little dumbstruck, as I wait for Sandia to get the wheelchair off the cart. It is a beautiful painting, a flowing waterfall on silvery rocks surrounded by lush trees and forest, flowers in a clearing, people—in some kind of dance or welcoming ritual, their faces full of compassion, their features and skin tones of every race and ethnicity. I've never seen anything like it, even in the days of street murals in the cities I once knew. We disembark and I am glad to be able to get myself down and into the wheelchair. A large door on another wall of the building opens and Sandia gently guides the four of us to the entrance.

There are cushioned chairs in a small room with skylights that open to the blue sky and a sparse tree canopy above. The Potter boy with the blood-soaked bandages is called in first. But Sandia appears with some pills. "Would you like any ibuprofen?" she asks. Catherine makes a garbled sound, a "god yes." We all are eager for the pills and Sandia offers them with slices of some kind of oat bread and ceramic cups of water. I suddenly want to ask Sandia, "Who are you? Who are you people?" Though of course I don't.

The front door of the clinic opens and JoJo appears. She's washed her face and redone her long braid, and wears a white lab coat. Sandia welcomes her and shows her in to one of the exam rooms. A few minutes later I'm called in and JoJo is my doctor. I feel enormous relief as she begins to gently remove my tunic, and then takes a glass syringe from a tray on the counter and injects a local anesthetic in my arm.

"Where's Ariel?" I ask as we wait for it to take effect.

"She's asleep. Rosa at the Mariposa House is looking after her and will bring her here if she wakes up before I'm back."

She works in silence for several minutes as I try not to flinch and wait for the pain meds to kick in more.

"It's a simple break," I hear JoJo say after she has palpated my arm which was painful, despite her wonderfully gentle touch.

She looks at me a second. "Are you ready for me to set it?"

I nod, and she makes quick work of it and I suppose I'm almost numb to pain at this point. I'm glad it's done. Someone has found a large splint and she wraps my right arm, bent at the elbow. She hands me a small cloth tie-string bag with more ibuprofen. "Every twelve hours. Can you ask Catherine to come in? Sandia had to go back down to the dock." JoJo gives me a brief gentle hug and turns back to the sink to wash.

I wonder what that means, what is happening at the dock—if more have arrived. I re-enter the waiting room and smile at Catherine. "Your turn," I say. We exchange a wry look. "I'll wait here." I know I should go up to the Mariposa House and check on Ariel but, I don't know where it is. I need to rest a moment. I'm not sure if I'm supposed to leave the wheelchair here to walk up the road or.... I feel suddenly a bit overwhelmed and I miss Catherine's quiet presence beside me; I hadn't realized how calming and reassuring it was. Of course I think of Star, I hadn't meant to because it is dangerous to do so. No, I tell myself and focus on the remaining Potter boy across from me. He looks both frightened and defiant. He's probably sixteen. Who knows where his parents are or if he has any. His left foot looks badly twisted, possibly broken. I can't think of what to say to him. I try to soften my mind, my heart, radiate calm and hope. What else is there to do.

"They said you dreamed it," he says to me out of nowhere.

I look at him. I smile, kindly, trying to think. Did someone overhear me telling Catherine my dream back at the creek behind the Muir House, the day we filtered water? He's still staring at me, angry or curious?

"I only dreamed of the storm, not the ferry," I say. "It was a shock, the accident. Such a hard time for us all."

"My brother drowned," he says. I remember then, the boys out on the deck with ropes, trying to save the Potters' wares.

I nod, my eyes tearing, despite myself. "I'm so sorry."

He nods, too. We are silent a moment.

"What was his name?" I ask.

"Ricky."

"He was a brave boy, wasn't he."

"I couldn't get him the rope."

"No, I saw how impossible it was. I saw through the window of the cabin. It was impossible."

He looks at me.

"There was nothing you could do. But you were so brave. You tried everything you could to help. Both of you. You were both so brave."

He looks down then. He's heard enough from me. I pray that he believes me.

"Ricky should'na gone out there," he finally says.

"It was a hard choice," I agree.

"He shoulda stayed inside like I told him."

"You tried to help him. And you did everything you could."

We were silent for several minutes. I could feel him seeing the drowning, over again, and again.

Catherine opens the door from the exam rooms. She has a bandage over her nose and another beneath her eye which is swollen shut. I feel leaden. I can't leave the boy here alone.

"Jason," Catherine says. "I'll wait for you."

"Naw, that's okay," he says to her. "I'll meet you at that house they told us about. The Mariposa." His tone is that of an adult now.

She hesitates but JoJo appears at the door. "Catherine, you need to lie down and take care of that concussion." Then she looks at me. "Sandia will be here in a minute to take you up to the house."

"Jason?" she looks at the boy with such compassion I feel its comfort. "Could you come in now?"

He pushes himself into a standing position and limps over to the door to follow her inside.

"He lost his older brother," Catherine says to me quietly when the door is closed. I nod.

"Does he have other family?" I ask.

"On the ferry," she says. "His mother and an older sister."

"You should probably go ahead and lie down," I tell her.

"A few more minutes doesn't matter. Besides, I don't know where it is." She sounds terribly weary. But Sandia walks in then and says, "Ready?" She looks flushed as if she's run from the dock.

"Is there any news?" Catherine asks.

"The sloops arrived. They're bringing back most of the passengers now. The crew of the yawl and some of your group are staying to try to save the ferry."

Both Catherine and I are quiet, our eyes welling with tears. "How will they save the ferry?" she asks as Sandia takes the handles of my wheelchair and begins to push me out the door.

"They're securing the branches to the hull so that it doesn't touch the water and the ferry can be towed, still listing. The yawl will tow it. They're removing the battery pack from the ferry and installing it in the yawl to give it the necessary power. They said there's a man on the ferry, an engineer, who said it can be done and is overseeing it."

Oh my god, I think, as I look at Catherine. Dix. She looks shocked, and then—is it elation?

"We won't know for several hours but the weather looks to be calm so it should be possible. One of the sloops will go back out to bring them in if they fail."

And then I realize, of course Star and Riga will be part of the ferry rescue team. I don't know what skills they can offer, but they will be there. I'm too tired to think. I pray I can sleep until the results are known.

As we come out into the bright sunlight I see two of the sloops tied up at the dock down the hill and passengers disembarking. Is that Shanika? And Kamala? I hope so. We need all the Caretakers. I hope some of the medical supplies were salvaged. I turn back to look at the street we are on and the buildings up ahead. Some of the two-story houses look like they're from the 19th century, but how, I can't guess. Others are adobe structures like the clinic. I wonder now if they even have a doctor at the clinic, but they must have. A surgeon who is tending to the slashed arm.

"Here we are," Sandia announces. She opens a low iron gate and we walk along another stone path through the remarkable garden. More brilliant colored flowers, dense ferns and some flowering trees. There is a sloping ramp up to a verandah, all wood, painted in mauve with yellow trim. There is a round wooden plaque above the large ornate double doors bearing a painting of a Monarch butterfly and the words "Mariposa House".

We enter a large foyer and Sandia introduces us to Mae, the "Dona" of the house.

"Can you share a room?" Mae asks after she greets us. "There are five beds."

"Yes, of course," we say. I can't place her accent. "May I see Ariel?" I ask.

"Ze is sleeping. Rosa is with zir. Can we get you settled now?" She smiles and then leads us to a large stairway beyond the foyer. We climb the stairs slowly with the help of the sturdy rail and then go down a hallway to a room in a kind of wing of its own, high ceilings and tall windows looking out on the back garden. I have a powerful wave of déjà vu.

"The Muir House," Catherine says.

"Oh, of course."

"It's so lovely, thank you" Catherine says to Mae.

"You're welcome." Mae smiles warmly at us. "You can choose your beds and there is a kitchen downstairs. You can share the food there. Help yourself."

"Thank you," I say.

"Let me know if there are questions. Also, Mikael can help you. Ze is downstairs in the office. You can call zir with that intercom, if you wish." She points to a simple speaker with two buttons on the wall that looks as if it may be a century old.

"I believe you must pull the curtains and have a dark room," she says to Catherine. Sandia must have told Mae that Catherine has a concussion. Mae quickly goes from window to window and pulls the long curtains closed and the room becomes dusky, almost dark. "Sleep well," she says. Then she is gone.

Catherine and I immediately choose two beds on the wall across from the garden windows. They are single beds with carved wood posts and big fluffy, goose-down pillows.

The bed covers are beautiful woven fabrics from who knows where—colorful and in traditional designs of birds, animals and flowers. A different world. A lost world. Or one I'd thought was lost. I lay down on my left side too tired to undress or even pull back the covers and despite how nervous and strange I feel I fall asleep in minutes.

Star

There's a Potter kid in the crow's nest at the top of the yawl's mast. I'm starin' straight up there and I can't believe how blue the sky is. There's no trace of clouds except far off to the south miles away. I've got my hand up to shade my eyes cuz the sun is a fierce glare, real hot.

"Jan," somebody yells to the kid in the crow's nest and Jan looks down and swings a long cable so gently, I'm amazed. A crew member catches it in one hand and takes it to the yawl rail to hand it to Riga here on the ferry. Riga walks it to Dix and the Captain who have the ferry's battery pack in a big basket on the deck. They spent all morning gettin' it out and rewired. We're all so grateful for Dix, it is a blessing ze is here—this is all zir idea.

I look east to the distant shore that is our destination. I wonder how Mom is. I feel so grateful ze got there. Everybody except Dix, the Captain, the boat crews and me and Riga and a couple Potters, already left on the sailboats they sent out from the shore. Someone told us there's a clinic there and that's where the injured people went.

"Star," Riga says. I go over to help and ze asks me to get everybody who's not workin' on the battery to take the slide over to the yawl and stand on its starboard side.

It took hours to get the tree branches under the hull of the ferry trimmed and tied tight against it so it's like a sled runner. That hull can't touch water or it could tip the ferry the other way and maybe sink it, I don't know. I'm just doin' what they tell me.

Our group joins the yawl crew to stand on the starboard rail and prepare to lean way over the water for ballast when the heavy basket starts swingin' from the cable.

I watch Dix for a minute and I gotta say ze's lookin' kinda tired and really red in the face. Ze must be past fifty, which is heart attack age my dad used to say, tho for Dad, it was his sixties. I pray for Dix. Ze has done so much good. I never really noticed zir 'til today cuz ze's a quiet type. I remember now how I saw Dix alone with a book in the orchard at the Muir House. Ze's sweatin' like crazy now. But I'm glad the mist burned off a couple hours ago cuz we couldn't see a thing in that fog. We were crazy shocked when those sailboats appeared and surrounded the ferry. I didn't think there was enough of a breeze to carry them along but these people are skilled sailors. I saw oars strapped on their boat decks so I guess that's what we'll be doin' if we get becalmed. Riga and I and the Potters are gonna go back on a sloop that came back here about an hour ago. Dix, the Captain and all the crew are gonna be on the yawl, towin' the ferry.

"Three, two, one...." the Captain's shoutin' and we lean way out over the water at, "Go!" as they winch the cable from the yawl mast and it rocks us like we're gonna sink and the battery's swayin' wild above the ferry, which rocks a little too. I can't see much cuz my body's twisted over the rail, and we are just willin' this boat to stay upright and hopin' the mast won't snap, but then the basket swings to the yawl wheelhouse and the crew grabs it and we do a kinda shimmy to distribute our weight for better ballast. Finally the battery's down and we relax. I turn around and see Dix, the Captain and Riga ridin' the slide here to the yawl. Two ferry crew stay behind cuz they're gonna have to stay on the ferry all the way to shore.

First the yawl has to have the battery pack hooked up. I hope Dix can keep on goin' but then I look at zir face and see ze seems pretty excited, like this is kinda fun. The Captain looks grim, tho, like the ferry is zir baby and it's hurt and may not survive. And I think of Mom again. I hope ze is holdin' up.

"Are you sad?" Riga says. Ze 's next to me, ze's like a cat that way. I look up and smile. "No. Just thinkin' about Mom." Riga's eyes get soft and I can see ze knows what I mean. Then ze looks back at the battery pack and Dix and the others gettin' ready to move it into the place where the small yawl battery was. There's some grunts and warnings, watch out, over here, and then they've got it down where it needs to be.

The Captain stands up, holdin' zir back like it hurts a lot. Then ze looks at the ferry, the yawl, and the sloop anchored fifty feet away. Ze straightens zir hat, a broad brimmed cap like what we all put on when the sun came out. Ze even has on sunglasses and so do the crew. Where and how, I'm wonderin'… Then ze walks over to Riga, and me and the Potters who are still in our ballast group.

"We'll keep Dix here with us and the crews of the Sunstar and Endurance," ze says, which are the ferry and the yawl. "But you all can go back on the Seadog." Ze looks up at the sun and then out across the sea. There's a good breeze that riffles the surface of the water but no whitecaps. "I'm not sure when we'll get everything hooked up, and we have to have a calm sea to make the crossing. If we need more rescuing later, the fewer of us the better."

"Of course," Riga says and we all agree and then the Captain goes to the wheelhouse and makes an announcement with a bullhorn.

We look around for any stuff we can take and one of the ferry crew brings some baggage to the slide and sends it down to us on the yawl. It doesn't take long for the sloop to put up its sails and come around. We toss the bags to the sloop crew and then each of us climbs down the rope ladder from the yawl and jumps on board.

I look back at the listing ferry and the yawl tied up next to it. I can't see Dix but the crew on the Sunstar wave to us as we set sail toward land. The wind feels good in my hair and I gotta say it's a relief to be off that boat. I say a prayer for them all who we're leavin' behind. What else can we do? I glance at Riga. Ze's lookin' at the ferry and yawl, then up at the sky and then across the water. Ze knows this sea a little, it's zir fifth crossing, ze said. And Riga knows the town we're goin' to tho ze hasn't told me much about it.

There's no clouds in the sky but that doesn't mean a lot cuz anything can stir up. I say another prayer. And I see in my mind Catherine's face and the blood from zir nose and cheek, and how ze looked at Dix before gettin' on the slide down to the yawl. I could just hardly see in the dim emergency light and that strange moon glow low in the south. It feels like days ago, but I guess it was just this morning.

We're clippin' along pretty good. The jib was luffed but now it's full out and we heel to starboard, goin' northwest. Then pretty soon we tack to port and we'll be tackin' all the way back, the crew says, and duckin' this boom. I can see the land to the east better now. In the west the sun's lower, it's probably late afternoon. I look at my watch but it must've gotten wet this morning cuz it says 7:00.

Riga's talkin' to the sailor at the tiller, and then ze scoots over to sit by me. "We'll be docking over at Old Town," ze says. "They need to keep the whole New Rose dock open for the ferry and yawl."

"What old town?" I ask.

"Roseville," ze says. "It was the big railroad station here a long time ago, no?"

"I don't know anything about it," I say.

"It started 200 years ago, and it became a small city. Then airplanes became the way to travel, so Roseville wasn't important anymore. Many people left. Then they built factories and the city grew again. But in The Fail the factories closed and everybody left for good. Also, now it floods when the winters are bad. Creeks come down the mountain overflowing water and silt. All the streets are covered in dried mud—you will see. But New Rose, it is on a bedrock hill two miles away.

"Is that where they took everyone else, to New Rose?"

"Yes. I'm sure."

"What's it like?"

Ze gets a big smile on zir face like I haven't seen since we got on that ferry. "It's beautiful!" Ze opens out zir arms wide in a happy way. I don't know how ze kept such good teeth, it makes zir smile gorgeous. I think it every time.

"Flowers everywhere in spring! Waterfalls and trees and stone paths and beautiful houses."

"Who lives there?" It sounds like a fairy tale.

"The people who built it before the war. Reformers and refugees moved big wood houses from Old Town before the floods would destroy them. Also they built new houses with adobe bricks they made. There is a windmill at every house. And the gardens! There is a bee farm and greenhouses." Ze smiles, kinda wistful, looks like.

"Why didn't you stay there?"

"I'm a Guide," ze says, like, case closed. I guess it's like the military where you do your role no questions asked.

"The people there have a mission," Riga says, "and I am part of it. The mission is to welcome and help refugees. I bring the refugees."

We're holdin' hands and I squeeze zir hand a little. I get it.

We watch the water for awhile. I'm wonderin' about this new town, tryin' to imagine it, and the abandoned city—Old Town.

"What'll we do in the Old Town if they leave us there?"

Ze laughs at first. "We walk!" ze says with a kinda happy energy. Ze's feelin' so glad to get back to this place, I see. "It's two miles. Only a little hill to climb."

I look at our packs and stuff and I gotta say I'm feelin' pretty tired.

"No, maybe they will come and get us in the electric carts." Then ze looks at me, more serious. "Old Town is a sad sight," ze says. "Many buildings are falling down and some are rotten from the floods. But people are living there."

"What? Whadda ya mean?"

"First it was like *favelas*—slums, no? There were poor people from before, but most were war refugees too old or sick to travel more. Almost all of them have died now, but they had children and people in Old Town now are children of the war, no? They do the best they can. They forage and grow food and wash their clothes in the sea. They live." Ze shrugs.

"But what! Why don't they live in the beautiful new town?"

"New Rose is for refugees who are traveling. It is a waystation. There are 100 refugees living in New Rose at any time, you will see. We will probably stay in Mariposa House or Walburg House. They are houses, like hostels, no? Refugees stay there until they take the train east.

There is room for only one hundred. But also there are houses for the people who do the work—hard work. They run the hostels, the clinic, the gardens, the train station, and the ferry. They have a town council of nine people who meet every month with the whole town. Oh you should see it!"

"What? See what?"

"The conservatory where they meet—it is all made of glass from everywhere in the world. It took years to build. There are so many colors and when the sun comes through it is a magic place! It is full of plants. It has a big reputation and when people come here, they bring a piece of colored glass from their homeland. Oh I love this place."

"But why can't they help the people in Old Town two miles away?" We both duck as the boom sweeps over our head with a loud clatter and the boat tacks again. I look out to the east now, just across from us and see the shore getting closer, but still so far away. It seems like miles of blue water, blue sky, kinda empty.

"They did help them when they first arrived. But they never left and there was no room. The new town was not built for a big population. It is a waystation."

"But...the people exist here now. How can they ignore them?"

Riga looks kinda exasperated, like I'm not being realistic, but I just don't get it. I see zir take a breath, and then try again, "They do help them. They take extra food there. They built windmills on the hillside so there is power now. They do all they can. But their first job is, and it always was, to welcome new refugees from lands that were destroyed, where nothing is left."

I guess I know what ze means. There are the workers runnin' the refugee waystation and they live in the new town. Then there's a lot of other people who aren't part of the helping operation who're just tryin' to survive. They live in the slum down the hill. Maybe slum's the wrong word. Maybe we're havin' a language problem. I just don't wanna believe it's like things were before. Second-class citizens, income inequality, all that stuff I saw when I was a kid and the way it was before the war. I wanna believe it's better now. I feel this like a burning in my chest. I'm grippin' Riga's hand hard I realize, and ze grips my hand back. It's better than words. We want the same thing. I believe that.

We watch the water. We both decide, without sayin', that's it'll be better for me to just see for myself. Plus we're so tired. I lean up against Riga and we snuggle in, layin' back against the bench a little and close our eyes. I pull my hat over my face, but the sun feels good on my tired muscles, even if it's crazy hot. And I gotta say, I have the thought that I wanna ask Riga about where to get some sunglasses.

Mom

When I wake I see my walking stick. It's propped at the foot of the bed and the top is wrapped in a bright red satiny fabric, a handle. I look around the room and there is Star laying in a bed on the other side, asleep, just visible in the band of light between the drawn curtains. In the next bed is Riga. I'm sure of it. And then I realize I'm dreaming. I lay my head back on the pillow. But no, there is only darkness. I am not in the dream world. I open my eyes again. Yes. The high ceilings, the Victorian windows. The Mariposa House. I use my left arm to raise my body and crane my neck around to the bed behind me. Catherine is still sound asleep. I edge quietly over and maneuver my feet to the floor to stand, then tip-toe to my walking stick and wrap one hand around the cool red satin. I lean on it a moment. I can hardly contain my elation. Star. My living heart.

Silently, I pad to the door of the room and ease it open. The hallway is light from the tall uncovered windows at either end. I see a door ajar across from me and am delighted to find a bathroom with working plumbing. Then I make my way down the stairs, and I hear voices from what I think is the kitchen, but no, it is a parlor, you might say, at the front of the house. It must be early evening. I couldn't have slept through to the next day, could I? The sun is low in the sky but whether it is about to set or recently rose, I'm not sure.

Where is Dix, I wonder. I follow the voices. There are three young people in the parlor. I stand at the edge of the doorway and listen a moment. They are speaking English, although two of them occasionally address each other in a language I don't know. For some reason I think of what Catherine told me on the Sunstar, before the accident, about Riga. How the Tinkers talking among themselves had called Riga "that gypsy." A young woman in the parlor looks over to the door and sees me and beckons me to come in. I do.

"Did you come on the Sunstar?" she asks.

I nod. "Yes. This morning..." I trail off, how to describe.

"We heard about the accident," she says, "and the rescue is going very well." She glances at one of her companions.

"There were two deaths, it's true," she says, and my heart stops in my chest. "Two young people who fell overboard trying to save their cargo. But everyone else is accounted for. The council has heard from the Captain. They're bringing the Sunstar in now."

Nonetheless, I feel my eyes tear up—the young Potters, Ricky... I think again of his brother, Jason.

"Will you sit with us a moment?" the first woman asks.

"Yes, well, I—thank you." I sit down. But I'm very hungry suddenly. "Who is the counsel?" I ask. I'm surprised there's a lawyer involved somehow but some things never change. My mind is feeling foggy, and I think of Catherine, her concussion. I should bring her something to eat or drink.

"Our city council," the Spanish-speaking woman says. "By the way, my name is Adrianna. This is Pyotr." She gestures to the man on her left. "And Chinua." She smiles at the other woman.

"Nice to meet you," I smile. "I am Mom." I say, since that is what they will hear me called, though I feel silly saying it.

"Our council is a collective of nine members. We were talking about the meeting last night and plans to install a windmill at each occupied dwelling in Old Town. But you must need something to eat," she says looking into my eyes with concern.

"Well, yes." I stand. "Can you tell me where the kitchen is?"

Adrianna stands, too, and then takes my elbow as she guides me out of the parlor, around the stairway, to the back of the house where there is a large kitchen. Every room we pass has dark wood wainscoting and tall leaded glass windows. All is beautifully maintained and polished, and, in fact, I see a young man dusting the furniture and artifacts in one of the rooms where there are several shelves with what appear to be historical items.

"Shanika!" I can't help but cry out as I see her standing in the kitchen with two of the children.

"Mom!" she rushes over to hug me, taking care not to touch my right shoulder.

Adrianna stands just behind us, smiling, and when I step back from Shanika's embrace, she hands me my walking stick. I hadn't realized she had it while helping me find the kitchen. I feel so cared for, it calms me for a moment; and I remember that Star is asleep upstairs, that we are here, in this house, in this remarkable town, safe for the moment.

"If you will excuse me I will return to my meeting." Adrianna smiles at us and as she leaves I realize she must be a member of the town council.

"Mom, let me make you something to eat," Shanika says. "Can you watch the kids a minute?" The kids have come up to me and are examining the splint on my arm.

"What happened?" Jasmine asks. Her eyes are wide and I feel how anxious she is, and yet excited—a sense of adventure she also feels, and I hope that is the feeling that wins out for her. Little Mikey, at her side, says nothing and just stares.

"Let's sit here," I say. There is a breakfast nook with bay windows and bench seats around a wooden table and we snuggle up on one side. Shanika returns with a platter of strawberries, cherries, bean cakes, lettuce and a dark brown syrup on a flat multi-grain bread. We have plates and forks and spoons and cloth napkins. We help ourselves. Late afternoon sunlight streams through the bay windows and I see the uppermost panes are colored glass, an interesting pattern of what appear to be tulips. We're quiet as we eat and I can't think when we last ate so well but it must have just been two days ago at the Muir house. The children finish quickly and seem revitalized. They start to squirm a bit and then go under the table to get out and run around the kitchen playing some kind of tag or hide and seek. They venture into the adjoining dining room with their game and we keep them in sight. I feel considerable relief seeing them play.

"Was JoJo at the clinic?" Shanika asks.

"Yes, she set my arm." I look closely at her and feel the urge to unburden myself of what's been concerning me. Shanika is a trained health professional and will understand.

"The Potter boy, Jason, was there waiting to be seen. His brother Ricky was drowned this morning."

"Yes." Shanika presses her lips in a tight line, remembering.

"He spoke to me," I say. "Told me about it. He was very traumatized, angry, sad, guilty. I made a snap decision to try to help him process it, his guilt. I told him it wasn't his fault, there was nothing he could do, he was brave, various reassurances. I suppose it was six months of therapy in six minutes. And now I wonder if I did more harm than good."

"What else could you do?" Shanika asks.

"I could have just sat with him, held his grief, without the reassurances. But I was afraid he would blame himself for the rest of his life."

"Ze might anyway."

"That's true. It probably doesn't matter what I said or didn't say in the scheme of things."

"We do the best we can. What feels right in the moment. We have to trust our instincts, and our compassion. It's really all we have. It's all we have left."

Shanika sounds weary, exhausted. And I know she is right. "Thank you," I say and reach out to hold her hand.

She smiles and keeps my eyes in hers a moment. Then we turn to straightening up the dishes and Shanika calls to Jasmine and Mikey to come outside with her.

"Let me take them," I say. "Have you had any sleep?"

"I was hoping to lie down... Let's go outside and see if there's somewhere for them to play and you can watch them while I rest." She helps me maneuver from the bench behind the table and get my walking stick.

There is a small porch out the back door of the kitchen with a few steps down to a large garden. Shanika holds Jasmine's and Mikey's hands as we walk into the sunlight and find a bench in the shade of two tall pines. It's very hot and the late sun is intensely bright. I can imagine what glaring heat must be on the Valley Sea now as they work to save the ferry.

"Have you seen Dix?" I ask Shanika, and again feel a moment of terror. Adrianna said two people died... But then, no, she said it was two of the Potter boys. I have to get my anxiety in check and make a much better effort at recall.

"Oh, it's great!" Shanika sounds delighted, suddenly. "Ze kind of saved the day. Ze oversaw the whole battery removal and reinstallation in the yawl. I saw zir working just before we were taken off on the sailboats and ze looked actually happy."

The children have started up their tag game again, but we call them back to the bench and say they need to play a quieter game. The garden is a maze of raised beds filled with edible plants, tomatoes, greens, root vegetables, squash, pole beans and runner beans, quinoa and cucumbers and berries and herbs and some things I don't recognize. Greens, golds, reds and white and pink blossoms in the sunlight. Not a place for chasing games right now. I reach in my bag and take out a little velvet sack of marbles that I sometimes let the children play with on special occasions. I stand and with my walking stick draw a circle in the patch of gravelly dirt in front of the bench. They know the game and Jasmine takes the sack reverently to dole out the brightly colored glass marbles between the two of them.

I sit back on the bench and suggest Shanika lie down, and she stretches out with her head in my lap. We talk desultorily for a bit—it's incredibly hot even here in the shade—about Dix and how he may have found a renewed calling. This town seems full of renewable energy technology: windmills, water mills, solar engines and we don't know what all. Shanika says that before the war, when the law was passed for a guaranteed income, it did little to help people, because when you take away a person's work, even if they get paid just to be alive, you have taken away their meaning and purpose. The small allowance people were given allowed nothing more than the most basic survival. Yes, it was a senseless time, I agree.

And now we have to work so hard, work together, just to survive. Shanika says, "there's no time for the decadence from before, all the shock jock, ugly talk and scapegoating—" I feel her getting angry and run my hand lightly across her forehead to soothe her. The kids start laughing when a marble shoots off the path and Mikey chases it as it rolls down a slight grade. Shanika watches and then is silent. A butterfly, a swallowtail, a rare sight, alights on a blossoming berry bush beneath a sycamore and then I can hear the sound of the creek nearby tumbling over rocks. There is nothing left to say and Shanika dozes off.

Star

I wake up and see Riga right away, ze's sleepin' in the bed in the corner. Mom's bed is empty. Ze was asleep when we got in last night. I guess ze's downstairs.

Riga's a silhouette in the gray light. Catherine is sound asleep in a bed on the other wall. I hope ze's okay. Zir skin looks white even in this dusky room and ze's so still. I get up to check and see. I lean in real close to look at zir face and ze startles a little in zir sleep so I back off. Ze's alive. I look around and see there's another empty bed, so Dix must still be out there. It's gonna take 'em forever to haul that ferry back here and I pray they make it. It's vital to the refugee trail. I go back and sit on my bed. I guess this town, New Rose, is pretty far above the water line. I remember we went up a couple hills in those electric carts they picked us up in over at the Old Town. I didn't see much of it cuz the boat docked on the outskirts. Riga says we'll go back and see it later, maybe today or tomorrow. There's some people ze wants to see there. I look at Riga now. I want to crawl into bed with zir, but some day, not now.

I kinda tiptoe outta the room, gotta find a toilet and I'd sure love a bath. Probably not in the stars, tho. The hallway's pretty dim and I look at the window far down at the end. It's past dawn I see, but there's not much light in this hallway. I come across a door that's ajar and peak in, blessed be, an old-fashioned bathroom! I don't know how their plumbing works, I just hope it does. I use the toilet and sure enough it flushes just like the one we had when I was a kid. I wash a little at the sink and there's some cloth towels piled up on a shelf and a hamper to throw them in. I don't know how much of our stuff got lost in the wreck. I know a lotta stuff slid overboard when we first tilted so bad. I'm back in the hall when I remember and I stand still a second—those two Potter kids. I think of them, and say a prayer for them, may they rest peacefully in love and light. It seems so long ago.

I hear voices somewhere downstairs and make my way in that direction. I find a wide wood staircase with a carpet runnin' down the middle, a red floral thing, looks like it's made of wool. There's more light as I go down and I wonder just what time of day it is. There's a large entry room at the bottom with doors to the side and an archway on the left and more rooms. This place is huge.

Someone comes thru one of the doors. "Hello, are you Star? My name is Mae." Ze smiles when I look surprised. I nod my head and we shake hands. Ze says, "I heard you on the stairs. Your mother asked me to tell you ze has gone to the clinic to help with the people coming in from the Sunstar."

"Is it back!?" I ask.

"No, I mean those who came earlier on the sloops," Mae says. I guess I look pretty sad then cuz ze says, "They expect the Endurance and the Sunstar to dock in an hour. They'll go to Old Town because there is a dry dock there for repairs."

I'm thinkin' whether I should go to the clinic or the dock or what when ze says, "You must be hungry. Let me show you where the kitchen is."

"Thanks!" I think to say and I wonder who ze is, exactly. "Do you live here?" I ask.

"I'm on the Mariposa House staff, but I live up the street."

Then we both look back as Riga comes runnin' down the stairs. "Mae!" ze says and they kinda run at each other and hug real tight, all smiles. I can't help smilin', too. You don't see happy people that much anymore.

"I guess you met Star?" Riga says to Mae and ze steps over to stand next to me and takes my hand. "Ze's a very special person."

Mae's face lights up. I see ze loves Riga, like ze wants zir to be happy. "I did meet Star," Mae says, "and zir mother and some of the Caretakers. They are doing so much good work! We are so glad you've arrived. And that...."

"The accident was bad," Riga says. "But almost all of us made it here." They look at each other like this is not a new story. Riga told me this was zir fifth crossing so I guess they've lost other people, like those two Potters. I feel like I need to cry but, not here.

"I'm going to Old Town after we eat something. I need to see Devi. Is there anything I can do for you over there?"

"Yes!" Mae says. "They're building a windmill at the old library and need some tools today. I'll go get them and bring them to you. Will you be in the kitchen?" Ze smiles at Riga.

"Yes." Riga laughs. "We're very hungry." Ze looks at me. "Star, you want to come with me?"

"Yes, I do."

In the kitchen we find a lotta fresh fruit and the colors are gorgeous. It looks much healthier than what we saw at Muir House. And there's grain cakes and ground mush that's probably plant protein. Riga heats it up on an electric stove and puts it in bowls for us. We sit at a sweet little window box table and I see a garden outside, really big with raised beds. The sun looks high in the sky. I guess it's late morning.

When Mae comes back ze's got two backpacks made of woven cloth like you'd see in a museum about indigenous cultures when I was a kid, only new, really colorful. I want one. I think about those sunglasses, too, but I don't want to ask.

"I better get my hat," I tell Riga after Mae leaves, but ze pulls it out of the little bag ze brought down from our room, and a pair of sunglasses, too! I look at zir like ze's a magician and ze laughs.

"I saw you craving these on the boat," ze says.

I don't ask how ze got 'em. I put 'em on and look at my reflection in the window tho I can't really see, just enough to know I look like someone from days gone by, at least where I come from.

We wash the dishes in the sink. I'm still in awe of the plumbing in this place, it's so…real. "How do they do this?" I ask Riga, wavin' my hand around at the stove and the pipes and all.

"They have hydropower, solar and wind power, no? Everything is electric. The watermill and pumps and panels and batteries—everything is very basic. They call it home-grown renewable energy."

"As long as the sun still shines and the wind still blows," I say, and shrug. And I guess it's not all over—all doomed. I guess I feel some kinda possibility for the world. It's a strange feeling and I can't really seem to hang onto it.

"Let's go," Riga says. Ze gives me that gorgeous smile again and holds out zir hand. This other feeling, of possibility with Riga, is startin' to stick tho. I kiss zir, I can't help it, and then we're kinda clutchin' at each other but then we stop right away cuz the feeling of respect we have for this house and the people who run it is even bigger than this fire between us. Riga grabs a colorful backpack full of something clunky and heavy and heaves it on zir back. I do the same.

We hold hands when we walk out of the garden to pick up a footpath thru the woods. But pretty soon we have to go single file plus we need both hands free to keep the heavy packs adjusted on our backs. When we get clear of the trees I stop. "Look!" Far away on the vast blue sea is the Sunstar, leanin' like crazy and bein' pulled along by the yawl like it's a tough little tugboat. I look where they're headed and see the flat old city below at the edge of the sea—a lotta sprawling buildings, only a couple tall ones. Tho I can't really see what's buildings or streets or what's vegetation all over things.

"They're gonna make it," Riga says. We hold hands again for a minute, kiss a little. God, I love Riga. I'm just feelin' crazy for zir. I try to move my body totally into zir but the big packs kinda stop me. I make myself pull away and look at the ferry and Old Town. Maybe, I realize, if we get goin' we can meet the Sunstar at the Old Town docks! I guess Riga's figured that out too cuz ze's already turned away, adjustin' zir pack and we head on down the trail at a pretty good pace with the metal tools in the packs clinkin' and dingin' like bells.

The grasses are high and I wonder if they've burned at all in recent years. It's only May but fire season has already started at the coast. I wonder if they have the Fire Rangers up here like they do at home. I don't ask Riga cuz I'm savin' my breath right now to make this trek.

It isn't long before we're down the hill and walkin' along an old road split up with weeds comin' thru the asphalt. The painted lines are long gone. A little farther down the hill we hit the flat plain and there's dried mud all cracked and ridged a foot thick. It's tough to walk on.

"This is the sediment," Riga says, "from the mountain streams flooding down and leaving silt. When there is rain for days it turns to mud. Then Old Town is cut off from New

Rose." Ze stops a second and looks around. "They are building a bridge. Maybe there." Ze points off to where there's some trees in the distance. I guess the muck isn't as deep there or something. I don't see any bridge. And I wonder if there are some people in New Rose who don't want that bridge. Who want a wall instead.

"Yes, they are. The town council voted." Riga sees my skeptical look, I guess.

"Well where is it?" I ask

"They have to survey to decide where it is highest off the flood plain. Then they will move the rocks to the site. It will be a stone bridge."

I nod. I do know stone is the only thing that lasts cuz everything else decays in the heat and rain, even plastic. Tho plastics got banned when fossil fuels did, and some, like bags and single-use, even before. A plastic bridge. I kinda laugh.

"There it is," Riga says. Ze's been lookin' out to the northeast where there's a rise and I can see a big box of a building on a hill. In front of it there's a suspension bridge—looks like one of those wobbly things in the jungle—goin' over a ravine to a stone tower pretty far across the way where there's the beginning of a stone arch. I wish I had some binoculars.

"We can go see it another day," Riga says. "Let's go to Devi's place."

The first buildings we come on have three feet of dried mud around 'em and inside too. They're abandoned, looks like, and some are fallin' down or completely collapsed. I can feel these tools diggin' into my back thru this cloth backpack and wonder just how far we have to go. It's not like I haven't seen flooded, empty, mud-covered towns before, I just miss that Mariposa House. And could it be any hotter? Yeah, I know it could. But I'm sweatin' so much now.

We stop and take out our bota bags and drink. The water's still cool in the bag, like right out of a clean mountain brook. I can feel it ease down my throat like a blessing from everything that's holy and I just stand there a minute feelin' so grateful, it's hard to even describe. It's like I was in that part of India that ran out of water years ago, and everybody had to move or die. I guess I didn't believe there could be a place like New Rose in the world now.

Riga ties zir bota bag back on zir pack but I hang on to mine as we keep walkin'. There are more empty old, wrecked buildings. The wooden ones are collapsed or caved in sometimes. "Where are the people?" I ask.

"We're on the outskirts. They're in the center near the old train station."

I guess I can smell the place before I see it. It's a bunch of old buildings in the town center—old hotels and bars, it looks like from some of the faded-out writing on the bricks. There's wash hangin' out to dry from ropes strung up and cookfires in the shaded alleys. It's too hot for many people to be out but I hear some voices, I don't know what languages. A few kids are runnin' around, not wearin' much.

"Riga!" I hear somebody call out. I look over and ze's sittin' leaned up against a building, not wearin' much either, it's that hot, and ze waves at Riga, so friendly. Not a lot of teeth when ze smiles, but enough I guess cuz ze isn't skinny and looks pretty healthy.

"Niko! Good to see you!" Riga says. "You know where Devi is?"

"Up the hill," Niko says, and laughs, like, poor you, you gotta climb up there, or at least, that's how I feel.

"Later," Riga says to zir and makes some kinda hand sign. Then we turn and start trudgin' up a side street toward that big building I saw near the new bridge. But it turns out we don't have to go all the way up there cuz Riga turns east and after awhile I see another tower gettin' built—it's the windmill I guess—and I am so happy cuz I can get rid of this pack of metal on my back. Nobody's workin' on it right now, it's probably too hot. I see there's train tracks nearby and I guess we must be near the station. I get a kinda thrill for a minute cuz pretty soon we're gonna be on that train. We're gonna be goin' to the Heartland. It takes me right out of this place for a second. But I feel a fear, too. It could be worse. I hear two people fightin' behind a closed door, real angry. But we keep walkin'. Riga turns on another street, wide like a main street, and covered with mud and silt that's seeped into some of the old storefronts. I see a lotta broken windows. There's one place tho that's kinda fixed up. It has curtains where the windows were and thin slats of recovered wood in a crisscross instead of glass. It looks dark and cool inside.

"Devi!" Riga calls thru the curtains on the doorway. We wait a minute. I wonder why Riga doesn't call again but then, sure enough, out comes Devi and gives Riga a big hug. Devi's shorter than Riga and me and rounder. I'd say zir accent is Asian of some kind, maybe Indian, but I'm no expert. Riga told me that after awhile the refugees pick up some of each other's words and speech and it's a new kind of English in a way. They're Westlanders now, all the people still alive in this area, so I guess Devi is speaking Westlandese. Devi looks at me and gives me a big smile. I'm pretty shocked to see a couple gold teeth as I give a happy smile back to zir and then shake zir hand. I think Devi is Mom's age when I look close, some lines around zir eyes and the gold teeth make me think so. Ze has on a toga like a lot of us wear but zir toga is made of that beautiful cloth people have around here. I wonder who makes it. And then it's so funny, cuz it turns out Devi makes it! At least some of it, I see, cuz we go into Devi's house and there's a couple people there and they've got some small looms, vertical and horizontal, and there's a big open part of the wall in back lettin' in the daylight. Riga and Devi are talkin' fast and I see Riga's tryin' to buy something and I'm pretty amazed when ze pulls out a couple of those coins I heard about to give Devi, who goes in another room and comes back with a beautiful kinda long shirt with buttons made of shells. I haven't seen anything quite like it before, it's got golds, and greens and I guess indigo blue. Riga turns and hands it to me. "For you," ze says. I just look at zir, and my heart opens up so big, I can't say anything. I just take it and look in Riga's eyes with all I feel and then I look at Devi and I kind of bow and say something, I think I say, "your work is pure beauty." Devi laughs.

"You want to see the dye pots?" Riga says. "Or the goats?"

I've put that pack of tools on the floor and I'm tryin' on this toga shirt.

"Come and see," Devi says, and pulls my hand to go in a little backyard area that's been cleaned of all the mud and has some plants in pots. Maybe they're plants for the dyes. But what ze wants me to see is a big piece of cracked mirror and I look at myself and it is a shock. This toga I'm wearin' is the happiest thing I've seen in awhile, and my face shows I love it, but I'm also a dirty mess. My hair is stickin' out all over and I guess I should try to wash it back where all that great plumbing is at the Mariposa House. But it doesn't really matter cuz Riga and Devi are laughin' and happy and so am I too. Devi takes my hand and pulls me over to a gate in the back wall and points to an open lot with a fence where about five or six goats are standin' around under a couple trees and eatin' whatever's on the ground. One of 'em has its hooves up against a trunk to nibble at the lower branches. It looks like native grasses have seeded up here in the rich silt that's everywhere.

"We have to go to the windmill," Riga says to Devi. "Tools from the Council." Ze rattles the pack that ze's still wearin'.

"Good. Good," Devi says. "You come back later. We have tea."

"Soon," Riga says. "Tomorrow or the next day. We have to deliver the tools and then go to the dock. The Sunstar is coming in."

"To Old Town?" Devi asks.

"There was an accident. They need to fix it at the dry dock."

"You come back," Devi says again.

"I will." Riga hugs zir, and then I do too. I'm wearin' my new toga but as soon as I get rid of these tools I'm gonna take it off and fold it up and carry it in the pack to keep it safe. I thank Devi again. Ze laughs.

It's another half hour before we drop off the tools with a worker and then head down to the big dock. We walk along the train tracks for awhile cuz it's easier than on the broken slabs of sediment in the streets. The tracks stop suddenly where they're covered with a wall of mud. I look at Riga. "Wait. The train…"

"It doesn't come here now. The new station is above the sediment, farther east near New Rose."

I guess we've walked three or four miles but I feel so much energy with that weight off my back. I take Riga's hand and we head down another street toward the sea. At the end the view opens out and we can see the blue water and sky, and there, still movin' so slow, is the Sunstar. It's pretty far from the old docks, where there's three electric carts and some people sittin' around waitin'. Riga and I look at each other.

"Let's go back," I say. So we turn due south toward New Rose. We're on a different route now than before. It's a wide road with old railroad ties laid across thick dried mud. After awhile it dead-ends at a wooded area.

"This is where the 19th-century houses were," Riga says. "The ones Reformers moved to New Rose for the waystation before the war. Like Mariposa House, no?"

"How'd they do it?"

"They had cranes and machinery from the rail yards. They took them all by train when the tracks were still here. Because they knew Old Town would be buried in silt."

"Seems like a strange use of resources," I say.

Riga shrugs. "It's hard to know what people will want to save, no? Some refugees during the war... It can hurt your heart to see how they suffer to save some things. They are things you just don't know why they care so much. But they are things from their homes."

I can't really imagine. Maybe older people who lived way back, like maybe before "stuff" became so cheap and meaningless. But then I think of the Potter boys, tryin' to save their wares.

We start goin' uphill. It's a slow rise up to the woods east of New Rose. Riga seems real happy now and takes my hand and kinda hurries us along. I don't mind cuz I can't wait to get back to that house and take some kinda bath, I hope.

It's a little cooler now and I see by the sun it's late afternoon. My watch still says 7:00. I'm wearin' my sunglasses cuz I took off my hat and put it in my pack, it was just too hot to wear. My hair feels like it's all stuck to my head.

And then I let out a yelp. "Look at that!" I take off my sunglasses and stare, my mouth wide open. Riga laughs. Ze leads me on the path across the clearing to the door of the most beautiful building I've ever seen. It's all glass, colored glass and the sunlight comes thru at an angle makin' rainbows everywhere in the grasses all around. Riga opens the door and we walk inside. It's hot, but gorgeous inside. And then I see so many different plants, I want to cry, palms and ferns and lilies, orchids and echinacea, magnolias and silversword and tampa vervain and holywood, I can't believe it. It's a botanist's heaven, like Kew Gardens for the 21st century. Someone brought all these plants here, some that I thought had long disappeared.

I walk down each aisle like it is sacred, and, yeah, I'm cryin'. Riga stands still at the door, lettin' me be.

Mom

It must be close to 8 o'clock. I decided to walk back to the Mariposa House from the clinic before it's too dark to see. I don't want any more stumbles or falls. Shanika offered to come with me but I said no. I see that if I move slowly and take small steps I'm quite safe and I feel so grateful to whoever put this satin wrap on the handle of my walking stick.

It's beautiful here, very quiet for such an active town of busy people. The electric carts make only a low humming sound but no one is about right now. I can hear the creek beside the road, tumbling and brisk, fuller after the rain. It is late. The clinic is still busy, there were so many injuries from the accident, large and small. They're expecting the Captain, Dix, and the crew who brought in the Sunstar to arrive here in town any minute. Word came that they had docked. I want to tell Catherine, although she must already know. Shanika and I looked in on her before we left for the clinic this morning and Mae promised she would make sure Catherine was well taken care of today.

It is so verdant here, even in this low light I can see how lush the creekside vegetation is, although I'm keeping my eyes trained on the path in front of me. Clop clop, the sound of my stick is louder than anything except the songs and calls of birds in the trees.

Jason, the boy who lost his brother, has gone down to the docks to help unload any cargo left, I heard. And even now I feel the tears, the aching in my heart. I suppose it's something about Dale. A grief so raw as his, Jason's, it can't help but bring up my own losses, too. I can't stop thinking about his voice as he spoke to me, the anger and bewildered sorrow. He's young to suffer such a shock, not used to such hurts, even in this world we live in now. The Potters are a close group.

Dale once said that aging is a kind of subtraction. The faculties decline, hearing, vision, every body function. There is a slowing down and...he loved to quote Emily Dickinson. "First—Chill—then Stupor—then the letting go—"

I don't know why it makes me laugh. Laughter doesn't seem right nor to reflect how I feel. I guess Dale was so...absolute? There was actually a bit of the Bell Jar, Plath more than Dickinson, about his view of aging and death. Like putting a glass over a bug until it squirms and finally dies. And then there is an absence. No more bug. Simplistic, perhaps. I don't know. I shouldn't blame Dale for dying so soon, so suddenly and without any spiritual preparation, that I knew of. He was a scientist, a rationalist of the old school. Not like Star, a naturalist who worships nature.

Oh thank goodness, a bench! I'll sit just a few minutes and rest; it can only be another short block but I am moving so slowly. I can see the creek in dusky light, a silvery black pouring over a wide and shallow rocky pool here. Of course it's uphill to the Mariposa House, no wonder it's taking me forever.

The creek, really, is how I see death, I suppose, rather than the Bell Jar. In the rationalist view, it seems to me, there is no continuity of life. It's—now you see it, now you don't. Here and gone, end of story. Where is the connection? The stream of life that flows through all of creation. I would say I see the self as one droplet, arisen from the stream in the light of the sun, brief and effervescent, and then submerged again into the stream. Connected, cyclical, ongoing in life and death. I'm a pantheist, I'd say, like Star.

I can't believe I still haven't seen Star since the accident! Except at dawn this morning, a shadow in the dim light. Someone at the clinic said she and Riga had gone to Old Town. Maybe they're helping with the Sunstar now. Or perhaps they've arrived back at the House. I push myself up from the bench with my walking stick and wobble a moment. I really should get back before dark. I've heard there is a patrol of New Rose citizens every night wearing reflective vests, yellow and orange, keeping watch of the town and this is reassuring. Still, do I really want to cause more trouble for people!? At least I was a help at the clinic today. Doing triage for mental health counseling. Mostly listening. People wanted to talk about the moment of the crash, the instant the ferry tilted violently and so much fell overboard. Where they were at the moment. What it was like. This is the kind of story they will tell now and again for the rest of their lives. Like, "Where were you in the earthquake of '28"? "Where were you when the Thwaites collapsed?" But there are so many of these catastrophes— maybe the ferry accident will fade to nothing in their minds. Yet this accident was more personally threatening to them than any natural disasters for which they were not at ground zero.

I see someone in one of the reflective vests now. Up ahead, where I think the entrance to the House is. I clomp along, picking up my pace; I don't want them thinking I'm lost or dithering about. I miss Dale profoundly, suddenly. And, too, I feel such a desperate longing for the company of someone my own age.

The dark figure in the dayglo vest turns to walk up the hill, away from me. They either didn't see me or think I'm harmless. Or maybe they're not on duty yet. It's not completely dark. I remember something Dale read to me so many years ago. It must have been just after we bought the house in the East Bay hills. It had started, the changes—the wildfires and floods and severe weather all over the world. But the sea had risen only a foot at that time. None of the true madness had begun, the total collapse of ice sheets and glaciers, societies, economies, The Fail. People still thought about social issues in the way they had for generations, with new twists every so often. But I can't forget the surprise we felt about a study that found attitudes had changed dramatically in favor of other races and gay rights; but what remained unchanged was the deep prejudice against the elderly! What? I didn't even know there had been such a prejudice. But then I noticed in myself at that time, how inclined I was to see elderly people as inconsequential, cute or annoying, and basically relegated to a psychic waiting-room for oblivion.

And now. I can't help but think, at least they had each other. What I would give to sit down with a group of fellow septuagenarians. And then I feel a quick thrill of excitement. Maybe in the Capitol? The Heartland?

Another person in a yellow vest appears, coming out the door of the Mariposa House. I've just put my good hand on the banister to ascend the steps to the porch.

"Hello there," the woman says to me.

"Hello," I greet her and smile, then focus on making my way up the steps. To my surprise and relief she doesn't offer to help me. They must see much worse cases than me among all the refugees passing through.

"Have a good evening," she says as she trots down the stairs and into the street. I do see that, kindly, she has left the heavy wooden door to the House ajar.

When I walk in to the foyer and glance in the open parlor, I am surprised to see Catherine sitting there alone. "Catherine!" I call out, elated to see her up. She still has bandages on her face and she is pale, but her eyes seem lively. She is sitting in an upholstered straight back chair and looking out the open door. I realize she is waiting for Dix.

"Mom!" She sounds pleased to see me and I walk in and sit on the settee across from her.

"Star and Riga aren't back yet, and neither are any of the crew of the Sunstar," she tells me. I sit back in my seat, realizing I'd been peering through the open parlor door as if I could see who was or was not in the House.

"How are you feeling?" I ask her now, looking at her more closely, although the light is dim. I glance around me for a lamp.

"They said we can't light the lamps until 8:30. Then they go off at 10:00. Electricity is rationed."

"Of course."

"I'm still a bit woozy," she says, and laughs, putting a hand to her temple and massaging it lightly. "But they said I could sit up for an hour or so in the dim light here."

"Oh of course." I don't know what I was thinking; she needs this dim light.

"How are you?" she asks me, concerned, I see.

"Tired but glad to have worked at the clinic today. What have you heard about the Sunstar and the crew? Dix?"

She makes a sound between a laugh and harrumph. I look at her quizzically and she says, "Dix is in tech heaven, apparently. Thank god. He refuses to leave and plans to work on the Sunstar's powertrain and all the rest of it until it's up and running. It could take days and we're going to miss that train to the Capitol."

"Oh! That's wonderful for him. And also, aren't you supposed to seriously rest for several days, or more?"

"That's what they say." She sighs.

I'm quiet a minute. It's a blow to think of going to the Capitol without them. And it's not just because they are closer in age to me by far than anyone else on this journey. Catherine has become a good friend.

"What are your plans?" she asks.

"Oh, I suppose Star will want to get on the next train. They only run once a week or....?"

"It's irregular, I heard. Sometimes four days apart, sometimes more than a week. It depends on the weather and the fuel supply."

I nod, thinking. A minute ago I'd been thrilled at the thought of boarding the train. Oh well. Adapt. Adapt.

"Though Star may be making her decisions in tandem with Riga now, don't you think?" Catherine asks.

"That's true," I agree. "They're inseparable. Love at first sight." I laugh. It seems so improbable and yet so symptomatic of the times. I don't want to be doubtful, or even questioning, about it.

"I saw them briefly this morning," Catherine says, "in the half-light with my brain on half speed. First Star—she came over to my bed and stood over me, then brought her face very close to mine, to see if I was dead I suppose." She laughs. "It startled me and I jolted a little and she backed up quickly and was gone."

"Well I'm glad she checked on you."

"But what was funny is that, five minutes later, Riga woke up and ze did the exact same thing. Only this time, I was more awake and I said, 'Hello'. And ze said, 'Hello Catherine. Can I get you anything?' And I said, 'No thanks, I'm still sleeping' or something silly like that and ze patted my arm and left."

"When was that?"

"I don't know. I was in and out of some sleepy trance state all day until an hour or so ago. I had some of the oddest dreams. And, oh!" She sits up a little straighter. "One was about Star and Riga. I mean I know that what I just described to you really happened, but later on.... Do you remember that soccer star, she was hugely famous, about thirty years ago? They won the World Cup."

"Oh, vaguely." I remember that time now; Star was just an infant, when the sea was still in its bed; when the changes had only just begun.

"Well I realized, if she'd had black wavy hair..."

"Wasn't her hair very coifed?" I laugh again. The idea of a coiffure so absurd in this new world.

"Oh probably, but if it had been black and her skin more olive, she looked exactly like Riga. Everything about her, her fitness and grace, and that expansive theatricality."

And then I do remember her, a vivid image of her. A beautiful smile. Her composure and bravery. It startles me. Is it possible? Is it possible Riga is female? I've been so sure he is a brave and charismatic young man. I inhale sharply.

"I know," Catherine says. "I've been sure he's a guy."

I'm still silent.

"You could ask Star."

"Never," I say.

"Of course, I don't know what I'm saying. I just wonder about my dream."

"I know. I can't tell sometimes. Was it even a dream. What is real now?"

Catherine closed her eyes a moment.

"Should you go back to bed?" I ask.

"Soon," she says.

"I can find someone to help you upstairs." I start to stand but she puts a hand on my leg to stop me.

"A few more minutes."

We both sit quietly.

"I wish we could travel on together," she says at last.

"I'll talk to Star," I say.

A young man appears in the doorway. He's dressed in the colorful cloth typical of New Rose and has a nice smile, the good teeth of the young.

"Dinner is ready. It's self-serve in the kitchen and the tables and chairs are in the garden and dining room." He looks at Catherine kindly. "I'm supposed to help you back upstairs. Someone will bring you your nutrient drink."

"Thank you," Catherine says without objection and the young man comes to her side to help her up. As they head up the stairs Catherine says over her shoulder to me, "Come and get me when Dix arrives."

"I will." I nod and smile.

I clomp my way back to the kitchen—thonk thonk thonk—with the walking stick on the wooden floors. Would it be crazy to see if I can attach some kind of rubber tip to it? Riga. Riga. Who are you? Oh well. A good person, I know.

There are at least a dozen people. I'm happy to see Shanika and the kids already sitting out in the garden. I hope JoJo isn't still at the clinic, though she must be. Maybe someone will take her something to eat. I recognize a few people from the city council, Mae and the others from the parlor this morning. They greet me warmly, make way for me and someone offers to help me fix a plate. I have to accept. I can't imagine right now how to balance a plate with my splint and stick, though I suppose it could be done, why bother. "Thank you," I say. I glance at someone else's full plate and say, "I'll have exactly what he has, only less." They laugh. Then I pull out the nearest chair in the dining room and sit. No need to make them traipse out to the garden.

The others at the large table are the town council members I saw earlier and a few other people. I hope I'm not intruding but they move to make room for me and smile warmly. One thanks me for the work I did at the clinic today. Word travels fast, around here, I gather. I wonder if they have any kind of devices, but I haven't seen any yet.

A young woman puts my plate and some utensils and a napkin in front of me on the table. Someone else pours water from a large pitcher into a glass. "Thank you. Thank you," I tell them as graciously as I can. I'm feeling a bit exhausted and wonder if I shouldn't have followed Catherine up the stairs to the beds. But I need some calories, I'm sure.

I sit quietly and eat. My fellow diners resume their conversation.

"Old Town is planting more fields to the east, corn mostly, some tomatoes," a young man says. "We need to get coordinated with them."

"I saw that, I was over there before the ferry crash. They're not tilling the soil first, just planting right into the cover crop."

"We are coordinating, Zabar, that's why they're using regenerative farming techniques."

"No, I know, Draymond, I mean…more formally. Let's all meet to decide which crops we'll plant and how to share food and start a joint market."

"If we can dedicate a huge tract to regenerative, get more natural fungicides and bactericides in the soil, absorb more carbon."

"We need to figure out which cover crops to plant for the most diverse microbiome."

I nod my head, appreciatively; I've heard of "regenerative farming", of course. Long ago, but not until it was too late for the coast. Could Riga really be a woman? This seems so, unexpected. But why, why does it affect me…? I wonder and then realize, to my shock, did I want a grandchild? In this world!? It must be some primal instinct, for every living thing, to reproduce ourselves. But there are so many ways people have children. Even though there aren't any fertility clinics now, there is definitely adoption, and donor sperm. But the Heartland, so famous once for homophobia. I want to laugh, how old-fashioned can I be? Riga and Star are already radical agents of change--

"... in East New Bay?" Draymond asks. He is looking at me. He sees my blank stare and I flush. But he simply repeats his question. "Were the Caretakers and Potters growing any food before you left?"

"Oh no. Just foraging," I answer. With a rush of adrenalin, I recover myself. "And I believe the Potters did some hunting. They lived south of New Bay, in the coastal mountains. The soil had become too salinized to plant food crops in East New Bay, especially after the second pulse— the sea level rise in '37."

"When was the first pulse?" a young woman, Nan, I think, asks.

"2029. Just after the final election. The sea rose ten feet that year. Millions were displaced, homeless, especially in New York, Florida, the Southeast. But also California, hundreds of thousands. Everything fractured. Government, cities. It was the first major migration to the Heartland. Isn't that when New Rose became a refugee waystation? Or was it the next year, during the war?" I realize everyone at this table is looking at me, and each of them was a child in 2029; some were infants, probably. I doubt if Nan was even born. I take a bite of some kind of hash that must be plant protein; it's delicious, and calming.

"Didn't the Chinese build a water desalination plant in New Bay just before the war?" Zabar asks.

"Yes. But it was bombed by the Guardians a few years later." I look away a moment, remembering that time. Dale's face when he told me the planes were coming and we watched out our large bay windows.

"It's the only thing they bombed," I say, "because very little of the San Francisco peninsula was still occupied or functioning after 2029. The first migration was ongoing and the sea was still steadily, although very gradually, rising then—until the second pulse. We were all using our own water filtration systems by that time."

"New Rose was founded in 2028, to answer your question," Mae says. "The old houses could never have been moved during or after the war since we had other priorities then."

"When was Roseville abandoned?" I ask.

"It happened slowly as the floods and sediment deposits got worse. But it was never completely abandoned, and there were some problems."

"I can imagine. Such a chaotic time. What specifically?" I ask.

"Well." Zabar glances at Mae who smiles, and he explains, "A lot of Guardians once lived in Roseville, but at the time we're talking about most joined the military or emigrated to the North or Midwest. The Reformers and pacifists stayed, and they developed New Rose in order to welcome refugees and help them transition. People from Westlands who weren't fighting in the war heard about us and came to help."

"Still," Mae says, "problems arose. People in Old Town are generally displaced persons of all kinds who chose not to move to new settlements in Mountains and Heartland. They just lost heart and stayed put. But there is no industry here for people needing work or currency. There is no livelihood."

"But there's farming," I say.

"Yes, now there is," Mae agrees. "But during the war there was only the one clinic here and it was rare that trained medical people passed through. The original residents of Old Town—when it was Roseville—had all left except for some elderly and a number of alcoholics and drug users who didn't have the wherewithal to leave. They resented us and the attention we gave to refugees. There was animosity from these people, retribution, some theft."

"It was pretty ugly some of the time," Draymond says. "That's what I heard, and saw. I was ten years old when my family came here to help with some people from our church."

"And then as time went by refugees who were too exhausted to keep going also began to settle in Old Town," Mae says. "They brought their ways from their homelands—farming, weaving, raising goats and even horses," Mae says.

"There were feral farm animals roaming around all over the foothills during the war," Zabar adds.

"Eventually the original residents who resented us and wanted to sow discord began to fade away. They moved on or, many died. Now Old Town is more of a self-sufficient community and we've developed good relations in the last decade."

"Riga helped with that," Nan says.

"Yes, and we're cooperating more and more. They don't have a town council exactly, in Old Town, but they do have different representatives who meet with us. We're building a bridge and pathway between New Rose and Old Town over the heavy sediment. We barter food, cloth, and other wares."

"A lot of things come through this town," Zabar says. "The war slowed it down but then after the second pulse, that second sea rise you mentioned and the migration from

Westlands then, we had maybe a thousand people a week. People coming on the ferry or down from the northwest—walking, horseback, some trains still ran from Oregon. The Valley Sea wasn't as big as it is now."

I shake my head. "So many changes. Huge changes. I can't keep track."

"You've seen it all," Nan says to me, a little awed, I can see.

"I've seen a lot," I agree. "And no one could predict it. Or at least, not accurately. Some people, like the Guardians, denied there was any climate change at all. But the meteorologists agreed with the environmentalists. They knew what was coming, sort of. But try as they might, with all their computer models and data sets... None of them foresaw the pulses. Only a small group of scientists, who studied the last melt-off millennia ago, even mentioned the possibility."

"That's true," Mae agrees. "They studied the coral shelves off Texas under 200 feet of water and found they were dramatically terraced. We studied that in my school in Taiwan. It showed the ice melted in bursts from sudden glacier collapses."

"Wasn't it the first pulse that buried fifty square miles of refineries and oil business in Houston?" Zabar looks at me.

"Yes, yes." I'm amazed they have to ask me. But he was probably a toddler then.

"The Gulf was already getting pounded even before that, by hurricanes," Draymond says and I nod in agreement.

"Right-wing governments came to power around the world and did nothing to prevent climate change," I say. "And that led to wars. That and the hostility toward immigrants. There were concentration camps and murders of non-white people."

"I thought the war in the United States started because of the U.N. ban on fossil fuels, when it split the population into who wanted to comply or not."

"Well, that's also true," I agree. "After the first pulse—after Houston was buried—the Oil Ban as they called it, gained a lot of traction."

"We called it the oil wars in Iran, after we were bombed by the U.S. and Saudis."

I look at the young woman who just spoke. "That was certainly part of it. The Reformers here were totally opposed to war with Iran."

"When the nuclear bomb was dropped, we left and came to Latin America," Mae says. "We were afraid China would get involved. We didn't realize the nuclear bombing would be contained."

"Well millions died in the Mideast."

"More than Hiroshima and Nagasaki."

"It was actually China that stopped it. They had the power to issue the ultimatum."

"The radiation is still in the atmosphere."

"It's in the soil."

"There's so much bad stuff in the soil," Draymond says.

"What else?" Nan asks. She seems upset and I realize she is still in her teens.

"Maybe the nitrates and phosphates from chemical fertilizers have washed out of the fields here by now, but it'll be after the next Ice Age before lead and mercury are gone, or cadmium—and the man-made stuff like PCBs and POPs. We'll have lower sperm counts than we already do." Zabar laughs. "It's not that easy to have a baby anymore." The others murmur agreement, and I see a sorrowful expression on the young woman next to Zabar. His wife, perhaps. And as I see her I realize I have seen no young children in this town since we arrived. Not one, other than the few who came with us on the ferry.

"People are still dying from the radiation and chemicals released in those wars," Mae says. "All of these years later."

"Wars go on forever. Their effects go on forever."

"There can be no more war!" This from Nan, who looks on the verge of tears. The others are more hardened. They were alive, even if they were just small children, during the wars. And I see how lucky I and my family were, to be marooned in New Bay, in our bubble, surrounded by rising seas.

"Mom!" I feel swept up from my chair and engulfed in strong arms. It's Star!

She and Riga have arrived like a fresh breeze of hope. There is handshaking and hugs, smiles and laughter as everyone shifts and makes room for them.

Star pulls up a chair close to me, practically sitting in my lap. I'm thrilled to see her and hold her hand tightly. Someone has brought her a plate piled with the delicious hash and vegetables. She begins to eat with her other hand, pausing to turn and smile at me.

"Where have you been?" Draymond asks Riga who sits down between him and Nan with zir own plate.

"To Devi's," Riga says. "And the conservatory."

Yes, I admit, I am studying Riga intently. Ze does look like that soccer star in a way. Except for the black wavy hair.

"Oh the conservatory!" Mae says.

"It is a dream. A botanist's heaven," Star says. "I never wanted to leave."

"It's heaven for all of us," Mae agrees. "We all work on it in shifts. And people from Old Town, too, many of them brought the plants. Word travels and I believe it is now famous around the world."

"I can imagine. You've saved so many species, some I thought were extinct," Star says.

"Are you a botanist?" Draymond asks.

"I studied it," Star says.

"We need a lot of help in the Conservatory," Mae says. "A little more expertise."

"And Riga," Draymond says. "We have a big favor. We need you to stay for our meeting with Old Town reps in a few days for some important issues on the agenda. Can you do it?"

I smile as they continue to talk. I can't wait to tell Catherine, we will stay until she is ready to travel.

"Where is Dix?" I ask Star.

"They're on the way. I saw one of the crew, they're comin' up here soon. They had to drag Dix away from his new baby, the Sunstar! It's too dark to see now, anyway." She laughs.

Star

"You! Where have you been!" Tania gives me a little slap and I turn around, ze's laughin'. I can see ze's tired, tho. It's only 9:00 in the morning but Tania's probably been workin' here at the clinic a couple hours already. I grab zir and give zir a hug.

"What can I do?" I ask.

"Talk to me," ze says. "Let's have some tea."

There's a hot plate in a tiny room they set up for staff. They got it wired up to a solar panel on the roof and it's workin' right now.

We lean up against the wall while the water boils. Tania's already put a big wad of yerba buena in a strainer.

"How's Riga?" Ze gives me silly googly eyed look.

"Ze took me to the Old Town yesterday. We've gotta go over there. You gotta see this conservatory that's on the way, it'll change your life."

"Oh, uh-huh. Okay."

"Tania, it's real."

Ze looks at me, sees I mean it. "Okay. But in the meantime, this clinic needs so much work—I don't think they've had any permanent staff in a year or more. From the look of things it's just been people like us who're passing through, and not that many."

"What about our supplies we brought?" I realize I don't even know if they were saved from the Sunstar.

"We took essentials off the ferry when we were rescued and, blessed be, the rest were in tact when the ferry came in. JoJo sent Jason—a Potter, plus Kamala and Chela to get the rest, but it's still not gonna be enough. Every sick person for miles has been coming in. Look out there."

I stand on my tiptoes to see out a little window and there is a line of people, maybe thirty, goin' out along the creek, standin' in the shade of the grey pines and sycamores. It's already that hot.

"They're coming in on bicycles and even horses. Somebody's been taming feral horses out at an old ranch, about ten miles east of here."

"Mom didn't tell me it was so crazy busy. Ze just said I needed to get over here today and help out. But I have to meet Mae and some of their town council people at that conservatory I told you about in awhile."

"Oh Star, the star. Pretty soon you'll be on the town council yourself." Ze's laughin'.

"I don't think so. You know how I am at meetings."

Ze laughs harder. "Yeah, New Rosians, watch out! The fire-breather has arrived."

"Speakin' of," I take the boiling water off the burner and pour it thru the strainer that's set on a ceramic teapot, a beautiful thing, I see, hand-painted.

"The people here are so real," Tania says. Ze's serious now. "I love it here."

"Really?"

"Yeah. Everyone seems to have come and settled here for a reason. I think the reason is values and they're like ours. This isn't a place where people put each other down or get obsessed with status. At least not from what I've seen."

"It's been so long since we've been around other people," I say. Not that I doubt zir.

"I know. It comes back fast though, how to be around strangers and new people. Really, like it was just yesterday—you know how some things are like that. You know," ze gives me that teasing look, "Like sex. Comes right back to ya."

"Ha ha," I say. I'm not gonna talk to zir about this. I pour the tea into two cups. I'm thinkin' how to change the subject, but Tania's already moved on.

"So JoJo's going to live here now. Ze's not going on to the Capitol."

"What!?" I'm really surprised and feel kinda lost for a second.

"Yeah, they need a doctor on staff here. Ze's been working fourteen-hour days. There were the injuries from the ferry the first day, and then word got out and people started pouring in here from other places yesterday. And here they are again today."

"When did ze tell you that?"

"Last night."

"Maybe ze'll change zir mind."

"Maybe."

"Mom and Riga and I aren't takin' the train tomorrow either. We're gonna stay 'til the next one, in a week."

Tania looks relieved, I swear. "Oh good, cuz I'm not going tomorrow either. None of the Caretakers are."

I guess I'm not surprised, with so much work to do here at the clinic, and some of us injured. "Good," I say.

"A lot of the Potters are leaving tomorrow, though. For one thing, they lost some of their cargo and they need to settle somewhere where there's plenty of clay, and not just the adobe kind. And Jason told me there's already a big crafts community here, mostly in the Old Town, so they don't want to compete with them."

"Is Jason the one who lost zir brother?"

"Yeah. Ze's having a hard time. Ze likes being around here, helping us out. Ze loves Mom."

"Of course," I say.

"Mom seems to be taking the accident hard."

"Really? I didn't get that."

"Or maybe it's about the two Potters drowning. Ze's asked me about ten times if I think Jason's okay."

"Ten?!"

"Okay, five, but either ze's a little fixated with it or....". I see Tania look at me like ze's thinkin' if ze should say something.

"What? Tell me." I say this softly.

"Maybe Mom's forgetting more. Sometimes ze forgets ze already asked me an hour before."

"Is it party time in here?" JoJo comes in and stares at us. "Did you see all those people out there?"

Tania puts down zir tea and starts scrubbin' zir hands at the small sink. I hold my cup of tea out to JoJo, "Want a little?" Ze takes it and sips for a couple seconds.

"Star, can you do an inventory of the supplies that are here? And when the rest arrive from the ferry add them in and organize them. There's an empty closet in the hall. The door sticks but if you can scrub it inside and fix the door we can store everything in there. Rags are in that box," ze points under the sink, "and paper and a couple pencils are in the desk in the office. Over there." Ze points to a door across the hall.

"Yes!" I squeeze past zir and Tania to find the office. I love havin' something so clear cut to do.

But I'm thinkin' about Mom, what Tania said, as I go in the little office they've set up and start to search the drawers in the desk. Paper is a precious thing but there's a fair stack of it here. Some of it looks homemade. I was shocked to see Mom's arm in a big splint when Riga and I got back from Old Town last night. I hadn't seen it when ze was asleep the first night when we got back from the rescue, and I almost squished zir in a big hug last night but ze seemed okay.

Mom said JoJo says it's a simple break and maybe ze can get a smaller splint soon in place of the big one, which is another good reason not to leave here yet. Tho it's a little hard for me to stay on. I can't wait to see the Heartland! There's two stops on the way there, one in the eastern Sierras and one out on the plains, I guess. The whole trip takes two or three days. It depends on fuel, Riga says, and there's great big stacks of firewood, acres of it, along the way, chopped wood from dead trees. That's how they fuel the steam engine.

It takes over an hour to inventory the supplies on hand and scrub the closet. I choose where to put things but I'll have to move it around when they bring more from the ferry.

I walk outside and see there's still a line, about the same. And there's Mom walkin' up the road with zir walking stick. I see the red handle shinin' in the sun.

"Lookin' good," I say to zir as ze kinda limps up. Ze's smilin'.

"How's it going here?" ze asks.

"Busy. Tania, Shanika and JoJo are with patients. Carrie and Liddy are doin' triage. Kamala, Chela and Jason are due back with clinic supplies that were still on the Sunstar. And I'm tryin' to organize the supplies here. I guess Jen and Caylee are with the kids."

"They are. I just left them at the Mariposa House, in the garden. Have you seen Jason?"

"Uh, no. Ze went to Old Town early this morning with the others, to the docks. The ferry. The supplies."

"Oh, I thought you might have seen him before he left." Mom looks around at all the people standin' in the shade of the trees. "I was here most of yesterday—with people who needed to talk. I thought I'd do a few more hours today, although I'm a bit tired. I don't want to make any mistakes!" Ze laughs.

Ze told me about yesterday when we talked late last night and I nod my head, but I remember, too, before that at the table in the kitchen with everybody and how they were all lookin' at Mom like ze was an oracle. Ze must be tired now tho. Talk talk talk. We weren't used to that at all.

"Mom," I say. "Do you still keep up your journal?"

Mom looks away from the people lined up in the shade and gives me a questioning look.

"I'm just thinkin'," I say. "Do you write about everything from before? Like everything that's happened in your lifetime since before the changes began? Cuz..." How to say it....

Mom laughs. "Cuz no one else is old enough to know."

"Yeah."

"I know. I was thinking about that. I have been, actually. But I realize I should be more methodical, set it out chronologically and fill in the gaps. There's no time, though."

"Cuz, Mom, I found a big stack of paper, and there must be someone around here who makes it cuz some of it's homemade. I'm gonna ask Riga to get you a lot and some ink pens or pencils, too, whatever they've got. Ze said there's a weekly market and we'll be here for that, or else ze'll know where to go in Old Town."

Mom looks pretty happy then, I gotta say. Ze smiles at me, zir blue eyes so warm, and says, "Thank you, Star."

JoJo comes out the side door then. Busted, I'm thinkin'. Ze's always finds me on a break.

"Mom," ze says. "I'm so glad you're here. There's someone who is very depressed—ze's in the front room where you worked yesterday."

Mom kinda snaps to. "Oh I'll be right with them. JoJo, I wanted to ask you, is there more valerian and St. John's wort on the ferry? We have chamomile here still and..." Ze turns to me. "Would Riga know if there are antidepressants in the Capitol?"

"I can ask, but I thought that there haven't been any for years. Remember that doctor in New Bay, way back, who told you about people who'd died when they all ran out."

"I don't know, Mom," JoJo says. "I'm not sure we should go that route here. Maybe in Heartland if they exist and are being manufactured, it would be a possible option."

"But, for anyone traveling on..."

"You're thinking of Jason?" JoJo says and shakes zir head a little.

"Oh, I don't know. He's so young."

"Honestly, Mom," JoJo says, "I think Jason is doing better with making himself very useful to us and to others. He's helping people and working hard. Sometimes that works just as well."

"Sometimes," Mom agrees, but I know ze's thinkin' that it works for you, JoJo, but not everybody. But I gotta say I agree with JoJo about this. It's too risky to get anyone hooked on any kind of pharma.

JoJo says, "One in eight adolescents were on antidepressants before The Fail. I don't think we should go down that road again. The objective of living isn't the absence of pain. And although yes, in certain cases—"

"Mom, what is it about Jason?" I ask. I want to know and I also want to cut off JoJo cuz ze's goin' too far.

Mom kind of flushes red, then says, "I....I just can't stop thinking about Dale when I see him. I don't know why."

"Oh," I say. "I can see it. I can see why Jason reminds you of Dad." Tho it's a stretch, I'm thinkin', but better validate it, as Mom might say zirself. But I'm wonderin' what's goin' on with Mom. I've been with Riga so much...

"Oh, Star, about the supplies. There's no refrigeration here," Jojo says. "I don't know if there's any in this entire town. Maybe you could find out? We'll need to create some kind of cold storage area, maybe in the creek?"

"That's right," Mom says. "Draymond said last night refrigerants are banned in New Rose. They cool rooms by pumping creek water through pipes, and there are storage areas built underground. We can ask him where the nearest cold storage to the clinic is."

"I'm glad to hear that. Thank you, Mom." JoJo glances at the people waiting. "We should get back."

Mom seems focused now and ready to work. I walk with zir back into the clinic and tell zir I'll go talk to Draymond.

When I get back later, Kamala, Chela and Jason have shown up with two wagons full of supplies. We all get busy and add them to the inventory in the closet and put some in a tiny cellar under a shed near the creek.

It's so hot in the sun, nobody's out on the street now. I'm wonderin' if it's time to meet Riga to go to the Conservatory. I look at my watch but it still says 7:00, so I sit in the shade with Kamala and ze shares some of the food in zir cloth pack. An apple and some kind of jerky, looks like. Ze lies back in the shade and I sit and eat, glad for the quiet. It's true, what I was thinkin' about Mom, how we're not used to all these people. I hope ze's holdin' up, talkin' to depressed people all day. Ze hasn't done that since I was a kid. Tania's keepin' an eye on Mom, tho—ze told me ze would when I asked about an hour ago.

I see Riga comin' up the road. Ze's got on a new toga of colorful cloth, probably from Devi, and some kinda necklace—looks like feathers and beads. I gotta laugh, ze looks wild and gorgeous. I jump up.

"Star!" ze calls out when ze sees me and we run toward each other. I grab zir hand but we don't kiss, here. "I'm ready. Are we late?"

"No, no. We have time. Mae said to meet at the Conservatory at 2:00." Ze lifts my wrist to look at my watch then laughs. "There's a clock in the tower of the Meeting House on the way."

I don't know how I missed it before but there's a big clock, maybe 100 years old, on a tower at the Meeting House, right past Mariposa House. It says one o'clock, so Riga and I take a path to the creek to follow it a ways. We run down the bank thru some brambles and shrubs, some is Scotch broom I'm sorry to see. But the sunlight comin' thru the canopy of sycamores, tan oaks and buckeyes feels clean and warm on my skin, like a warm massage, and I start to relax. We stop at the creek to watch its musical flow—it's runnin' high this spring, Riga says. It's crystal clear.

"Is that a fish!?" I almost scream it. We squat down to look. The fish die-off after Rancho Seco melted down spread for hundreds of miles, but I guess this is far enough upstream. All the other reactors are underwater now, and anyway, most of 'em got shut down during the war cuz the feds were scared of nuclear terrorism. At least they'd done that right, shut 'em down! But there was still so much radioactive waste all over. I look hard at this pretty creek. We watch the silvery little fish glide thru a ray of sun on the water. Then there's another. "There are more," Riga says and ze points downstream. "They're coming back."

And then I swear I hear the song of a warbler. Songbirds. They're comin' back too, I've heard. And I feel just a flash of hope again. It just streaks thru me like the sun rays on my back as Riga and I watch the fish, like we're seein' species come back to life before our own eyes. A miracle. And I feel something fierce, too, like a crazed Mother Bear, that if anyone starts dumpin' toxins in this creek I could kill 'em. Riga feels me tense, zir hand is on my shoulder.

"What's wrong?" ze asks. I tell zir, tho I tone it down cuz ze already knows about my temper.

"I don't want it to ever happen again. All the poison. I just wanna protect this creek."

"We will," ze says, real quiet. And I guess I could believe it.

We stand up, feelin' kinda urgent to get to the Conservatory now and the meeting. Riga'd said ze sensed something important was up and that's why they want us to stay around. But we keep walkin' along the creek most the way. We see more birds and wildflowers. And then Riga puts out a hand to stop me and we stand still, quiet as stones—there's a juvenile cougar 100 feet up the creek standin' stark still, too, starin' at us. Zir tail's raised a little and I see the black marking at the tip, and then I look back at zir gold eyes, starin' us down. After another second or two, ze turns and walks back into the trees on the hill across from us.

"Blessed be," I whisper to Riga like a prayer.

"It's rare to see one in the middle of the day, even at the water," ze says. "But the juveniles—they're full of possibility!"

We're laughin', happy, when we get to the Conservatory. It's still early but Mae and Pyotr are already there. They're at a white iron table I didn't notice the other day, in a small side room thru a glass door.

"It's room temperature for native plants," Mae tells us, and this is where they have their meetings with the Old Town reps. We sit down and they give us sun tea and fruit and bean cakes. Mae says three more are comin', but since we're here ze'll tell us some background stuff.

"You know about the Eden Network?" ze asks. Riga says yes and I say no, so Mae says to me, "New Rose is part of it. You know how we've been a waystation for refugees since the first migration before the war? Well, there are many other waystations, too. When Earth Corps replaced the United Nations, they began establishing contacts among refugee waystations and eventually we formed the Eden Network. Our polices and values are coordinated through Earth Corps on every continent still inhabited."

I gotta say, I am shocked by this information. I had no idea there was any global anything left. "How do they communicate?" I ask.

"Slowly," Pyotr says and laughs. "There are still sailing ships and steamships, and there are trains, as you know. And lately some solar vehicles are being created. But also there are still a very few functioning telecommunications satellites with occasional signals for the fraction of internet that remains."

Ze's explains more about what's left of the internet and tech and I think of JoJo. Ze told me this morning ze'd emailed a clinic in the Capitol about supplies. The clinics up there used to be a hospital and a medical school where ze did zir residency after the war. Now they're only clinics cuz of the migrations and a kinda brain drain. But JoJo's on that tiny internet all the time it seems like to me. At least ze can charge zir phone now, if the battery holds up. But JoJo gets around, ze's "connected" as they used to say. And ze didn't have to come back to New Bay after zir training but ze did, to help zir family, and us, the Caretakers.

Riga's askin' Mae about the Heartland Convention, if it's happened yet.

"No, not yet. Not for another month. That's what we want to talk about..." Mae looks at zir watch. It's still before 2:00. "Let me show you something." Ze's smilin' and I feel how excited ze is as ze gets out one of those colorful cloth packs they make here and puts it on the table. Ze takes out a big book, like a textbook, and turns the cover toward us so we can see it.

The Americas, it says. There's a map of North and South America but they look real different. I reach for the book, I gotta see it, and Mae passes it over.

Riga and I lean over it. North to south the map shows:
Canada.

Westlands, Mountains, Heartland and *Eastlands* for what used to be the United States

Mexico

The Isthmus. That's where Central America was, and not only is it a skinny little strip now, just a mountain ridge, but it looks like there's a strait thru it. The continents aren't connected anymore.

Then where South America was:

El Norte

Peru

Brazil

El Sur

There's a big sea in *El Sur* and another really big sea in *El Norte* above *Brazil*.

Mae's watchin' us pore over this map. "This book was printed two weeks ago," ze says. "It's published by Earth Corps. Ayala brought it from Boulder, our biggest Eden station in Mountains. Ze was there for a month. It was a long journey. This is the first history book of The Renewal."

"And Ayala heard some of those "white only" enclaves up north are already burning it." Pyotr laughs.

"Do you believe that?" Mae turns to zir.

I'm just listenin', kinda speechless.

"If there are still Guardians up there?" Pyotr says. "Yes, I do," ze says.

"Where was this, you are talking about?" Riga asks.

"Mount Rushmore."

As they talk about the Guardians, I turn a few pages of the book and see the Table of Contents.

The First Pulse Sea Rise—Greenland Melt
The First Major Migrations
The Wars
    Domestic (Reformers and Guardians)
    Foreign (U.S. and Mideast allies vs Iran and Mideast allies. India vs Kashmir.)
The United Nations First Fossil Fuel and Plastics Bans
The Global Fail
    Economic crash and currency failures
    Government and institutional collapses
The Pandemics
    SARS-mutated viruses from Asia
    Aural candida in the Americas
    Global influenza
The Dissolution of the United Nations
The Founding of Earth Corps
The Second Fossil Fuel and Plastics Bans
The Second Pulse Sea Rise—Thwaites collapse
The Second Major Migrations
The Resurgence of the Guardians at Northern Latitudes
The Founding of the Eden Network
The First Heartland Convention
The Third Pulse Sea Rise—Antarctica
The Third Major Migrations
The Earth Corps Accord
    Clean Air and Water
    Renewable Energy
    Artificial Intelligence Regulation
    Species Protection
The Renewal

"The Renewal," I say it out loud. Mae looks at me. "Where's this book kept?" I ask.

"Right now? It's in a safe in our library. You can read it there if it's available when you come in, but there's a line." Mae laughs. Then ze looks out the door and waves.

Lucia and Chinua are walking in and behind them is Jorge.

I'm still so amazed about what's in this book and wanna see more, but I get up and shake everybody's hand. I wonder where the rest of 'em are. Riga said there's nine members in the council. I guess this is a quorum, tho. I gotta say, I feel nervous, but excited too. What do they want from us?

"A little more background for you Star," Mae says as I sit down again.

"The Eden Network has a Covenant of values in addition to the Earth Corps guidelines. They are values of inclusion, diversity, and cooperation. Some of the Covenant uses language directly from the Reformers documents because they are who started most of the Edens in North America. In Europe the Eden movement was led by the Green Party, and in Latin America the Liberation Theologians, and they joined with other humanitarians, progressives and socialists in Africa and Asia. You can read the history in this book." Mae taps on the book and then takes it and puts it back in the cloth bag.

"We communicate like Pyotr explained," Mae says. "Sometimes weeks can pass before we hear word from our allies in Asia or Africa or Europe. I guess you know, Australia is now uninhabited."

"Well, I..."

"Except some Aboriginal peoples may still live in the interior. In fact, we think they probably do," Chinua says. "Because they survived there for 60,000 years before."

"We live for the hopeful news," Mae says. "For the accounts coming in of The Renewal. The return of forests in Canada, Eastlands, the region of the Amazon basin not yet underwater, the boreal forests of Russia and Europe."

"And the flushing out of chemicals in the waterways. Draymond knows a lot about this," Lucia says. "Some will never leave—enriched uranium, for example, but a lot was done to sequester radioactive waste during the war."

"There is hope," Mae repeats. "The levels of radioactivity in the atmosphere may still be tolerable. We won't know about genetic mutations for decades yet."

"There are some reports of mutated species in Asia, particularly in the mountains of what remains of Japan," Pyotr says.

"But," Mae slows down the stream of words. "There is renewal. This is our first focus. The Renewal." Ze looks around thru the glass behind her at all the lush green plants of this beautiful place and I do the same. It calms me.

"We see ourselves as harmonious ecovillages," Lucia says, "welcoming migrants, creating communities, nurturing each other and the Earth."

"The further east you go, the more technology you will find," Chinua says. Ze turns to Mae, "Ayala told me there are fuel cell buses in Salt Lake."

"How can that be?"

"We don't really know all the changes and the ways of the various pockets of humanity left on this Earth," Pyotr says. Ze doesn't seem as optimistic as everyone else here.

"What is the population of Earth now? Any ideas?" I ask. Everybody laughs, includin' me. I'm still in shock at all the things they do know, if it's true.

"Between one and two billion," Mae answers, "according to Earth Corps estimates."

"Even with all the people in the north and inland?" I ask. Riga's sayin' nothing I notice. Just listenin'. I'll find out what ze thinks later.

"The tropics are depopulated, Australia's mostly uninhabited, the southern region of Eastlands is underwater. Wars, pandemics, floods, crop failures and starvation—"

"People are not giving birth," Jorge says. "And infant mortality is what it was two centuries ago."

"A lot of things are like they were two centuries ago, and some of that's good," Mae says. "The population in 1850 was 1.5 billion. There was clean water and air then and enormous biodiversity."

"And slavery," Chinua says. "We have to protect some of the advances. There have been advances." We agree and they start to talk about that.

"Like the wind and solar farms, and electric vehicles, and new clean batteries from Asia," Lucia says. "And the solar-powered desalination and water purification devices."

"The robots in Heartland—those cleaning and service robots—we need some of those here," Jorge says and everybody laughs.

But Mae says, "We do. We can trade for them." Then ze looks at me and Riga, and then at the others at the table who all kinda shift and look at Mae and then at us. What? I'm thinkin'.

"Riga, and Star, we want to ask you if you will be our representatives at the Heartland Convention. Every Eden village is sending representatives to advocate for our values and Covenant in the new constitution. We need strong representation, although I believe there are far more of us than former Guardians."

"They did lose the war," Lucia says.

"Not completely," Pyotr says. "You could say The Fail won the war."

"There are the Centrists now, though. You never know what they'll agree to," Chinua says.

"This convention is profoundly important," Mae says, "much more than the first one which was called to assess the conditions at that time. This one is called to write a unifying constitution for the four regions."

"It's a long journey," Lucia says, "and none of us can get away for the months it could take to go there, and represent us there, and then return here to our duties in New Rose. We are the farthest Eden village from Heartland Capitol, where the convention will be. Ayala needs to recuperate from her trip to Mountains. Ze returned with a fever and needs rest."

"To be truthful," Chinua says, "it could be dangerous. The trains are irregular and have accidents. There are long delays when fuel runs out. They rely on acres of firewood stacked at each station that are not always replenished. And there are thieves, and up around Salt Lake some renegade Guardian bands come down to sabotage the Eden couriers sometimes."

"Wars never really end," Riga says. The first thing ze has said since we sat down, seems like.

"Chinua's right," Mae says. "That's part of why we are asking you, Riga, because you have been on these routes as a Guide, although not to Heartland for several years, but you know the dangers."

"I do and I am honored to represent New Rose and the Eden Network at the convention." There are tears in zir eyes. Ze is dead serious. And everyone starts to murmur, sayin' thanks and they're grateful and you can feel appreciation, and relief, I guess. My head is just swimmin'.

"Star," Mae says to me. I look at zir. "We also want to ask you to transport our plants, the endangered species we are cultivating here." Ze looks around the conservatory then back to me. "To some of our Eden villages en route. They will require constant and complicated care. We are hoping to reintroduce the species that are especially important to birds, butterflies, bees and other pollinators, as part of The Renewal."

Now I almost start to cry. Then, "YES!" I say. Everybody laughs, but I gotta say, I can't help it, I'm so excited, this is like a dream come true. "Blessed be."

PART III

Mom

The train is more comfortable than I'd expected, although old and well-used. There are some cracks in the vinyl bench cushions with stuffing popping out. Luckily I was guided to a seat that is intact. There are ten of us making the trip after all, six Potters, including Catherine and Dix, and then Star, Riga, JoJo and I. JoJo is coming only to buy supplies for the clinic and she'll return to New Rose on the next train that goes west. All the Caretakers, except for Star and me, have decided to continue working at the clinic in New Rose for the time being. Shanika and JoJo think the children, Ariel, Taddie and the others, need a rest from the journey and they are happy in the beautiful and tranquil town of New Rose. A few of the Potters have stayed, recovering from their injuries from the ferry accident, but I suppose they will move on fairly soon. There is no work for them in New Rose and they need to settle where the soil has more clay content.

I see these windows open and I shove at the one next to me with my good arm, managing to gain an inch or two of air. My broken arm is getting better. A week in a large splint has been very helpful and now I have a smaller splint from the supplies from the ferry, and better use of my hand. I'm not feeling rested, though. I worked at the clinic every day, though only four or five hours; it's draining. Unbelievably draining. How did I do this kind of work eight hours a day in my practice for so many years? After Dale died, I thought it was grief that made me so tired. But maybe it's simply age.

I've never seen Star happier, and this gives me joy. She and Riga are inseparable, of course. Except when they're performing they're separate duties as directed by the New Rose council. Riga spent a lot of time with residents of Old

Town and on infrastructure work there. Star was forever in the Conservatory which she eventually took me to see. It is a marvel. Something to make the heart sing. She had a field notebook someone on the council gave her and I was thrilled to see her making her botanical sketches and taking notes again after so many years. And she and Riga seemed to spend every spare minute in the little town library reading some book that, I have to laugh, we used to call "hot off the press." A new history book issued by something called the Earth Corps. I hope these things are true. I haven't seen a history book I trusted in fifty years. But then, I haven't seen any history books at all in many years. I would love to have spent time in the little library but the truth is I can't see to read now. I'm hoping there are glasses, some kind of eye care in the Capitol. Mae had a few pair of readers, lost or left behind by people passing through, but none were right for my eyes. I suppose I could adapt if I struggled with it. But more likely, I'm afraid, I have cataracts and JoJo said as much. Mae also produced a magnifying glass and that was kind of her. It may have helped but I didn't manage to get over to the library. Now I dearly wish I had a bag full of paperbacks for this long train journey. Perhaps the natural light through the window and a magnifying glass would work, and I'm sorry I didn't experiment more in New Rose.

But in fact, the train will take only half a day or so to get to the Capitol. The "or so" is highly variable, I was told, depending on all kinds of things. Available fuel, debris on the tracks, et cetera et cetera. The thought of branches, swaying branches, unnerves me for a moment, but I push the thought aside. I turn to see if Catherine and Dix have boarded yet, but then I see them outside my window still talking with some of the Potters staying behind. Dix looks a bit sorrowful.

There were several new people in town yesterday. The ferry is running again, but it only recently left for Muir House, which seems vastly far away to me now, although it was just over a week ago we left there. The new migrants are from the northern coast of Westlands, and they came down by way of rafts and boats, along the Columbia River to the Deschutes, and then took weeks traveling the old I-5 corridor on some kind of solar/electric vehicle, bicycles and horses. I didn't quite hear the whole story, I confess. But they were exhausted and in great need of care and the clinic was going full out when I left. This added to my mixed feelings on leaving somewhere as seemingly idyllic as New Rose. Aesthetically it's paradise. Socially, it is exemplary. But these people work very, very hard. I don't know what I could contribute. Truthfully, I don't know if I could continue the daily work I was doing at the clinic. My mind wanders. I forget. I am tired.

I slump now in my vinyl seat, trying to lean my head back, craving sleep. Wishing to somehow recharge from this exhaustion that starts as a hard pressure behind my eyes and sinks through my body, making it limp. No wonder Star asked me the other day, privately and with considerable concern, if the antidepressants I asked JoJo about were, in fact, for me. I shrug now. Of course that wasn't my motive, but I can see her point. I'm going to miss Shanika and the children so much, all of the Caretakers! and I can't imagine how Star can leave Tania after twenty years as best friends. It's bewildering and yet somehow it seems inevitable that we must move on. Either you're part of the solution in New Rose or you end up in Old Town. I wonder for a moment, if that would be so bad. But yes, it would. Star is my only family. And she is more determined now than ever to get to Heartland.

Star told me some things she'd learned about "Earth Corps" and "Eden Network" and "The Americas" book and what excites her the most: "The Renewal." She told me what she and Riga were asked to do although I can tell no one. And her sense of purpose makes her incandescent. I have never seen her like this. I wish Dale were here to see her. Thinking of Star now gives me a kind of contentment that I had thought to be lost to me.

Am I a believer, though? I wonder. Part of the hope and excitement Star talked about was all the new technologies that would be in Heartland, and even the Capitol, and I am deeply wary of the "world according to engineers." One minute she was talking about all the recovered rivers and waterways from dams breaking down and the renewed riparian lands and species, and the next minute it's the engineers—who built the goddam dams—we're supposed to be excited about. It's a mix I don't know how to think about, how to weigh the pros and cons.

I see Dix and Catherine coming down the aisle with several people behind them, Potters and Riga, Star, JoJo. I even, to my amazement, hear the words "All Aboard!" from somewhere outside. Catherine looks at me and smiles then, with an ironic wink. She and Dix pile into the seats behind me. Catherine leans forward and puts a hand on my shoulder, talking into my ear as I turn my head, though my neck seems a bit stuck.

"I am so glad we're making this journey together," she says.

"Me too," I say, with heart. We've talked often this past week, although Catherine still had to spend a good deal of time resting and sleeping. She's much better now, the bandages off her face and the swelling almost gone. But still she has to take it easy, be careful, for months.

Star plops down next to me, to my surprise. "I feel like I never see you!" she says. Riga and JoJo get into the seats in front of us.

I hear the loud huffing of the steam engine. We're the first of the three cars it will pull up the mountain, after the tender, of course, which is piled high with firewood. Slash from dead trees. The rear car is all baggage and cargo. After a minute a deafening whistle sounds and then the chugging along the track begins. I feel an unexpected dropping of my heart, a sudden grief, another home left behind. I look at Star. Her eyes are shining like she's on a ride at an amusement park. Pure exhilaration.

I turn to talk to Catherine but see she is dozing, or at least her eyes are closed. The demands of packing, riding in the carts to the station, boarding the train, the emotion— I'm sure it's tired her, as it has me. Sleep still eludes me though and I gaze out the window as we begin to pull away from the small station. We're in a woodsy place, although Riga tells me the land outside Roseville is mostly open fields, except for a few reforestation projects that have begun. I glance at Star who is leaning forward talking with Riga and JoJo who are making some kind of list, and now she turns back to me. And again I think of Dale, how, right now, I see Dale in her. And this reminds me, urgently, of something I'd felt I must tell her but had since forgotten.

"Star," I say. She looks at me with some concern. Had I shouted? I don't think so. But more quietly, I say, "Star, I wanted to tell you something about Jason." I can feel her tense, and her face takes on a look of — not this again.

"I just want to tell you." I've lowered my voice to a whisper and I see this alarms her even more. But I go on, "I realized why he's been so much on my mind."

"Why?" she whispers back to me, her eyes searching mine now.

"It's his guilt. His unbearable guilt. I've tried to help him with it. And I think I understand it because I've felt it myself. After Dale died. It's not rational. I suppose it's survivor's guilt, but sometimes it's more than that. Like there was something I could have done--"

"No, Mom," she starts to say, but I put my hand on her arm.

"I want to tell you, Star. My deepest request to you is that you never feel that guilt. That you remember what I've said today, and that you never feel that guilt if you lose someone you love." I add all the weight I can to these words. "And most especially, if something happens to me. Do not break my heart by feeling guilt." I hold her gaze in mine until I see she has taken this in. I don't know that she totally understands me but she gives me the gift of not arguing. Then I sit back against my seat, looking ahead, with a tremendous, inexplicable sense of relief.

Star stays quiet beside me, until in a moment JoJo turns around and says, "How much quinine did we have?"

JoJo seems oblivious to the brief conversation Star and I just had, which does not surprise me in the least. But I wonder about Riga. Riga's sensitivities astonish me sometimes. I wonder if ze heard every word. And I realize I hope ze did. Because ze will remind her of what I've said someday. At least I hope ze will live long enough to do so.

Star is talking with JoJo about supplies again and Riga is helping keep notes or occasionally looking out the open window.

I turn to the window, too. Warm air gushes in as the train is picking up speed. It ruffles my hair, is soothing one minute and enervating the next. I shove the window closed just a bit, with some effort. Luckily no one notices or tries to help. I sit back and make myself comfortable, training my gaze on the passing landscape.

It's not long before we're out of the pretty park-like woods and into a dry scrubland. There are occasional clumps of bright green and yellow scotch broom, and then acres of hardpan, arid packed dirt. I see trees up ahead but they turn out to be heavily logged with dead slash still scattered across acres of damaged pines. I close my eyes.

I can feel the currents, like micro-wires softly buzzing beneath my skin, like a hive of bees, that has made sleep so difficult. What I wouldn't give for some old-fashioned pharmaceuticals, ambien, xanax, opioids, whatever. Even a glass of sauvignon blanc. I can hear Dale scoff, who do you think invents those things? Engineers. Really? I would say. Fermented grapes!? Though of course he would be right, about Big Pharma, which has died the death of all huge mass production facilities and factories, and I don't care. They killed off their own labor force. Although there are robots, I've heard, in surviving urban centers in some of the inland temperate and polar regions. But not enough power to run them all. Fossil fuels are no longer extracted, refined or transported and haven't been for years. There is wind and solar. But energy is rationed and there are curfews. Just as some places in poor counties cut off power at 10:00 PM even at the height of the global oil glut. So no, no more flood of oil, or pills, or any products, in our brave new world.

I wonder if anyone reads Huxley anymore. Where would they find his books? Maybe the New Rose Library and again I'm sorry I never even entered the building. Where is my curiosity? I asked JoJo if she thought the clinics in the Capitol did cataract surgery. We'll be staying there a few days, I was told, before taking the train on to Heartland. But she said no, any surgeries would be at the hospital on the other side of Mountains, the Capitol there. What used to be Denver, I gather. This joggles something I haven't thought of in years. A cause Dale and I worked hard for, long ago, in more innocent times. There was a nuclear waste dump there. Still is! Will be until the end of time. Rocky Flats, next to the airport. They made plutonium detonators for atomic bombs. It wouldn't be underwater, like all the nuclear reactors on various waterways. Mustard gas, napalm and nerve agents were manufactured at Rocky Flats. It was eventually shut down and the plutonium was shipped to South Carolina, I think it was. Now safely underwater, poisoning the seas.

I do remember the half-life of plutonium—24,000 years. For it to completely dissipate would take...? Forever? Like enriched uranium. Before they closed it, Rocky Flats stored its nuclear waste, thousands of drums of plutonium and uranium, outside on the bare ground. They leaked radioactive oil. And when this was discovered, asphalt was poured over the whole mess. Eventually it was all scraped off and the drums shipped to South Carolina, too. The South, so willing to embrace everything toxic, figuratively and literally. I should not have these "bigoted" thoughts about our southern neighbors but, in fact, that beautiful subtropical region really is underwater now. Except the Blue Ridge Mountains. And the Shenandoah. That haunting song. Hundreds of years old. I can hear it so clearly in my mind now, "Oh Shenandoah, I long to see you...." I glance quickly around to be sure I haven't sung this aloud. Star is sound asleep. Well, of course. JoJo is reading something on her phone. Only Riga sits, gazing out the window. Well, Riga will know all my secrets.

I have no idea where this song has come from.

Rocky Flats. That's right. That, unlike South Carolina, will live as long as the Earth. Dale and I read that engineers proposed 25-foot tall granite monuments be erected with warning signs in many languages including glyphs and pictures for future civilizations, anyone who might haplessly decide to do an archeological dig and come up with an underground blazing hell of radioactivity.

I wonder what forty years of extreme weather and erosion have done to the "secured" radioactive waste at Rocky Flats. And the other sites, the underground salt domes in New Mexico. We lost track of nuclear proliferation and contamination decades ago. It seemed too abstract once the changes started. But if "The Renewal" is really possible, man-made contaminants like enriched uranium, cadmium rods, mountains of plastics—where will they go? Draymond talked about the nitrates and phosphates finally flushing out of the soil, but where did they drain to? I heard there were huge dead zones in river deltas, killing all the wildlife.

But these are things we knew about decades ago. And we organized and donated and fought to protect our planet. And then it was too late. And instead of rising to the challenges a great percentage of people turned to nationalism, scapegoating, and war. And this is why it is hard to hope. This is why I have to wonder if humanity deserves to survive.

I open my eyes, conscious even now of what a dangerous thought that is. Of how I must never say it aloud. Even now. It is my private despair.

And, too, it seems, to my amazement, that youthful idealism still exists—in New Rose, and now Star and Riga, and even JoJo and the Caretakers. It's contagious, just like hatred and despair were contagious before. "Love it or leave it!" is shouted in my ear by some voice in my head. It's the guilt again, for thinking such anti-human thoughts.

Did I say it out loud? Because Star wakes up next to me with a start. "Oh, the plants," she says. "I have to check on the plants." I turn and watch her make her way down the aisle and disappear through the door between the cars. I know there are eight crates of endangered plants she will be distributing, like Johnny Appleseed, at Eden communities from here to Heartland Capitol.

Catherine is awakened by this sudden movement in our sleepy train car and opens her eyes. I smile at her, my head still turned as I watch Star. "How are you feeling?" I ask her.

She straightens in her seat and Dix stirs beside her and wakes up also.

Catherine looks at me, "Is it time for lunch?" she says, half-joking. Only she and I and probably Dix recall the concept of having "lunch" every day, instead of "a meal" at any random time when food is available.

"It could be," I answer and happily reach for the cloth sack at my feet and hold it up for her to see. It swings a bit wildly as the train jolts and I tilt off balance as a squealing of brakes brings us to a stop. We all look out the window. "We can't be there already," I say.

Riga turns around. "It's a fuel stop."

And indeed we can see through a screen of trees an acre or more of firewood stacked high.

"They will load fuel here because the next wood supply is high above. We will climb in steep mountains now," Riga says. "I'm going to help load." Ze and JoJo, too, head for the door of the car. Dix follows them. Catherine and I watch them go. Some Potters are getting up, to help or to go outside and stretch their legs. Catherine and I exchange a look, as in—this is going to take a very long time. She pats the seat beside her. I slowly stand with my walking stick and cloth pack in hand and maneuver around to sit next to her.

"Any idea of an ETA?" she asks.

"Well, I'd hoped by evening. I believe that's what Star said. I'm hoping it's before dark."

"I'm not even clear on where we're staying, are you?"

"A refugee waystation of some kind, an old hotel, I think. Something Riga knows about and will take us to."

"Mae told me the next train will have sleeping cars, although I'm not sure she really knows," Catherine says. I'm a bit surprised because, if I were to believe anyone in this age of uncertainty now, it would be Mae. And possibly Riga, although I saw ze had plenty of doubters back at Muir House, about zir map. But maps—a very unreliable artifact now.

"I wonder about us," I say. "You needing to sleep and sleep and I can't seem to sleep at all."

"Still?" she asks, looking concerned.

"Oh, well, of course I do, a few hours here and there." And then I remember what it was that woke me this morning. It was something about the Eden Network. But I can't remember if I'm not supposed to mention the existence of the Eden Network.

"What do you think it is? Stress and anxiety and all the usual culprits? Or something else," she asks.

I'm still trying to recall the dream, my eyes narrowing as I stare out the window. Catherine turns to look at whatever I'm seeing, but it's only an image in my mind. A wall of old logs, like a cabin and a large stone fireplace. A warm fire in the hearth. And then a feeling of happiness.

"What's out there?" she says still looking.

"Oh—oh, I'm just remembering my dream. That's what woke me up this morning just before dawn."

She tenses a bit, turns to look at me. "What was it?"

"Nothing. Nothing frightening. Quite the opposite. A warm scene, safe, in front of a fireplace. A feeling of happiness. Even bliss." For a fleeting moment I can feel it. What can it be?

Relieved, Catherine laughs. "Good. I don't want any branches crashing down on the train tracks."

"No, no. I certainly hope not. Riga said the service has improved dramatically in recent years and the tracks are well maintained, and the fuel supplies stocked. So far so good, anyway."

"Maybe things are starting to recover," Catherine says. Her voice is quiet, as if daring to hope. "I never would have dreamed there would be solar ferries, and steam trains, and especially the level of organization required to keep it all running."

"Well, yes, but I wonder where the ferry would be if Dix hadn't been on board with us."

"That's true." Catherine looks out the window, craning her neck to see the people outside, looking for her husband's tall frame, his head above the small group of people. She turns back to me. "He hated to leave New Rose. And, the Council actually asked him to stay. They would love for him to be the Chief Engineer of the ferry, the windmills, the solar farm, the whole town. Can you imagine?"

I can, and I feel a sudden fear. Not them too. New friends, yes, but dear, and my only friends now. "Why didn't he agree to stay? He did seem so much happier when he was working there." Does he think there will be even better opportunities in Heartland? I wonder. Is he just too curious about what lies ahead?

"He wanted to stay," she admits. "They offered us a beautiful little suite in one of the historic houses past the library."

"Oh my god." My heart sinks.

"But Dix felt I would need better medical care than they could offer and we should go on, to at least Mountains Capitol, where there's supposed to be a well-equipped hospital, whatever that means now."

"But a concussion..."

"He's convinced something worse might have happened, I don't know. He wants me to have a CAT Scan and apparently that's possible on the other side of the Sierras where there's more access to supplies from Heartland. Don't tell JoJo he thinks the medical facilities in New Rose can't take care of me!" she says, half laughing. "But to be fair, at the time he decided we had to go on, he didn't know JoJo would stay in New Rose, or any of the Caretakers."

"Is part of it...Is any of it that he's curious? That he wants to see Heartland? There are so many stories of fabulous robots and automated factories churning out electric vehicles, and miles of wind farms...."

"Maybe a little," Catherine agrees. "There would surely be work for him there."

I nod in agreement.

"Unless there isn't," she says. "Unless the rumors are false or at least inflated. Unless every engineer in the world has come to Heartland, too. Remember Silicon Valley?"

"Vaguely." I'm not really joking because it was so long ago and was employment high or low?

"Anyway, we've decided to continue."

"And you?" I look at her closely. "What's your heart's desire here?"

"Aren't 'heart's desires' a luxury of the past? And the affluent?"

"You know what I mean."

"Oh, well," she sighs, and turns to the window again. "I don't know."

I see, then, that she'd wanted to stay.

She turns back to me. "I'm tired," she says. "I wish I could've stayed. And that you would have, too."

I press my lips together, silently, realizing that she's right. I wish that, too. We look at each other, a bit ruefully.

Star

We're gonna get there pretty soon, you can tell, cuz the land's opened up to wide rolling hills and there's some buildings here and there, old barns or houses, looks like they're in pretty bad shape. Then there's miles and miles of windmills, I had no idea! And acres of solar panels. I was talkin' with a couple people in the car behind this one after I checked on the plants back in the baggage car. They asked what I was doin' so I told 'em and then we started talkin' about the Capitol. They live there. They just went down to New Rose to buy some goods like cloth and seeds and some ceramics. I asked if they were doin' barter or what, and they told me an earful. They said the Westlands Regional Council operates in an old church, a basilica, they said, on the west side of the city. The center of the city got flooded from the Truckee River way back when and it covered a lotta roads and buildings in a layer of silt like in Old Town Roseville. But in the last couple years more people've been comin' there to live. The Council—they call it WRC—is pretty new, just a few years old, and they're workin' right now gettin' currencies regulated. We got onto this subject when I asked about barter, and these two said there's still a lotta barter but there's also gold and silver and that new coin minted in Heartland that I saw—Riga has some. The WRC wants to get cryptocurrencies goin', too, especially for government purposes, but you need internet for that and the domestic infrastructure for internet is still gettin' rebuilt so it's inconsistent. There's crypto everywhere in Heartland, these two said—they look to be about my age. They also said the WRC doesn't collect any taxes from people or provide any public services yet, cuz they're just tryin' to rebuild infrastructure and trade right now. They organize trade groups and rules for the trains, farms, wind and solar energy, city maintenance, garbage, utilities—and money, like I said. The WRC does collect fees and dues from these trade groups, tho, to pay for all they do. I asked them how many people they thought live in all of Westlands now. They said the WRC says about half a million people, but really they've got no idea.

"You all should come see us," they told me when I started to go and they even gave me a phone number, so I guess the infrastructure's workin' for them. I get the idea they may be richer than some. A funny thing to think of, like something from the way back past. I don't have a number to give them right now and thought about givin' 'em JoJo's but I didn't. They were pretty friendly after I told 'em about the endangered plants we had and I'm glad I talked to them. Back in our car I told Mom and the others all about it, and then we started seein' what looks like the outskirts of the Capitol. I'm feelin' excited but nervous, too. Something about talkin' with those two in the other car about this city, something that feels different than New Rose. I don't know. I haven't seen any city or even a town since we got cut off in New Bay so many years ago, except New Rose.

A voice comes on crazy loud in a bunch of static and Mom kinda jumps out of her seat and I gotta laugh. I put my hand on her arm to calm zir, and I guess to calm myself, too. The voice says we'll be at the station in a few minutes! Everybody starts scufflin' around and gettin' themselves ready. Riga steps around JoJo into the aisle and I stand up and take zir hand. I feel like we've been apart forever and I rest a minute, closin' my eyes just to feel Riga with me.

We get off the train and Riga's helpin' me with the plants while the Potters unload their cargo from the baggage car. Some other people, like the two I met, have some crates they're gettin' too. We've got a wagon the Potters gave us that they don't need cuz they lost a lot of their cargo in the Valley Sea. We're loadin' the plant crates in there but we're gonna have to carry a couple too. We're all dressed in that New Rose cloth, Devi's clothes I think of it, tho there's a few different people who make clothes in Old Town. Mom and Catherine are sittin' on a bench nearby. There's a lot of people walkin' around on this platform to greet other passengers and help with their baggage, and others are waitin' to get on the train, cuz it'll continue over the Sierras. It's so busy I feel like I gotta hurry but I don't know why. And then I see they're all wearin' different clothes than us. I don't see togas or Devi's clothes, except maybe on one or two people. It's like we have Westlands clothes, but most everyone else has Mountain clothes or Heartland clothes. I see a lot of green shirts or tops with patterns, and dark pants and skirts, and leather shoes and boots. They're darker clothes—city clothes. And everyone here is about my age or younger. I realize how old Mom looks, and even Catherine, sittin' on the bench, Mom with zir cane and splint. I see a couple kids starin' at zir even. One of 'em looks like ze's seen a ghost and turns to zir friend and whispers something. Or maybe ze's makin' fun of Mom. I swallow hard, something that rises up in my throat. I'm glarin' at this kid when ze looks over at me. Ze gives me a kinda—I don't know—a "fuck you" look, we woulda said when I was a kid. I turn to Riga and ze doesn't say anything, just raises one shoulder about an inch, like—shrug it off, and I turn around and get back to work. We gotta get this stuff packed up and outta here. One of the Potter's rigged up a dray to drag stuff cuz the three wagons are full. Riga says where we're stayin' is real close, it'd be like a three minute walk if we didn't have all this stuff. And I feel something odd, like I haven't felt since I was a teenager—I know people're gonna look at us all, the Potters and their dray, Riga and me and our wagons, our bright, loose clothes, Mom and Catherine limpin' along, and I don't like what I feel. Embarrassed. Something I thought I'd forgot how to feel. I close my eyes and I pray to all that's holy to remind me what's important. I go over to see how Mom is and ze and Catherine get up to start the walk, and then I see to the plants with Riga.

The street's kinda dirty as we walk to the Waystation Hotel, it's called. There's some trash blowin' around. It's windy and I'm squintin' to keep dirt outta my eyes and I reach in my pocket and get my sunglasses, even tho the sun's gonna set in about half an hour. I feel safer with them on, and I don't like that feeling either. I say another prayer. Then I offer to carry the crate Riga has and ze hands it to me. It weighs a lot, we're tradin' off. Dix is carrying one for us, too. The other crates are in the wagon and JoJo's pullin' that.

Just as we're comin' up to the door of the Waystation—it's a tall brick building with a heavy wood door—a parent with two little kids, really dirty and sad lookin', come up and ask us for food or money. We all look at Riga. What's the custom, we're thinkin', cuz those of us over twenty remember homeless people and all that goes with it. Riga reaches in his pack and takes out a couple apples and some flat bread and hands it out. The older kid says, "Thank you." The others just look down at the food, and they start eatin' like it's been a long time. Dix sets down a crate and tries to open the big wood door but it's locked. There's a corroded brass bell with a clapper by the door and Riga rings it loud.

The door opens finally from inside and a kid about fifteen lets us in. It's dark inside, and I know I heard there was a curfew on electricity but there are no electric lamps in this place. The kid turns and picks up an oil lamp from a table and I see we're in a hallway. There's a staircase to our right and a long narrow passage goin' straight back. That's where the kid takes us, blessed be, cuz I don't wanna be climbin' any stairs with all this stuff and I don't wanna leave it down here. And there's Mom and Catherine, it was hard enough goin' up and down the stairs at Mariposa House.

We get to the very back and there's two rooms for us. One is for the Potters and one for us Caretakers and Riga. Dix says Catherine should stay with us so it's five and five and we agree.

The room's about as big as the one at Mariposa and has four cots. I say I'll sleep on the floor and JoJo and Riga say we'll take turns. We don't know how many nights we're gonna be here. The train east is supposed to leave in three days if it's on time, so that's only two nights here and I'm startin' to feel real glad about that. The next stop is another village in the Eden Network, about a day's train ride from here, and the thought of that makes me so happy I forget about how strange, in a bad way, the Capitol feels so far, mean and lonely. I start movin' all the plants over by the window and then make shelves with the crates to put each plant where it'll get the best light it can for its needs.

JoJo's found a room with a toilet and a sink with running water down the hall. There's a line of us already, but I'll get some water for the plants as soon as I can. It's dusky out but I can see from the window of our room that there's a vacant yard out back, just dirt, and the backs of some old buildings. There's some trash out there too, and then I make out in the corner on the far side a lean-to thing made with old blankets, looks like, and some more trash and clothes or I don't know what layin' to the side. One of the kids we saw at the entrance to this place is down in a crouch in front of some sticks and wood like ze's gonna make a fire.

I turn around as a light comes from across the room, it's an oil lamp Riga's just lit. It casts a pretty golden glow that soothes my nerves. JoJo's pulled a blanket off zir bed and some stuff from zir pack to make a bed on the floor for me next to a cot that has Mom's stuff on it. We've got enough food in our packs to make a dinner and Riga says we should wait 'til tomorrow to go out into the Capitol. I'm guessin', tho ze didn't say, that's it's not safe after dark.

Mom

When I open my eyes there is only gray, like the inside of a rain cloud, a misty fog. I see nothing yet I hear voices. The voices that woke me. If I had a light to shine I could see through this gray fog but where would I find a light? And where am I? I turn my head toward the voices and there is a dark outline, two figures standing, one stooped, talking. The bed is hard. I hear Star's voice and my mind calms. As I lie still I can make out the two figures standing by a window where the gray is lighter. It must be dawn. The stooped figure is Star. She's hovering over something. "Oh." I smile. Her plants. And the other voice. Of course, it's JoJo. We're in the Capitol. I must have slept very soundly despite the circumstances. It's quiet in this old morgue, at least, I think. It's not really a morgue, I don't know why I would say that, but it is an old gloomy building. So far, the Capitol reminds me of the Civic Center in San Francisco circa 2010. Dirty, depressed, the homeless camps. I wonder where the rich live. Is it possible there are no rich people anymore? But how does the adage go, there will always be rich and poor. But wasn't there another adage? "…death makes equal the rich and the poor." *Pearls of Eternity*. That was the book. But we're not dead…yet. I wonder how we refugees, our little band of Potters and Caretakers from Westlands would rate on the rich and poor scale of this cataclysmic decade. I'd thought catastrophe, like death, would be a great equalizer. But of course not. The rich always fare better in disasters, for the most part.

New Rose. It was different there. Although they had their rich and poor in a way. Those with important meaningful jobs, and those just trying to survive in Old Town, like villagers eking out an existence. Yet they make beautiful textiles and ceramics. Possibly American indigenous communities, pre-contact, would be a better analogy. And even they had their rich and poor, their royalty. But no homeless people, I don't think. Catherine and I were impressed with many things about New Rose, especially how egalitarian it seemed, despite its uptown, old town divide. Because of the values. There was no one-upmanship, that we could see. Compassion, and shared identity in diversity, was what they cultivated. That's part of why it was so hard to leave. I sigh, audibly, unintentionally.

"Mom?" Star looks at me. I can see her more clearly now. The room is lightening. I smile at her and maneuver to a sitting position.

"Good morning," I say in a quiet voice, seeing that Catherine is still sleeping, or resting, in the cot across the room. I don't see Riga anywhere.

Star comes to sit on her palette on the floor next to me. "How did you sleep," she asks.

"Very well," I answer as I realize I must have because my mind is working well this morning, once I realized where I was. "Where's Riga?"

"Ze went out to meet with some people from the WRC, I told you about, and ze's gonna arrange our train tickets goin' east, too. Ze wants to get a room in a sleeping car for you and Catherine. Ze says it's possible with a little effort." She doesn't say it but I think we both wonder what "a little effort" means. Money, I assume.

"JoJo and I are goin' to the clinics to buy supplies."

"Buy?"

"JoJo has some crypto on her phone from the Eden Network. Dix is comin' with us. And ze and Riga asked the other Potters to stay here and take shifts to guard our stuff, and also Catherine who wants to stay here and rest. Do you want to come with us? Or stay here?"

"I'll come," I say and get up from the bed. Star picks up my walking stick from the floor and hands it to me.

"We're gonna leave pretty soon. Dix is with Riga gettin' some food and ze'll bring it back to us. After we eat, we'll go." She grins at me, and I see she is glad I'm up for this venture. I know I'll be able to carry some of the supplies in my backpack. I'm especially glad Dix will be coming with us, otherwise I probably would have declined so as not to make us more vulnerable in the streets. I don't know what I was expecting of the Capitol. Something less reminiscent of the past, I suppose. Something more hopeful or experimental. I put it out of my mind as I head to the small bathroom, which is a luxury, in fact, to wash and dress.

It's fully light outside as we close the large wooden door of the Waystation Hotel behind us. The street is only slightly less dingy in the morning sunlight. I wonder how much longer we'll get by before a rainstorm. It's been over a week. I look up at the sky and I do see some clouds in the horizon to the west. But at the moment, the sky above is blue.

It's a two mile walk to the clinics, JoJo tells us. We walk in silence, taking in the sights. I remember this city, from decades ago. Dale and I came here once or twice for a weekend. There were homeless then, too, and people stumbling out of bars. But this is different. How can one describe the before and after? It's not just the abandoned buildings or thick layers of dried mud covering so many streets. Elevated boardwalks have been constructed over some and by the look of the wood, they are new, within the last decade. But it isn't just this and the occasional panhandler and encampments inside abandoned buildings. It's something in the air. Or not the air, because the air smells only of woodsmoke here and there and otherwise is very clean.

It's something in the attitude, or, a feeling of barely hanging on. There are few people about now, just after dawn; maybe the streets come to life as the day warms. But right now, the place feels doomed.

We're walking quickly, because I think we all want to escape this gloom, and I'm keeping up well. I'm glad Catherine didn't try to join us; this would be much too difficult. I just wonder how long my energy will hold. I'm counting on those bursts of adrenalin that have gotten me through this journey so far. I was flagging after the accident, but the week in New Rose revived me, I believe.

The neighborhood begins to improve as we continue due north toward the clinics and I feel myself relax. I didn't realize how tensely I've been gripping my walking stick. I glance at the others and notice Star isn't wearing her Devi clothes but instead an indigo sleeveless toga. She's got a bright Devi cloth sash tied at her waist and she's wearing her sunglasses. Her hair has grown longer. I wonder how I haven't noticed this before. It's brushed back from her forehead and flowing like a mane down her back. She looks like a figure from a bygone era. Stylish even. There's a French word for it.... I can't recall it. She's walking ahead with JoJo, and Dix and I take up the rear. Dix is very solicitous of me for which I'm grateful. I know he's worried about Catherine but the Potters are caring and responsible and they have JoJo's cell phone number. I didn't see Riga this morning, but as I recall ze usually wears zir Devi clothes now. Riga's black wavy hair is still wild and ze has a new totem necklace, as I've come to think of it, feathers and beads and colored glass. Ze and Star make a striking couple, these days. The phrase seems almost foreign in my mind. It must be this city, what's left of it, the urban setting, that makes me think in terms of how people look, instead of how will we get through this day and survive.

The clinics are in view up a slight hill, imposing buildings. They appear to have been kept up better than the train station and old downtown. Star didn't mention healthcare as a priority for the WRC, but perhaps it is.

We arrive and find ourselves among a large group of people standing and sitting on all the available benches, outside as well as inside the lobby. And so, I see. No, healthcare is not a government priority in this city. It is in New Rose.

JoJo moves forward toward the entrance, checking her phone, as we follow, when we hear a voice beside us. A man has come up very close to us, I smell him before I see him, and says, "Well, if it isn't the bizzzy beeze."

I flinch, I can't help it. Star and JoJo turn to him and Dix moves closer to us. I had thought we would never see Mitch again. Or any of the Tinkers. My thoughts rush to Millie, and Dot, and I want to ask him how they are. But his manner is beyond off-putting. I see he has a gash in his cheek that looks infected.

"Mitch," JoJo says flatly, holding his rude gaze. "How are you?"

"Pretty good," he says and laughs, looking at each of us. "When did you all arrive?"

"Last night," JoJo says. "How about you?"

"Oh I beat ya here. I've been here a couple days. Long enough to get this." He laughs again, a hollow laugh as he touches his inflamed cheek.

"What happened?" Star asks.

He looks at her, curious, and then his eyes mocking. "Where's the gypsy?" he asks.

Star's eyes narrow. No one answers him.

"It was a gypsy guy who did this," Mitch says, more belligerent now. "A dark guy, a little bastard with a big knife. I got him though. He's dead now," Mitch boasts and laughs. None of us know whether to believe him and I feel shocked to silence. He's frightened, I see, and in pain. Dangerous.

"Is that so," Dix says now.

"That's right, big guy." Mitch laughs the threatening laugh. He shifts on his feet and looks at JoJo. "Why don't you get me up to the front of the line. You're gonna work in here, right?"

"No. I'm not," JoJo says. "We're here to get supplies for another clinic. I'm sorry, I can't help you. Good luck, Mitch." She turns to go into the building but he reaches out and grabs her arm. Star moves so fast between them that Mitch steps back and as a group we forge past him into the clinic.

"BZZ BZZ. Bizzy beeze!" We hear Mitch mocking behind us, and the cruel laugh.

We say nothing as JoJo leads us down a hall and then up a set of stairs. Star and Dix are walking behind JoJo and me now, glancing behind to make sure Mitch isn't following us. Though why would he be. We're of no value to him. For spite, perhaps, but that's probably too much trouble. I wonder if he's running a fever. Wasn't his behavior just now worse than before? I don't know. I can't remember. It's so disheartening. A reminder of the worst of the past, and the war.

"I didn't think we'd see him again," Dix says finally. We're walking down a wide corridor, an old hospital ward, on the third floor. It's empty, the doors mostly closed. The few that are open show rooms stripped of any furniture or equipment.

"No, I didn't either," I say.

"I suppose there will be more Mitches down the road," Dix says. I know what he means, and it's an unhappy thought. We had found hope in New Rose. I glance at him and see his mouth set in a tense, downturned line.

We turn a corner to another wide corridor and then JoJo stops in front of a double door and knocks. Then she sends a quick text on her phone. A door opens and a young woman in a lab coat says, "Dr. Hernandez, happy to meet you. I'm Rashida Dahl." She shakes JoJo's hand. She's the pharmacist, I gather.

It's an hour before all the supplies have been gathered from the shelves in this large storeroom. They are better stocked than I thought they would be. What they are missing, apparently, is staff. Trained doctors and nurses and pharmacists. JoJo promises Rashida to ask the Caretakers if any of them can come to work here, even temporarily. I think of Shanika then. I miss her. And Tania. All of them. I glance at Star who is busily packing supplies into our backpacks. In addition to the large packs, everyone but me will also carry a duffle bag. It will make us vulnerable, I think. Lumbering along the streets like human packhorses. But that's a negative image, isn't it. I must have a hangover from the encounter with Mitch. I'm fearful, I realize, of running up against him again when we leave. But JoJo is asking Rashida if there is another way to exit the building and to my relief, there is. She also asks if there is any kind of public transportation. Something else that must be low on the WRC agenda.... Rashida tells us there are only private companies, which can be very expensive. She shows JoJo how to summon a car or van, if we decide we need to.

Rashida leads us to a freight elevator that is functioning. None of the other elevators run, not just because of disrepair, but to conserve energy. We load our gear and slowly descend to what seems like a basement, and then walk along another corridor that has pipes running the length of the ceiling. We arrive at a large heavy metal door. Rashida opens a metal box on the wall and punches in a code. The door begins to rise, slow and noisy, as we watch in some amazement, having seen nothing like it in decades. Outside is a ramp, for vehicles, I imagine, and at the top, a street. She tells us to turn left at the top of the ramp and follow it to the west a few blocks, before heading south again. We thank her and she and JoJo embrace quickly. Rashida has renewed my faith and I look around at the tree-lined street as we trudge along with our baggage. I'm glad we'll have the Potters' wagons when we take JoJo to the train station tomorrow midday. She will be taking all of this back to New Rose by herself.

We walk slowly, pacing ourselves, and I feel myself flagging a bit, leaning on my walking stick heavily with each step but I keep my back straight. I know Star is worried because she keeps glancing over her shoulder to look at me. The houses here seem lived in and well kept. There are even gardens, native plants, and mature trees. There is no one about. It's mid-morning but already very hot, and humid, like a storm is coming. I glance up at the sky; it's beginning to cloud over.

We head south after only two blocks. JoJo and Star decide we can't go too far out of our way with all of this weight to carry. We're walking downhill now, making better time and before long we come to a more rundown area.

The houses are older, some abandoned. There is an occasional storefront—used clothing, produce and bagged foods, a sundries shop with candles, ceramic dishes, homemade paper on a vertical display through a dingy window. Dix stops a moment to look at the ceramics. We all stop to catch our breath. None of the shops has opened yet and no one seems to be on the street. We walk on and the next block has even more abandoned buildings; I suppose we're nearing the decrepit area we came from. A flash of red catches my eye and I see three bodies in bright red are running toward us and the next second they are surrounding us and grabbing at our bags—they wrest a duffle bag away from Star and JoJo swings wildly with her own duffle bag, knocking a boy over as he's thrown off by the weight. But the other two, a girl and boy are grabbing Star. Dix and I were behind and now run up to the melee as I jab my stick at the boy's arm while Dix grabs his other arm and Star shoves the girl off her. JoJo has something in her hand and sprays it at the fallen boy as he yells and jumps up and the three of them run fast around the corner and they're gone. All of us are breathing hard and we back away from the dusty cloud of mace JoJo sprayed. We all work to straighten the packs on our backs as we look around us. I realize we've formed a circle, each of us looking out to the north, west, east and south, with the duffle bags piled in the center. JoJo gets out her phone. I hear her exhale of relief when she sees it works.

"There's a café two blocks up that hill," she points behind us and to the west. "Rashida told me about it, I can see it here on the map." She holds up her phone. "We can call for a van from there."

"JoJo why don't you walk up front, Mom behind you, then Dix and I'll keep up the back look out."

"Sounds good," JoJo says.

We all regroup and get in line. We are hyper vigilant now. I still feel the adrenalin pumping and I need it to get up this hill.

"Were those Guardian uniforms?" Dix asks.

"I don't think so," Star says. "Some gang though. Riga said there are gangs. Those kids were probably, what, fifteen?"

"I'm just glad they weren't armed," Dix says.

That makes my blood run cold. We would have been sitting ducks if they'd pulled knives on us. I don't think JoJo's mace would have helped.

"Do they have guns? The gangs?" I ask. I look around, right to left. Beyond alert.

"Riga says there's plenty of guns everywhere but there's no ammunition, or it's hard to get," Star says.

"A lot of it was blown up during the war," Dix says, "or used up. No one manufactures it now on any scale, I've heard."

"It's around though. It can be gotten," Star says. And I wonder how she's so sure about that.

"Does Riga have a gun?" I ask her. Something I've wondered for weeks.

"Yes."

We stop talking. We're out of breath. And we're demoralized. Or at least I am.

It seems forever before we get to the "café." My heart is pumping. It's really probably only been about ten minutes of hard walking.

There are two small tables outside, and four or five inside. It's just a storefront with a counter and some fresh food, pots of tea, lemonade. We take the two outside tables and stack all our packs and bags at the wall behind us. There are only two other people here, inside, drinking hot tea and talking animatedly. A young girl at the counter takes our order from Star who pays with the Heartland coin she must have gotten from Riga. JoJo is busy on her phone making calls and finally seems to have arranged for a van to pick us up. A company from up the hill she says, in the wealthy neighborhood, I gather.

I try to relax as I sip the mint tea Star has put in front of me. I look farther up the hill and see we are on the edge of an affluent neighborhood now. I'd forgotten how that happens in cities. One minute you're in a slum, tripping over people on drugs, and a block later in the Hilton Hotel with women in jewels and men in natty suits.

"They're called Red Riders," Star says. We know who she means. She must have asked the girl in the café. "They work the streets from about there," she points to the block we came from, "on south for about a mile. After that it's some other gang down to the train station, then another one down to the river."

"Are there police?" I ask.

"Only in the rich areas. We're safe here cuz this is the beginning of the Northwest district."

We all keep looking around, though, alert. The sky is overcast now but the sunlight is diffusely bright.

"It's going to cost a lot to take this van," JoJo says, and I can see even she is a bit discouraged. "I hope the Town Council can afford it. I don't want to drain their crypto account."

"We don't have any choice," Star says. "Riga should've come with us."

"Ze couldn't have done much more than we have. It's better ze wasn't here when we saw Mitch. And those kids--if Riga shot somebody, even in self-defense? Who knows what the police here would do," JoJo says.

Star accepts this. Afterall, I think, they were unarmed children and we fought them off. It didn't really call for a gun. The key to safety here, as always, is money. And I feel profoundly grateful JoJo can pay for a van. I look at Dix and see that tight frown on his face again. At this point, I feel the same.

The van arrives. It's an electric six-seat model circa 2025, I think. But as the door opens and we start to climb in, I see there is no driver. Oh no. My heart starts pumping again. A self-driving van. JoJo seems unfazed as she heaves her duffle bag up. Dix helps with her pack and then helps each of us get our baggage into the van. He seems to have revived and as we take our seats I see him look with great interest at the dashboard of the van. JoJo suggests he sit in the driver's seat in case there are any manual back-up controls. Dix is happy to do that and begins examining the instruments, but the door suddenly closes with a bang and we're off. Star laughs. She's sitting next to me. And she and JoJo look at each other, laughing some more. None of us has been in any kind of car for years.

It's been remotely programmed to take us to the Waystation and is remarkably efficient. We arrive in under ten minutes. There's no traffic, of course. Dix didn't need to do a thing. We unload all the gear and in moments the van closes its door and drives off. Well. Technology. If you can afford it, I suppose it has its place.

JoJo has a key to the big wooden door and opens it and we lug all the bags in. Star puts her hand on my shoulder. "Mom. Why don't you go see how Catherine is. We'll get all the bags." I let her take my backpack off over my splint and then I make my way down the hall, looking forward to my bed.

Star

Riga's there when we get back. JoJo and I tell zir everything that happened in a rush and ze hugs us both and says ze's sorry ze wasn't with us. Ze got the sleeping car passage for Mom and Catherine, blessed be, and I know ze got the other things ze went to get too— currencies and information, ammunition—I could see by the look ze gave me when we first came thru the door.

We're in the hallway now so Mom can rest and we don't disturb Catherine anymore, tho ze was sittin' up talkin' to Mom when we came in. The bags of supplies are locked in the rooms which is a big relief. We've got our daypacks and some food and water cuz we're gonna walk to the river, Riga, JoJo and me, and follow it east out of town to look for herbs. JoJo wants to see if ze can get some that don't grow in New Rose before ze leaves. Tomorrow we're gonna take JoJo and all the clinic supplies to the train that goes back to New Rose at noon and then the rest of us'll take the train east tomorrow night.

Riga's pretty surprised we saw Mitch. We can't figure out how ze got here before us. Tho the ferry was runnin' again before we left New Rose, so ze must of got the ferry across. Maybe ze was in Old Town after ze crossed, but how'd ze get up here?

"Mitch was a Guardian," Riga says. "Ze told me ze fought in Montana during the war, so ze knows mountains. Maybe ze came on horseback."

"I guess Mitch could've bought a horse in Old Town," I say. We all look at each other—or stolen one, we're thinkin'.

"I wonder where ze's headed," I say.

"Heartland, probably," Riga says.

"I hope ze's not on our train."

"Not with that cut," JoJo says. "Ze needs to get that cleaned and sutured, and ze probably has a fever. Ze'll be waiting in that line at the clinic for awhile. They need more doctors here."

"Shanika wants to stay in New Rose," I say. "Tania, too, I think. But do they need so many staff there?"

"Probably not. But I'm not so sure Tania wants to stay." JoJo gives me a look like, ze's your best friend, don't you know? I remember how Tania and I were talkin' about Heartland back at Muir House. I miss zir so much right now.

"Tell Tania—give Tania all my love," I say to JoJo. "Tell zir we'll see each other in Heartland, or somewhere on the way."

"I will," JoJo says. Ze knows what I mean.

We're walkin' pretty fast. It's easy without any bags or Mom or Dix. We hear the river before we see it. It's runnin' strong this time of year and it's so wide. I guess it overflowed its banks a long time ago and never went back, tho I'm sure it waxes and wanes.

We find a path along the hard-packed sediment headin' east thru some abandoned streets. There's camps and I see some people with fishing poles up ahead. We don't spend much time here lookin' for herbs, tho there's vegetation, we decide to hike a couple miles 'til we're outta the city.

The river's loud and we don't say much. It feels good to be by such a beautiful river, even with the ugly old buildings around. I get a feeling I haven't had since New Rose, like I'm part of this and I breathe in the mountain air.

We walk in a line. I'm in front in case I see a plant we wanna collect, but it's mostly asphalt rubble and sediment on the path. The river's so high, whatever grew here is mostly underwater now. We see some tops of shrubs and trees stickin' up outta the swirling eddies.

It's hot, not sunny but humid and there's big gray clouds behind us in the west. They were there this morning and they're comin' this way, but it'll take awhile, I hope.

Finally, we're climbin' up a rise and then we see open land out in front of us, miles of rolling hills covered in sagebrush. I think I see some yarrow out due east by a rock formation and I take out some binoculars as we keep headin' east. When we're up a little higher we stop a second and I take a look and say, "Oh there they are!"

"What?" JoJo says and Riga looks hard out to the eastern horizon.

"Horses," I say. I hand the binoculars to JoJo and ze puts them up to zir eyes.

"Oh my god," JoJo says. Riga's got zir binoculars out now and see's 'em too.

"Let's go out there," JoJo says. It looks to be about a mile.

We start to walk faster. At the rock formation, we stop and drink some water from our bota bags. Then JoJo and I collect a little yarrow, tho it grows in New Rose, I'll take some with me goin' east. We walk around awhile and find gumweed and mesquite and we cut some with our collecting knives and stow it in our packs.

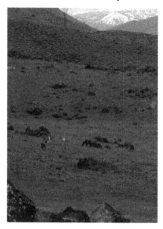

I look out again at the snow on the mountains far in the distance. I haven't seen snow since I was a kid. It's just a wonder. It's a wonder to be on this journey and I feel like I could start runnin' and singin' and I can't wait to see what's next. This world, it still exists! We're still alive! I turn to JoJo, who was stuck in New Bay for years and years just like me. "Look at that!" I say. "Can you believe it?"

"That cell tower? I knew there had to be some around here, the transmission in the Capitol is pretty good."

I look at zir, and then just bend over laughin'. "JoJo," I say.

"Well." Ze laughs. "I guess you mean the mountains. Yes, I see it." Ze sweeps out zir arm across the panorama, all dramatic now.

But then ze's quiet. "It's magnificent." Ze feels the awe.

Riga's watchin' us with a big smile. "It's good to have an old friend from long ago," ze says. I can see ze feels how JoJo and I go way back, like all of us Caretakers. I wonder where Riga's old friends are. I look down the hill at the horses.

"Let's go!" Riga says. We start pickin' our way down the rocky hill, quiet and careful. It doesn't take too long before we get near a family of grazing horses and we stand back, just watchin'—they're so beautiful. Healthy and wild.

There's some crazy big rocks in this meadow and we walk back silently to a high formation so the horses won't see us and spook. We haven't said a word for awhile so it's a surprise when Riga kinda shouts, "What is this?"

JoJo and I look at zir as ze leans into a crevice in the rockface next to us. I go over to see and there's a triangular opening, and a smell of, I don't know, damp earth or—a mineral smell. Riga's already squeezin' zir body into the bottom of the crevice where it's widest, like a gymnast, all contortions, but ze does it. "It keeps going," I hear zir voice say from inside. JoJo's next to me now and shoves zir daypack inside after Riga, who takes it and pretty soon JoJo's squeezed inside too. "Oh my god," ze calls out. I'm pretty quick gettin' in myself and we're standin' on a wide ledge lookin' down into a cavern about the size of a barn with all kindsa wild formations. JoJo has the flashlight on her phone movin' all around and we see stalactites and stalagmites, a rainbow of colors—gypsum, azurite, garnet—then down on the rocky floor is a tiny stream, just a trickle of water, and we can hear a drip, drip from the walls. When ze shines the light way to our left it shows a step that goes down, looks like, to a second, smaller ledge. And then we see the stairs carved into the rock. They're eroded and probably ancient, but real. We are silent and in awe. Then ze turns off zir phone, and I say, "JoJo!" But ze says, "The battery's way down." We stand there in darkness. I can hear us all breathin'. Real slow, I turn to look at the crevice we came thru and from this angle there's only a hairline of light. Riga puts zir hands in zir pockets, searchin' around and then, "Oh, we are lucky," ze says. "Matches." Ze takes off zir daypack and pulls out something. I can feel what ze's doin' more than see. It's crowded on this little ledge.

"For emergencies." Riga turns and grins at us. I can't see zir face but I can feel that smile. Ze strikes a match and then lights a short fat candle and holds it high. We laugh, and then first JoJo, then me, and then Riga pick our way down the narrow rock stairs to the floor of the cave. As careful as we can, we get to the tiny stream of water that's runnin' thru the cavern and sit down beside it. We're in a circle and Riga puts the candle at the center like we're at a campfire. The shadows from the little flame are dancin' like giant birds and animals on all the walls and rock around us. I'm shiverin' from the damp cold and the feeling like I'm on another planet. But now, this is Earth, like the center of the Earth. We're lookin' around, watchin' it all. It's so silent here, like a tomb must be, except for the water—the trickle beside us and the drip, drip from the walls.

"It feels like the beginning of time in here," JoJo says in a quiet voice. It echoes, just a little.

"Like we are the first human beings," Riga says.

"We are in a way," I say. "The first in this new world."

"I wonder who lived here before," JoJo says. "Was it ten years ago? A hundred? And thousands of years before..."

"It could have been people from the ice age who carved those stairs."

We're silent again.

"It's like a womb," JoJo says finally. "The womb of the Earth."

"Or the belly of the whale," Riga says. "We are Jonah."

"Going to the Capitol to turn people from their evil ways," JoJo says.

I don't know the Bible, but I say, "I wish we could turn people from their evil ways. But the Capitol, it looks just like the past with all the homeless people who have nuthin', not even a bed or a coat. And then rich people in the hills with all the money and tech. It's not any different than San Francisco when I was a kid."

"New Rose is different," JoJo says.

"The Eden villages are different," Riga says. Ze looks at me. "We can be like Jonah, and bring their values. That's why we are going to Heartland."

Of course. I feel it again, that purpose. I look at Riga and our eyes meet in the strange candlelight like we're spirits who seek some truth in each other.

"But *homo sapiens*," JoJo says quietly, and I hear the echo again, "has such an ugly past." The candle flickers and sputters a little, then burns stronger. A shadow leaps behind JoJo like a scary thing as ze keeps talkin'. "Of all the species, none torture and murder each other, or have wars, or destroy their own habitat with greed. I wonder if extinction...." Ze stops.

We don't say anything cuz we all know what ze means. We just watch the spirit dance around us and breathe in the damp smell of rock and dirt deep underground.

"But so creative, too, no?" Riga finally says. "So much knowledge, like tech and...that phone," ze nods at JoJo, "it's a new appendage we grew—another brain. There is one brain in our head and a bigger one growing on our hand."

JoJo gives Riga a look like ze's startin' to get who ze is now. "*Homo electronicus*," JoJo says. "You're right. We've evolved into a different species."

"So we can live as a different species now. *Homo sapiens* is extinct after all," Riga says.

"Not quite," I say, thinkin' of Mitch, and the Red Riders, and the homeless family livin' in the lot behind the Waystation Hotel.

"Not yet," Riga agrees. "But it's possible."

"Or we could become so robotic we're even more heartless," I say. Riga wasn't with us this morning, seein' what JoJo and I saw of this new world. What did ze see, I wonder.

"Look what *homo sapiens* has done to the Earth," JoJo says.

"And look what the Earth is doin' to us now," I say and I feel it at that instant, in this ancient cave, the power of the Earth—the livin', breathin' power of it.

"Yes, it's true," Riga says. "And also it's true for us, us sitting here." Ze looks around at the dance of spirits as we listen to the water in the tiny stream. "We can decide who we will be. We are starting over. We are being born here, in this womb, no? We can give love to the Earth, like this stream of water. We can become the energy of love for what is here, the Earth now."

"Yes." JoJo looks at Riga and at me. "Yes. Let's commit to that."

I nod my head and so does Riga. Then JoJo reaches out for our hands and we all sit, hand in hand before the flame, in silence, and make a vow so profound I can feel it in my blood.

Mom

I see the gray cloud again when I wake but there are no voices, just the sound of breathing, sleeping bodies. And then some shapes come into view, the window on the far wall, Catherine in her bed nearby. It's dawn, although no real light comes into this dark building here on the ground floor. Then I can hear it, the drum of rain, muffled but steady and hard.

I admit I worked myself into quite a frenzy last night. It was after dark when they finally came in, drenched to the bone, but in such high spirits. They had run, it seems, several miles in pouring rain. They had stories about wild horses and an ancient cave, their knapsacks were full of native herbs which they carefully laid out on a cloth on the floor to dry out. Even JoJo, usually so practical and no-nonsense, seemed transformed with buoyancy. Although she did plug in her phone as soon as she walked in the door, I noticed. I was so blessedly relieved to see them, I wanted to weep. Catherine had been so kind to me, seeing how beside myself with worry I was. But she has not left this hotel yet so has not seen what we have in this Capitol, the antithesis in many ways, of New Rose. She couldn't know its dangers as we experienced them. Although I did tell her about our encounter with Mitch and she was amazed, and not pleased, to hear he was around and, presumably, on the same emigre trail we are, heading ever east.

I'm glad to see Catherine is feeling so much better. The day alone, resting, did her a lot of good after the disruption of leaving New Rose. She was even reading a book yesterday in the late afternoon while there was still light. I have to admit, I envied her that. She said she would give me the book when she finished and, who knows, if I can get the cataract surgery in the Mountains Capitol, or the Heartland, maybe I will be able to read like that again. Riga brought her the book, she said, when ze returned here to the room after zir morning errands. Ze'd brought in several parcels and stashed them under zir bed. It was a book about the West in the 20th century, a novel. A huge paperback that would last her for an entire train ride, Riga joked. It was sweet of Riga. And then I saw ze had left some handmade paper and new pens on my cot. I barely had time to thank zir before ze and Star and JoJo went off on their herb-gathering adventure. I was too agitated to sleep so spent the afternoon writing while Catherine read. Dix and two of the Potters went out to look for batteries and tools and windmill parts. When Dix returned in the early evening, ze asked Catherine to come out with him for a walk. She was eager to go, I saw, feeling so well that she'd begun to feel cooped up. So I was left alone with my journal and thoughts for the evening, writing and munching on nuts and dried fruit that Dix had brought us. It was pleasant until I heard the rain begin at sunset and from that time on, I worried. My heart pumping. The usual anxiety. I simply could not keep it checked. I was about to look for some of our precious valerian supply when the young people came bursting in, and Dix and Catherine returned soon after. They seemed subdued, compared to the young people, and said very little. Dix returned to the room he's sharing with the Potters and Catherine went to bed, lying quietly while the rest of us talked. It was an hour before everyone settled down and I finally fell asleep. JoJo has a long journey today and we all have to help her take the packs of supplies to the station and get them on the train. Then the rest of us must regroup to board our train east this evening.

I rise as quietly as I can from my cot. I slept in my clothes, like we generally do. I tiptoe to the door and ease my way out and spend some time in the small room with the sink to wash. There's a cracked and mottled mirror above the sink which is barely visible in the shaft of light from the tiny window above the toilet. But it's enough for me to see that I look like a very old woman. The sun has left its mark, and my hair is nearly white now. My eyes, once striking, are watery and shot with fine lines of red. The skin beneath them sags in pouches and there are deep grooves in my forehead that may as well spell out the word anxiety.

Laugh lines crinkle at the corners of my eyes as I smile at this and shrug. Yes, I'm very old. Well past the life expectancy in this current era. Rumor has it we've returned to the early 19th century in that regard. Forty-five being the average age of death now. Four decades, the time the human body was designed for. Before teeth get loose, rot, fall out. Before vision begins to fail. Without our man-made aids, we lose our faculties so much sooner. Although there are still wealthy people around the world who have the usual surgeries and hearing-aids and pharmaceuticals. As Star said about ammunition—it's still out there. The means of prolonging life, or cutting it short.

When I slowly and quietly open the door to the room, Catherine is up and dressed. She seems to be waiting for me. She looks concerned, even anxious. She puts a hand on my arm to stay me and whispers, "Can we talk? Let's go outside."

I turn and leave the room with her behind me and stand in the hall.

"Dix and I found this parlor last night," she says and leads me down the dark narrow corridor, then opens a door to a room near the front. It is a parlor, although not a charming one. There are some worn chairs, a low table, two oil lamps. Catherine takes a seat in one of the upholstered hard-back chairs and I sit in the other, an end table between us as we turn the chairs to face each other. I'm wondering what has happened. Has she had a relapse? Or is there a problem with Dix?

She leans forward, her face closer now and says, "I want to tell you that Dix and I have decided to return to New Rose."

This hits me hard, like a sharp pain in my chest. I should have seen it coming; I can see now, in my mind's eye, the grim downturn of Dix's mouth yesterday after the encounter with Mitch; but I didn't see it coming. "Oh, I see," I say now and look away from her to the small battered wooden table between us, then back to her. "But what about the CAT Scan? Your health?"

She sits back in her chair a bit. "It was Dix who wanted that, and then he talked to JoJo about it yesterday, apparently. She said it wouldn't do much good now. If I'd had a serious bleed in my brain, I would be dead." She gives a little laugh. Shrugs. "And if there is a slow bleed, it will have to heal on its own. There's nothing to be done except rest. In the past they would have said I should stay off airplanes for several months and Dix wonders if the trains, the moving from place to place…. It's obvious I could get more rest in New Rose."

"That's true," I agree.

"And JoJo is hoping to expand the clinic. She's even talking about some of the Caretakers going to the Mountains Capitol to buy more equipment at the medical facility there. It's supposed to have some of the latest tech imported from the Heartland, part of the recovery making its way west."

"And Dix could do so much good in New Rose. I know you'd wanted the two of you to stay there."

"He was horrified by what he saw here yesterday," Catherine says. "Mitch. Then that near mugging from those kids in red uniforms." She widens her eyes, a look of both astonishment and dismay. "Who knows what lies ahead, despite all the supposed marvels and economic recovery in the Heartland. As usual, recovery for who exactly? The rich, it appears. That's Dix's fear. He doesn't want any part of it if we can live somewhere like New Rose."

My heart feels heavy, hearing this, because I think they are probably right. And she knows I think this.

"But, Mom, listen," she says and leans forward and takes both my hands in hers, looking closely into my eyes. "Come with us. Come and live with us in New Rose."

Of course I want to and when I smile at her, to thank her, she can see that. But I shake my head, no. "I can't leave Star," I say. "She's my only family. Losing Dale was devastating for me. I can't lose Star, too."

"But Star and Riga will come back to New Rose. They're liaisons for the Town Council."

"They may, months from now. But what if I lose them, what if I can't find them?"

She squeezes my hands and then lets go, sitting back in her chair. She knows she can't promise that I would see Star again.

"And I don't know what I would do in New Rose, where I could live, as much as I'd want to...."

"You could live with Dix and me!" she says.

"I might feel like the proverbial third wheel," I say, trying to be light. Although I realize, with a sudden sad sense, that now I will be exactly that for Riga and Star.

Catherine ignores this and presses on, "There's so much work to be done in New Rose. The clinic—"

"No, no," I say. "It's exhausting. I can't do the work the way it needs to be done. And, honestly, my sight is not good. It's getting worse, and it's very hard for me to listen well to people when I can't see them, their eyes and expressions. I need to get the cataract surgery, if I'm to be useful to anyone."

This stills Catherine. She sees the truth of it.

"I won't have work there either," she says with sadness. "There's no clay in the soil, not like New Bay, or what little there is the Old Town crafts people need."

"But the gardens and greenhouses..." I don't finish. Yes, gardening is creative, but it is not Catherine's first love.

But she brightens, "That's true. And Dix will be so happy there."

"I wonder if Tania and Shanika and Kamala and the other Caretakers will stay on there. I'm sure some of them will be coming east, there's so much need for health workers. There certainly is in the hospital we saw yesterday."

"Dix told me how understaffed they are. It depressed him, as well as everything else he saw."

I know Catherine fears Dix's depression returning. The most important reason to go back to New Rose, perhaps. There is nothing more to be said, really. We would part ways. A wrenching thought to me, another tearing away of family, friends, home. I feel so weary, I close my eyes a moment. Then quickly sit forward, looking at Catherine who is watching me, her eyes sad.

"You'll be leaving in a couple hours, let's get something to eat. JoJo will be wanting help packing. Does she know you and Dix will be with her? You'll be a tremendous help to her." I stand up and look around for my walking stick and see I've left it in the room. We say nothing, knowing we may never see each other again.

It's nearly 11:00 a.m. when Star, who has a new watch Riga has given her, says we should leave, and our group and all our carts and drays and duffels of baggage head out of the Waystation Hotel to make the short walk to the train station. Savvier now, we have all the goods in the center with Catherine and me, and then an outer circle made up of Dix and the Potters and Riga, Star and JoJo. It was yet another surprise to me that the four Potters will stay on here in the Capitol and not be boarding the train east with Riga, Star and me tonight. When they learned Catherine and Dix were returning to New Rose, they decided to stay here to look for work. They want to wait to hear from the Potter group that went east on the train last week, to see where they've chosen to settle, and what it's like. They'd made arrangements for phone contact. And so, plans change again as I'm sure they will repeatedly on this journey. Although we started out with so many, the Caretakers and the children, then the Potters and then the Tinkers. I think of Millie again, and her little dog, Dot. And for the first time, I feel I might understand why she decided to stay behind rather than leave her little dog, her companion of so many years.

It's arduous, but we make it to the station without incident; although there are a number of people milling about on the streets near and inside the station, and we've had to do some maneuvering to get around the large puddles from last night's torrential rain. Fortunately, there is a boardwalk part of the way over the sediment layers that are muddy sludge now. With all the obstacles, it's taken us half an hour and I'm grateful we had the good sense to allow plenty of time.

Dix is in the lead as our troop and cargo march toward the departure area. The train is there, waiting. Dix seems eager to board and manages to corral a rail worker who allows us access to the baggage car after looking at the tickets JoJo has on her phone. Very few people are heading west and it took only a few minutes for her to book Dix and Catherine's passage this morning. JoJo was very happy and relieved, I could see, when she found out she would have their company and help for the journey.

We all pitch in now to load the medical supplies safely into the baggage car. The young people heave it up to Dix and two Potters who stand in the open doors of the car. Catherine and I and a young Potter are standing guard over the things waiting to be loaded as well as the personal baggage JoJo, Catherine and Dix will have with them at their seats. Do I long to go with them? These dear friends. Yes, I do. I turn away. And I see Dale walking by with a worn leather satchel slung over his shoulder and cry out his name before I can stop myself because I see then it's just a shadow, a reflection in a window of someone walking outside. No one hears me in the commotion except the Potter boy. Catherine was trying to get Dix's attention about something. I smile at the Potter boy. "I thought I saw an old friend," I say. He gives me a sweet smile, kind. But I can tell he is on to me. I pull myself together, wondering if it was an actual hallucination or a *trompe l'oeil,* some effect of my failing vision. Or just what is going on with me! I feel suddenly angry and impatient with myself. And the accompanying rush of adrenalin clears my head. At the baggage car they're finishing up. Dix and the Potters have jumped down from the boxcar onto the platform and the rail worker shoves the heavy sliding door closed, making a huge clatter, then locks it in place.

I feel us regroup now that the work is done, and it is time for good-byes. The four young Potters are each embracing Dix and Catherine and talking about how they'll make do here and be in touch. And then Dix comes over and to my surprise, embraces me warmly. "You are always welcome in our home," he says. "We would love you to come and stay, to live with us." I'm very touched, and I know it is his love for Catherine that moves him to sincerely make this invitation. As he steps back I see Star and Riga and JoJo standing in a circle nearby, hands joined, talking fervently among themselves. Then Catherine is there and we embrace. Her warmth and kindness and good humor seem to emanate wordlessly and we say nothing. She steps back and we smile, sadly, at each other. Tears blur my vision now as I see her turn and Dix takes her hand, leading her to board the train. I follow them to where JoJo is joking now with Star and Riga, their intensity gone as JoJo says, "You're going to bring us that cleaning robot from Heartland, right?"

Catherine turns and says, "Yeah, don't forget!" as she embraces Star and Riga and Dix shakes their hands, offering some kind words to each of them. JoJo envelopes me in a tight hug. "You take care, Mom. I love you."

And I say, "You too, JoJo. My love to you, and all the Caretakers." The words seem so inadequate. And then they're gone.

Star

Riga's gone out for some last minute supplies and then we're gonna head to the train station as soon as ze gets back. Mom's been real quiet since the others left. I understand. It felt pretty lonely after JoJo and Catherine and Dix got on the train and then the Potters went off somewhere. I can't believe it's just Mom and me and Riga now. I didn't really see that comin'. Mom's been in zir bed writin' in zir journal for hours, and I'm glad for that. I've been washin' some stuff and I packed and re-packed the plants so they'll all survive this journey.

And I'm thinkin' now about how far we've come. Not in miles so much, but in our plans—our intention, as JoJo says. Cuz I gotta say, back in New Bay I used to think, when I was in school and I'd learn about all the species that'd gone extinct—600 plants and 300 animals and 30,000 more endangered—it made me crazy. And now there's so many more gone! Forever. But nobody knows what cuz nobody's countin' cuz everyone's just tryin' to survive, I guess. I used to think—if it's humans that cause species to go extinct at 1,000 times the usual rate, why should humans be the ones to live? Back then there were 8 billion humans at least, just crawlin' all over the Earth dumpin' trash and toxins and bein' mean to each other. That's how I saw it, and that's part of why I "acted out" as Mom used to call it, cuz I didn't care. The changes had started and you could see what was comin'—tho I gotta say, no one knew it would happen so fast, that stuff would collapse—Bam Bam Bam—one after another, the economy, the ice cliffs, the government—I can't even remember in what order.

We were just survivin' in New Bay, all of us who hadn't left. Some of us formed the Caretakers and that became a reason to live. We tended the gardens in the hills and took care of the children and helped people who were sick and old. Part of how I became an herbalist was that work. Everything was day to day, and it still is.

But I feel like something happened to me in that cave with JoJo and Riga. I was already a little more hopeful after New Rose, that's true. But then in the cave we felt the Earth talk to us. We all did. We saw the spirits with our own eyes. And the spirits told us to be strong, and to feel the power and dance with them and heal ourselves and care for all that lives. To be a Caretaker, for me and JoJo, or to be a Guide, for Riga—it has so much more meaning now—a kind of great holy vision that I didn't see before. It's what it means to care for the sacred Earth. Blessed be.

I pick up a milkweed seedling to make sure its new leaves aren't turnin' yellow and then set it on the window ledge 'til it's time to go.

I see Mom's lyin' on her bed with her eyes closed now but I don't think ze's asleep. I feel worried about zir eyes. I didn't realize how bad they were until today when it seemed like ze was seein' things on the way back from the train station. Maybe it was all the puddles and mud and tryin' to get around 'em, or the shadows looked like—I don't know what—to zir. Ze was kinda jumpy and then ze was just sad when we got back here. Riga and I were talkin' and makin' plans and that's when Mom started up with zir journal.

I'll be glad when we can get on that train, get movin' again and be around some more people. I look at my new watch. It's 5:00. The train leaves at 7:00. Riga says this train is a lot fancier than the one we took before. It has some old Pullman cars from a train museum, and we can have a meal at a table cuz we'll be in a sleeping car with a diner. I gotta say, I'm not sorry ze got that extra sleeping compartment for Catherine cuz now we are gonna stay in it instead. I can't wait! We haven't been alone since I don't know, days and days.

The door opens and Riga comes in all fresh and ze smells like the outdoors. Ze's got a big sack of stuff, more for us to pack. I laugh. The Potters said they'd be back in time to help us get to the station. I love these Potters, they're so willin' to help. I will miss them.

When it's time, we get to the station pretty quick. It feels funny to be comin' back here in the same day, but we're glad most the puddles are dry now and Mom seems like ze's got zir energy back. I'm focused mainly on the plants. Dix and JoJo aren't here to carry any and we got 'em all balanced on the two wagons, but thanks to the Potters everything gets to the station and loaded in the baggage car.

This train's longer than the one goin' west this morning cuz it has the sleeping and diner cars and Riga says we'll have to stop more often for fuel to pull the weight. We're not due to arrive 'til about noon tomorrow tho it's only just over the mountain—the next Eden village we're goin' to, called Elk. They have an old town, too, I guess. I'm excited to get there, hopin' it's like New Rose at least in some ways. This Capitol sure is not.

We get on board and I can't believe this old Pullman car! It's like heaven, the seats are even velvet, looks like, kinda worn but somebody's keepin' 'em clean. Maybe a robot. This train'll go all the way to Heartland Capitol, but we're gettin' off in Elk and then we'll get the next train that comes thru to the next Eden village and make our way east like that.

Mom's in zir cabin lyin' down. In Mountains Capitol we're gonna see if ze can get the cataract surgery, tho I'm afraid it can't really happen 'til Heartland. I didn't tell zir yet but JoJo called the hospital in Mountains yesterday and they said, yes, they do the surgeries but there's a long waiting list. So if Riga and I are gonna get to the convention in time we're probably gonna have to move on and wait for the surgery in Heartland, plus the best care will be there. I can't wait till Mom gets zir eyesight back, ze'll be so happy.

I'm runnin' my hand over the velvet when Riga comes back from checkin' on the baggage and says it's time to go to the diner car cuz it won't be open long. We get Mom from her cabin and walk down a narrow hall and between cars to the diner. We're rockin' side to side and I keep my hand on Mom to keep zir steady.

The diner looks nice. There's little wooden tables, bolted to the floor, I guess. We're only just creepin' along right now, gettin' thru an area where Riga says there can be trash or sometimes wild horses on the tracks. The whistle screams every now and then and I guess they see an animal, equine, bovine or human, I don't know.

The three of us sit at one of the tables next to a big window. There's a few other people in here, and they're dressed up, like the people I met on the last train, rich people from Westlands Capitol, I guess. Maybe they're on their way to Heartland, like us, to make their case for how they want the future to be. A couple next to us give Riga a funny look, it seems to me. Maybe it's zir bright colored Devi clothes and wild necklace. I think ze's so beautiful. Maybe that's why. I turn and smile at them, nice and friendly, and by the powers that be, they smile back! Earth spirit, thank you.

Mom says, "Look at that," just as there's a loud squeal of the brakes and we slow with a shudder and stop. Outside is an acre of stacked wood.

"A fuel stop," Riga says. And then a kid, maybe fifteen, brings us a ceramic pitcher of water and three glasses.

"Do you want your dinner now?" ze asks and we say yes.

"This train is so comfortable!" Mom says. I feel so relieved to see her comin' back to life.

"Who runs the trains?" ze asks Riga

"Heartland government. It is part of their economic recovery starting four years ago. Westlands Capitol is their only Westlands stop." Riga looks out the window. "We are already in Mountains, I think. But all roads lead to Heartland, no?" Ze smiles.

I'm glad the train's stopped while I'm pourin' us all a glass of water. We saw 'em loadin' the barrels of filtered water back at the station and I'm gonna fill our bota bags. It'll be a relief not to work our filters for awhile, and I heard more rain's comin' so we might not be able to recharge our solar pumps.

We're halfway thru dinner when there's a jolt and some loud noise and the train starts up again. It picks up speed pretty fast but we don't even say anything cuz we are lovin' this food. It's hot, I don't know how, and it's delicious. Some kinda root vegetable mash with tofu and salsa and fresh greens.

"Do most climate refugees migrate all the way to Heartland, do you think?" Mom asks Riga.

"Yes, I think they do. In the first wave, many went to Buffalo and Duluth, and to Canada. Many still prefer Canada and go there, especially after the epidemic in the south of Heartland. You remember?"

"No. We didn't get much news," Mom says.

"It was *Candida Auris*," Riga says, "a fungus that no medicines could kill. The ranchers had used so many fungicides on their crops that nothing worked to stop the epidemic. It is the same as how antibiotics they used on their animals don't kill the bacteria anymore."

"Oh yes," Mom says. "I do remember, of course. I think...was it before the war?"

"Before and during and after. Finally, the cattle ranches—they are all gone. Now it's wind and solar everywhere." Riga stretches out zir arms wide like the prairies. "I saw this when I was there four years ago," ze says. "And now there is more... I hear stories, no? There is so much new tech we can't even imagine it."

"And underground cities?" I say.

Ze grins at me. "Yes."

"I'm surprised anything could survive the extreme winds and storms they were getting," Mom says.

"Some places, it's true, they can't build anything. There is only flat land wiped clean like the moon."

I look out the window next to us. "Will we see that?"

"This train goes north. We won't see that."

"It must be where the dustbowl was," Mom says.

"Yes, I think so, but a much bigger area."

Out the window, I'm seein' a lotta green tho. "Looks like things are growin' here," I say. "It's pretty lush."

"It's beautiful," Mom says, watchin' the trees go by while the train follows a river.

"What's this!" Riga says and we see something fly by, a flash of red and black and white.

"A woodpecker!" Mom says and laughs. "It must be."

"There are so many birds, now. They told us in New Rose," Riga says, "we will see a lot of birds in Elk."

The train veers left and we can see the river runnin' fast beside us, deep green with white caps where it runs over a stretch of rocky bed.

"Maybe there are fish, too," Riga says.

We just sit and watch. The train's climbin' and it's slow enough we could see if a fish were to jump outta the water like a steelhead trout. I wonder if they died off, last I heard they were endangered. But sittin' here right now, lookin' at the river and the forest beyond for miles, without a human in sight except us on this train, I believe it's true: the Renewal. I feel Riga's eyes and I look up, into zir eyes, green as the river, and we feel it. We feel the spirits, tellin' us what to do.

Mom

I don't think I've slept in a bed this comfortable since we left New Bay. Oh, perhaps the bed at Muir House. But it didn't have this gentle rocking motion and the soothing clack clack clack sound. We never go very fast, whether because of the rough terrain or the lack of power in a steam engine, I don't know. I feel very happy in this safe little bunk, looking out at the night sky. The moon is full. Clouds come and go. The expected rain has not started yet. There's no forecast, of course, it's just what people feel and say from experience that has led to talk of rain. As far as I know. Perhaps there are weather stations that are operative again in Mountains and they broadcast their findings to the train engineer.

Someday, I'm sure, this will be a self-driving train with enormous batteries and electric motors powering it along, pulling refurbished transit cars of light metals and god knows what. I can't help but feel grateful for this interlude of low-tech activity in the recovery. I'm starting to get the idea, to see how there really is a recovery taking place, although not in the Westlands, to my knowledge. The Valley Sea presents a large obstacle to transit. But more important is the Renewal they spoke of in New Rose. Reforestation, endangered species now flourishing. Clean air and water. I would have thought it all rumor if I hadn't seen it for myself, in New Rose and now on this train journey.

But will it be different. Will humans behave differently now?

I remember before The Fail rumor had it that a band of astronauts and tech billionaires lifted off in a spaceship headed for Mars. Some even said secret missions had already established a colony there with biospheres and microbial foods of some kind. I didn't believe them. But I was so naïve then. Yet can I fault myself? The national news was full of trash, ridiculous stories. And the true stories were of atrocities that would have shocked even the Romans under Nero.

I hear a sound, something other than the clack clack of the train, more of a steady thrumming and now I see dark drops hitting the window. The rain, at last. We've driven into it, it seems. The train slows, but does not stop entirely. Visibility might be a problem. I heard someone in the dining car say they had seen a bear by the tracks. I refuse to think of rising rivers or the kind of flash floods that created the silt and sediment layers in the Capitol not far below us. But of course, the familiar adrenalin burst and heart palpitations start up. I take several slow, deep breaths and clear my mind.

It was a joy to share a delicious meal with Star and Riga. They have so much energy and hope. I admire them. I'm especially happy that Star, beyond foraging for herbs, will be cultivating plants and working as a botanist with the Eden Network. There are books in the Eden village libraries and the horticulturists will share their knowledge with her. She said there are conservatories in each village around the world. Some are using seeds from the Svalbard Global Seed Bank in Norway. And many of the greenhouses simulate climate conditions necessary to grow medicinal herbs. They're growing Mastic trees in one of the Elk greenhouses! She said she heard it feels like a sauna inside. And, I don't know if it's rumor, but they said new species of herbs are being discovered and their medicinal properties investigated. New medical practices are evolving. It's tremendously hopeful. I hope all the

Caretakers become involved in this transformation, a nature-based, cooperative way of living and healing. And I assume they will, even if they stay in New Rose; although it seems the closer one gets to Heartland, the more innovation and resources there are. Such an irony—the Westlands a lost and abandoned civilization, now; its greatest cities under the sea.

I wonder what's happening at Muir House. And why we haven't yet encountered any Muiristas. Although didn't Riga or someone say they had all deployed to protect the hundreds of National Parks and Monuments that still exist? Maybe some have returned to Muir House. But no, Riga said they had completely abandoned the coast and even the home of their hero. In the Tinkers control now. A hotel! Or did Kelly manage to keep it a refugee waystation, like the Mariposa House? The old man, what was his name? He agreed to cooperate with Kelly, Star told me, after some contentious meeting they had. And now that Mitch has left. That was a surprise. It may be because of that very agreement about cooperation that he decided to move on to where he could assert his dominance, violently if he wished. There must be many others out there, I cannot kid myself about that. Former Guardians, resenting their losses in the war, feeding their resentments as the Germans did after World War I, producing the Nazis. Or for that matter, how the Confederates did after the Civil War, leading to the KKK and, eventually, the Guardians. But in Germany, there was a national atonement after the atrocities of the Nazis. The United States never atoned for the atrocities of slavery. It's appalling, really, how white southerners defended it until the very land they lived on sank into the sea. But nature plays no favorites. The Westlands, the Old South, so opposed, both gone.

Is it even possible that Millie and the old man Tinker started a relationship with each other? Was there something I didn't see between them that made Millie stay? Though it was for Dot, they wouldn't let her take Dot. That's right. But Millie and the Tinker...why not? Maybe that was the last straw for Mitch. A Guardian and a Reformer, so opposed, joined together.

Nature plays no favorites but can't we make some kind of difference ourselves? Can human behavior change?

I turn in my narrow bed, wrestling with the thin blanket. The cabin is warm, heated by electric power generated from this moving train. I wonder if we will ever return to New Rose. And I know, if I let myself, that I will not. When I quiet myself and feel this question deeply, the answer is no.

I believe in this, "the knowing." That we can know beyond our material selves. That science cannot preclude this. I believe it is possible to see beyond the "thin veil" as Catherine calls it, the scrim between our bodies and existence far beyond. You could say the internet proves it, although what I believe does not involve machines. It involves perception. I wonder if the library in Elk has Huxley's books. I would love to reread "The Doors of Perception." He described the knowing as "the Mind at Large."

Tonight at dinner Riga spoke of using radios during the war because the cell towers had been sabotaged and internet communication wasn't possible much of the time; but no one bothered with the radio towers. Ze said radio waves emanate forever into space, like light, and travel at the same speed; and that the human mind emits electric impulses similar to very low-frequency radio waves. Our thoughts emanate out from us creating an energy flow. Riga believes that we are all cells in the mind of god. As I do. But ze went on to say that the energy we emanate joins a stream, an energy stream, invisible and one of many. These streams flow through the universe, the love stream, the hate stream... And how we choose to live our lives contributes to these streams, making one or the other energy more prevalent on the planet.

I was amazed by this view of existence! Perhaps I was amazed that Riga...what? Believes it? Told us? It was a gift; Riga's gift to me, perhaps, because I could see Star and ze had discussed these things. Ze was telling me zir deepest beliefs and values. Personal and, to me, compelling. Star, I had thought, is more of a pantheist, in the tradition of Gaia philosophy. That the living Earth is one self-regulating system. But they're not so different, these beliefs.

And I? What do I believe now? I suppose what I have really been wondering, these days, is what will happen when I die? And the truth is, I believe the Earth is a living whole being, as Star believes, and that we are cells in the Mind at Large, as Huxley wrote, and that there are energy streams creating an emotional climate in society, as Riga believes, just as there are jet streams that create the global weather. But I, as an individual.... I believe I will dissipate and the thoughts and feelings I've cultivated will flow into the eternal energy streams, for better or worse.

I wonder what values will dominate at the Heartland Convention. Profiteering, greed, the "free market." Socialism. Communitarianism. Gaia. Or something new?

I feel enormously curious. And considerable dread. And hope and joy that Star and Riga will be part of it. How I would love to be part of it, too! But my body is not up to the task. Even if I were to get the eye surgery, if the problem is in fact cataracts and not macular degeneration as I sometimes suspect, my stamina is fading. Everything is fading! I'm old. And truth be told, I don't mind. I am grateful for my long life and all I have seen and known. I am truly grateful for the blessing and gift of my existence here. And I am grateful, too, to "lay my troubles down" as the spiritual says. And I sing this song silently to myself as I begin my nightly prayers. "I will lay my troubles, down by the water, Where the river will never run dry."

I awake to sunlight streaming through the window. I feel its warmth on my face and turn to see bright daylight outside. The rain has stopped. It must be nearly mid-morning. I sit up. Why didn't Star wake me? Maybe we're behind schedule. Weren't we supposed to arrive at noon? I stand and open the door to the narrow hallway.

I don't see anyone else out of their cabins. I turn back and sit on the bed. I'll look in the diner car in a minute.

The trees have thinned and the land is more open here. We pass a log cabin by a dirt road, and horses in a corral nearby.

Then I see an unusual settlement. Some kind of teepees on hardpan. And nearby, an outdoor oven. A windmill.

I try to remember what Star said they told her in New Rose, about Elk...I remember the greenhouses that are said to be there, but did she mention a hotel or waystation? I decide to find her and get my walking stick to head to the diner car as I feel my heart racing again.

There they are, at the same table and they look up and smile at me and pull out a chair.

"I didn't wake you up, Mom," Star says. "I thought maybe you should get all the sleep you could."

"Yes, you're right. I appreciate it," I say as I take a seat.

Star puts a bowl of grains in front of me, some fruit. "We're gonna be there in about an hour, we heard," she says. I can hear the excitement in her voice. I feel it, too, and decide not to burden her with my anxious questions about hotels.

I needn't have worried. As the train pulls into Elk I see a small wooden building, the station. And on the other side of the platform a charming town set beneath tall trees. Like an oasis in what had been a high-desert landscape of handsome mesas and dry scrub. The high snowy mountains in the distance are magnificent.

As we descend from the car the air is a shock. Dry, thin and freezing. Star jumps down and turns to help me step onto a small stool and then solid ground. She laughs. "It's cold!"

"We're expecting snow," a man next to her says. He's waiting for someone to deboard.

"Oh!" I say. Well, snow in May. Why not.

"We're gonna have to put on every stitch of clothes we've got," Star says to me as she walks us down the platform toward the baggage car where I see Riga reaching up for a crate of plants. A young woman approaches Riga and they start a conversation. Then she gestures at an electric cart farther down the platform. Riga nods enthusiastically, smiling, then turns to get our backpacks. The young woman, a teenager, I'd guess, retrieves the cart and drives it to Riga and they load our packs as Star and I join them. "Mom, Star," Riga says, "this is Imani."

"Welcome to Elk," Imani says. "We are so happy you have come. And thank you for bringing these plants from New Rose." We smile in greeting and shake hands. I feel a warm glow despite the freezing air.

"Can I take you to the lodge?" she asks me. "Another vehicle will be here shortly for the plants. They must go straight to the receiving greenhouse. They can't be in this cold air long."

"Yes, please," Star says. "Mom and I will come with you." She turns to Riga. "I'll be right back."

From the electric cart we see the town. It too has dried sediment layers extending out from the Elk River. There is a boardwalk, new, traversing the small downtown and a narrow flood plain, then climbing to an uphill residential area. Beautiful mature trees tower above us and many new ones have been planted. Conifers and deciduous. The downtown buildings are occupied in their second stories while their foundations are packed high with what look like sandbags behind walls of mud. The buildings must be well over a century old; they have the tall rectangular wooden facades of the old West.

Up the hill we turn, and what I hope is "the lodge" comes into view. It's in the style of the great WPA lodges in the National Parks but on a much smaller scale. Imani brings the cart to a stop at the entrance and helps me step out as Star gathers the things we've brought with us.

"That's a very beautiful tabard you're wearing," I say to Imani as she let's go of my hand. It looks wonderfully warm, wool probably and knit in an intricate pattern.

"Thank you. You can find some wool clothing in your rooms. We have lots of knitters here!" She laughs. "We've been knitting clothes for refugees for years. We have our sheep, and spin our wool."

"How wonderful!" I wonder if I could remember how to knit. I took it up as a young woman when it was a very popular pastime for awhile. Of course, this splint might get in the way now.

Inside the lodge there is a lobby and a grand stone fireplace with a large hearth. A fire is burning and comfortable stuffed chairs and wooden rockers surround it. No one seems to be sitting there at the moment and I gaze at the flickering flames.

Star is looking at the staircase leading to the rooms above. "Mom," she says. "Why don't you sit here and get warm while I take our packs up and get our rooms ready. "Riga!" she calls as we turn and see Riga coming in the entrance with two large duffle bags.

"I brought your other bags in case you need something. Now I will go to the plants."

I walk to the fireplace, my stick clomping on the wooden floor, and sink into one of the large stuffed chairs that embraces me like a down coat. "Ahh," I say. I stretch one hand to the warmth from the fire, feeling it thaw.

Star walks up to the hearth to warm her hands, too. "Mom, we're gonna take the bags upstairs and then Riga and me'll go to the greenhouse and get the plants set up. And we'll get some food and water for us all. It shouldn't take too long."

"That's a good idea," I say. "I'd love to sit here and rest for awhile."

She puts my small cloth handbag on the floor next to me. "Are you warm enough?"

"Yes, it's wonderful here. It feels so familiar."

I'm rifling through my cloth bag to find some dried fruit, when Star and Riga come back downstairs. I put my bag down.

"What a beautiful fire," Riga says. Ze stands closer to the flames, studying them a moment.

"You are still okay here, Mom?"

"Yes, it's perfect."

"Should we get the cart? Or we walk?" Riga asks Star.

"Let's get the cart," she answers.

Riga leans down and kisses my cheek. "You look so happy," ze says. "See you later." Ze lopes off across the lobby as Star leans down to also kiss my check and I reach and take her hand and hold it in mine. "I love you," I tell her.

She squeezes my hand. "I love you, Mom." Then she looks in my eyes, and we rest there, in each other's eyes for a moment. "Enjoy yourselves," I say, and I let her go.

When I look back to the fire, I feel enveloped by déjà vu, as if I've entered a room that I'd visited in a dream. My eyes still as I watch the flames, and I settle my vision in the dancing light, letting my mind rest, as if put to bed under a warm feather comforter. I am content and so thankful for Star and Riga and their new life and hope. My faith in them fills my heart. The warmth here and stillness are deeply calming. I feel no need to even think, and though I slept long and well a drowsiness overtakes me and I close my eyes. Images stream like scenery in the window of the train, the clinics, the Caretakers, Muir House, Millie and Dot, Mitch, his family, the hospital, the courtyard there, the homeless, the conservatory, Mae and Catherine and Dix, blending like a dream; perhaps I am dreaming. I feel it behind my left eye. And I tip to the left. Just a hint of wooziness, a sound, fzztt … a jolt, electric, then a gentle flow and giving way. Like an ice crystal, falling from a glacier and melting into the sea.

Star

We buried Mom last week, zir ashes, from the pyre. Me and Riga, in the garden at the lodge in Elk. But I have some with me. I keep 'em in the little red satin pouch, the one I had for herbs and then put on the top of Mom's walking stick for a handle for zir to grab onto. I'll take it with me wherever I go. I have zir journal, too, but I can't read it yet. Riga did. Ze loved it and says it's an "historical document" and should be in all the Eden libraries. I can't think about that now.

We're goin' on to the next Eden village right now. And then the next and next and then Heartland. I don't know what it'll be like. It's hard for me not to keep thinkin' about Mom. Ze would've loved the Eden villages. Each one is different so far but it's what they're tryin' to do, the Renewal. I try to think about that. But I don't know about Heartland. I guess I'm scared it's gonna be like the Capitol, and the past, and I gotta say, ever since we saw Mitch there I'm kinda lookin' over my shoulder, where's ze gonna show up next. Or somebody else, some other person the same as Mitch and that way ze has of makin' fun of people. Greed, and what else, the hurt, inside and out. Riga says I need to forget about Mitch. Ze says Heartland is different than the Capitol. Yeah, there are Mitches wherever you go, ze says, but there's all kinds of people in the world, like there always have been, and different ways to be. And we can be whoever we want. We can be part of the healing and the Renewal. I guess. I feel so sad now.

I wish we'd never seen Mitch that day at the clinics, and I wish those crazy kids never attacked us that day. And I wish Catherine and Dix would've come on with us on this journey, then probably Mom wouldn't of felt so lonely or sad. Maybe Mom wouldn't of had the stroke. Maybe ze'd still be here. I cry now, again. Riga holds my hand, then puts zir arm around me. Ze's used to my cryin'.

I look out the window at the half light. The sun's already set. There's more rain comin' in, someone said when we got on this train.

I wish that last day in the Capitol hadn't been so bad for Mom. And I wish I'd stayed with zir when we got back to the hotel instead of goin' off with Riga and JoJo. My head drops down with the shame I feel about that.

Then I hear Mom's voice, like ze's sittin' right here next to me, "Don't break my heart by feeling guilty." It's a shock to me, and I look up—because then I see. I see Mom knew. Mom knew! It fills me, this knowing. Mom knew ze was about to die and ze as good as told me. And I feel light inside for the first time.

Then I remember something else Mom used to say, when I was a kid. When I'd say, I wish this or that, like...it wouldn't rain. Or I wish my teacher wasn't mean. Or I wish I had some candy. I wish it were different. And finally Mom would say, "You know what's in the middle of a wish?"

I'd say, "What?"

Mom'd write the word on a paper. WISH. And then ze'd circle the two middle letters. This made me so mad, I hated word games and jokes like that.

"IS is in the middle of a wish," Mom'd say.

And I'd say, "What!?"

"Take care of what IS," ze'd say. "That's all you need to do."

I hear zir voice again, sayin' that, "Take care of what is." Love what is. Existence. Take care of it.

And then I thank all that's holy for these plants I'm gonna take care of. I'm gonna take care of plants wherever I go. And I thank all that's holy for Riga, here by my side.

"I'll do it, Mom," I say.

Supplemental Reading

Baldwin, J. (1962, January 1). A Letter to My Nephew. Madison, WI: *The Progressive.*

CBS. (2018, October 4). 85 Million Americans Eat Fast Food Every Day, New Study Reveals. *San Francisco CBS Local News.* https://sanfrancisco.cbslocal.com /2018/10/04/85-million-americans-eat-fast-food-every-day-new-study-reveals/

Cho, R. (2018, July 25). How Climate Change Will Alter Our Food. *Earth Institute, Columbia University* (Blog). Retrieved from https://blogs.ei.columbia.edu/ 2018/07/25/climate-change-food-agriculture/

Cornell University. (2017, June 26). Rising seas could result in 2 billion refugees by 2100. *Science Daily.* Retrieved from http://www.sciencedaily.com/ releases/2017/06/170626105746.htm.

Elmire, S. (2018, November). Septic Systems Vulnerable To Sea Level Rise. Miami-Dade Country: Florida Department of Health. Retrieved from https://www.miamidade.gov/green/library/vulnerability-septic-systems-sea-level-rise.pdf

Frazier, I. (2018, October 29). The Day the Great Plains Burned. New York, NY: *The New Yorker.*

Harvey, C. (2017, October 20). Oceans Can Rise in Sudden Bursts. *Scientific American E&E News.* Retrieved from http://www.Scientific American.com/oceans-can-rise-in-sudden-bursts/

Huxley, A. (1954). *The Doors of Perception.* New York, NY: Harper

International Maritime Organization. (2020) Maritime transport is essential to the world's economy as over 90%

of the world's trade is carried by sea. *United Nations.*
Retrieved from https://business.un.org/en/entities/13

Kaur, H. (2019, August 18). Scientists bid farewell to the
first Icelandic glacier lost to climate change. If more melt it
could be disastrous. *CNN.* Retrieved from
http://www.cnn.com/ 2019/08/18/health/glaciers-melting-
climate-change.

McKirdy, E. (2019, February 11). Massive Insect decline
could have "catastrophic" environmental impact, study
says. *CNN.* Retrieved from
http://www.cnn.com/2019/02/11/health/insect-decline-
study-intl/index.html

Mooney, C. (2019, February 6). Today's Earth looks a lot
like it did 115,000 years ago. All we're missing is massive
sea level rise. *Washington Post.* Retrieved from
http://www.washingtonpost.com/climate-
environment/2019/02/06/todays-earth-looks-a-lot-like-it-
did-115,000-years-ago-all-we're-missing-is-massive-sea-
level-rise/

Penniman, L. (2015, August 11). Four Ways Mexico's
Indigenous Farmers Are Practicing the Agriculture of the
Future. *Yes Magazine.* Retrieved from
https://www.yesmagazine.org/environment
/2015/08/11/four-ways-mexico-indigenous-farmers-
agriculture-of-the-future/

Robertson-Wilken, M. (2018). *Kumeyaay Ethnobotany.*
San Diego, CA: Sunbelt.

Surrusco, E. K. (2019, October 28). How Climate Change
is Fueling Extreme Weather. *Earth Justice* (blog).
Retrieved from http://earthjustice.org/blog/2019-july/how-
climate-change-is-fueling-extreme-weather.

Weisman, A. (2007). *The World Without Us.* New York,
NY: St. Martin's.

Wilson, E.O. (2016). *Half Earth*. New York, NY: Liveright

Witze, A. (2019, January 9). Earth's magnetic field is acting up and geologists don't know why. *Nature*. Retrieved from http://www.nature.com/articles/d41586-019-00007-1